ANACONDA

CHOKE

Published 2016 by Jeremy Brown

Copyright © 2015 by Jeremy Brown

All rights reserved.

Cover design by Michael Nagin

Printed in the United States of America

ISBN 978-0-9983933-5-3 Paperback

978-0-9983933-4-6 eBook

10 9 8 7 6 5 4 3 2

Second Edition

For Ellen

ANACONDA CHOKE

CHAPTER 1

I KNOW HOW TO SAY GO FUCK YOURSELF IN PORTUGUESE.
What you do is have four guys in cutoff fatigue pants and dirty T-shirts stand outside the Arcoverde Brazilian Jiu Jitsu Academy in Rio de Janeiro and block the entrance when me and Marcela and Gil and Jairo pull up.

The four guys watch while we pull our training gear out of the van.

Jairo says, "Don't look at them."

Marcela takes my hand and gives me the look: Don't be stupid. She's used to giving it.

When we try to go through the door the men don't move.

Jairo barks something at them in Portuguese.

One of the guys opens a duffel bag hanging over his shoulder and shows us the military-grade assault rifle with the grenade launcher mounted under the barrel.

He looks at me and smiles and they stroll away.

Go fuck yourself.

———

My trainer Gil Hobbes and I had flown coach from Vegas to Rio. This was on a Wednesday. We landed at the Galeão International Airport and hunched over to look out the porthole at Banzai Eddie's private Warrior Inc. jet sitting at the APO. That was a go fuck yourself as well, but I already knew how an American said it.

We were in Brazil for the first international Warrior event, my third fight under Eddie's thumb and Jairo Arcoverde's professional mixed martial arts debut. I'd warned him Eddie was a snake. Jairo's response: "Snake tastes good, you cook it right."

The fights were a distant second on my list of reasons for going to Rio. I'd talked to Marcela nearly every day since she'd left Vegas but hadn't seen her or touched her cheek or smelled her hair.

Over half a year.

I scanned the crowd at the arrivals gate, looking for Jairo's shiny brown head among the colorful hats. At six foot four, he was easy to find. He grinned and leaned down to talk to someone. The people between us saw me coming and got out of the way.

There she was.

Marcela.

She shot the gap and ran toward me, her black hair trailing.

"Brace yourself," Gil said.

I set my feet. Marcela was five foot three and had to carry loose change to break 105 pounds; I'm a foot taller and walk around at 240. I took three steps back when she hit me full speed, jumped and wrapped her arms around my neck and legs around my waist, and locked her ankles. Like all the Arcoverdes she had a black belt in Brazilian jiu jitsu. I couldn't have peeled her off if I tried.

I did not try.

I squeezed and smelled and kissed her. She was warm.

"Hi, Woody."

"Hi."

"Welcome to Brazil."

"It's the best place I've ever been."

"You're still in the airport."

"Right."

She laughed and gave me a light smack, buried her face in my neck.

Gil and Jairo might have hugged, shaken hands, set something on fire, and danced around it. I couldn't say. At some point they got tired of waiting and wrapped their arms around us, a group hug that turned into an intervention.

Jairo plucked Marcela off. She dropped down and ran her hands over my face, the new scars and some of the old ones. I looked into her tan eyes, touched the tiny bump on the bridge of her nose.

She frowned. "What did you do, stick your head in a cannon and shoot it?"

"How else could I get my hair to look this good?"

She looked skeptical of my head in general.

As we walked she welded herself to my right side. If I'd worn baggier pants I could have put her in my pocket. We collected our luggage and made our way outside.

Gil stopped on the curb, closed his eyes and breathed it all in. He'd moved to Rio when he was eighteen, stayed for nine years while he studied under Jairo's father Antonio Arcoverde and earned his own black belt. He was almost forty now.

"How does it feel?" Jairo asked.

Gil smiled. "Man, it feels exactly the same. Nothing's changed."

Jairo and Marcela shared a look.

If I had figured out what that look meant right away, I would have piled all of us onto a plane and flown it out myself. Screw the landing part—it still would have been safer.

CHAPTER 2

THE GALEÃO AIRPORT WAS ON AN ISLAND IN GUANABARA Bay. Jairo drove the Academia de Arcoverde van with Gil in the passenger seat and the windows down. Marcela and I took up half of the middle seat, her head against my shoulder while she named some of the birds flying over the water and sitting at the tops of trees. She said something in Portuguese to Jairo, who shrugged and switched lanes.

"I told him to go this way so you can see where the hospital is."

I shrugged too. It was a good idea.

Marcela said, "And I want to show you something else."

We rode south on a raised highway through the center of the city, above the flat roofs of one-story buildings, past windows of taller concrete buildings. There was some impressive graffiti on display. So far it wasn't much different than Vegas, just wetter.

Gil turned in his seat and pointed ahead, grinning. Green mountains humped over the horizon. All right, that was different—the mountains outside Vegas are brown.

Gil said to Jairo, "You're looking solid. You ready for Preston?"

Tim Preston was from the States, a big farm boy with a few Warrior fights under his belt. In addition to ground-shaking, world-class wrestling, he had an overhand right that demolition companies in Vegas rented when he wasn't fighting. It was cheaper than C-4 and did twice the damage.

Jairo snorted. "That guy, he's going to have a bad time in Brazil, man."

Jairo was thirty-one, two years older than me. I had almost thirty professional fights under my belt, couldn't imagine starting out at his age. But he'd been grappling since birth, as comfortable with the mats and tournament lights as he was with blinking.

I'd sparred with him leading up to my first Warrior fight, getting ready for Junior Burbank. We'd also tussled for a while in an illegal fighting pit, something I'd been doing since I got chucked into an empty swimming pool as a kid and had to scrap my way out. Jairo more than held his own.

Now he said, "I have concern for Woody though."

He looked at me in the rearview. I waited for a wink, but he was serious.

I was going against a tall, lean Brazilian jiu jitsu specialist named Rafa de Jaguaribe. He went by the nickname "Aviso," because he warned his opponents which submission he was going to do, counted down, and did exactly that.

He was undefeated, ten–zero, nine of them won by armbar. Of those nine arms, he'd broken seven. You could hear him in some of the footage, slipping and leaning away from punches, telling the guy, "I going to break you arm. You ready?"

Snap.

Asshole.

Aviso was also the name of his clothing line and cologne. He modeled for both of them, serious black-and-white shots that highlighted cheekbones sharp enough to cut through the knuckles of anyone bold enough to take a shot. After we got word who I was fighting, Roth, the crazy Australian fighter at our gym, slapped magazine photos of Aviso all over the place and ordered a jug of the cologne. Doused my headgear and gloves with the stuff, which, according to the bottle, smelled of sandalwood and confidence.

It was intoxicating.

For the next few weeks Roth walked around with the best-smelling black eyes in history.

In the van Gil said, "Why the concern?"

"Aviso is tough, man. He's slick, hard to hit and grab."

"You fought him?" I asked.

"No, just what I've seen and heard."

"We heard he doesn't like to get hit."

"Well, he has the pretty face," Jairo said. "He don't want to mess it up."

I smiled at the mirror. "Aviso's going to have a bad time in Brazil too."

"Shut up about your work and fighting," Marcela told us. She tugged my arm. "Look, that's the Feira de São Cristóvão."

It was a huge open-air arena shaped like a Pringle chip.

"We can go there for dinner and dancing," she said.

Now I was concerned.

———

We drove south and the dense city thinned out. Lush green filled the spaces between the buildings. I wondered if I'd ever seen so much of it in one place before. Marcela bounced.

I tilted my forehead to hers. "What?"

"It's coming up, what I want to show you."

We came out of a curve into a straight shot and she pulled me to the passenger window.

"There, look."

Maybe a half mile to the right, past a bunch of trees, a narrow green hill rose above the landscape. On top was a huge statue of a guy spreading his arms, like he was taking it all in.

"Neat," I said.

"Neat?"

"Who is it, some soccer player?"

Jairo and Gil kept quiet, but if they'd eavesdropped any harder the NSA would have hired them.

Marcela said, "Woody, that's Christ the Redeemer. It's Jesus."

She crossed herself and kissed the golden cross hanging around her neck.

"Oh yeah, I see it now. How did they get him up there?"

"That doesn't matter, just look at him."

I stared until my neck hurt from cranking around, hoped it was long enough to make up for whatever I'd said wrong. When I sat back Marcela had her arms crossed and was looking out the far window.

Redeemer my ass.

CHAPTER 3

WE HIT THE COASTLINE AND CUT WEST, DROVE along the waterfront with mountains and jungle on the right. I was starting to get what Gil and Marcela had run on and on about leading up to the trip. The smell of the ocean mixed with damp earth and something light and fruity. My lungs weren't used to the heavy air, but they seemed to like it.

Compared to the Vegas landscape, some of the trees and plants looked like alien invaders. It was a whole new color palette, no buzzing neon or strobing billboards or puke stains.

"This is paradise," I said.

Marcela punched me in the ribs. "What have I been telling you?"

I pulled her close. She put me in a brief wrist lock, then held my hand in both of hers like two birds carrying a buffalo between them. Her hands were strong, pulling and spreading mine while she examined the kettlebell calluses, busted knuckles, tooth and glass scars.

Look close enough, you get the whole story.

I told myself I wasn't nervous about how closely the rest of the Arcoverde clan would look.

The year before, Jairo and his brothers Edson and Javier had come to Vegas to train at Gil's gym. That was when I sparred with Jairo. Marcela had tagged along. We ignored each other at first, because I'm an idiot and she had good taste. Once we got past that, we fell fast.

Then I kind of got her kidnapped by a psychopath named Kendall Percy.

Banzai Eddie Takanori, President of Warrior Inc., had been working hard to keep the Yakuza out of Vegas MMA. A corrupt organization called Shinto wanted to shove a small promotion into the scene so it could spread. Shinto was run by the Dojin-gumi, a family of Yakuza assassins. The head of the family was a scumbag named Omori.

It was looking hopeless for Eddie when an ex-operator in the British Special Air Service named Burch let him know about Vanessa Brandenberg. She was the daughter of Vegas real estate kingpin Tim Brandenberg, who had lost his daughter to Omori in a card game. Vanessa's mother hired Burch to get her back, and Burch laid it out for Eddie:

He told him to set up a meet with Omori about getting into Vegas. While that went down Burch would kick doors in and find Vanessa, take her away from Omori. Omori would lose face and the Shinto promotion.

Worked like a charm. There was even a bonus—Omori committed seppuku, ritual suicide that ends in decapitation. His eldest son, a monster named Shuko, swung the blade.

The Yakuza came to Eddie for reimbursement, a little something for their trouble. He couldn't pay it, or wouldn't, so instead he gave them a fight.

And along with it, a fighter.

First Eddie found a buffer to wedge between himself and the Yakuza: Kendall Percy, a Vegas bookie who liked a dose of juice with his wagers. Kendall took on Eddie's debt to the Yakuza with the promise he'd get his own payday, and Eddie found the closest thing he could to a fixed fight: heavyweight poster boy and destined champ Junior Burbank against the one guy who beat him years back, some scrub still floundering on gas money fight promotions.

Me.

Eddie snagged me and Gil in the net and hauled us into the hype. A short-notice fight against a top-three contender. Eddie knows how to talk to fighters, warriors who believe they can beat any man set before them. Check out the lumps of scar tissue around my eyes for proof—I actually thought I could take Burbank on.

Everybody else was too busy laughing, ready to get paid and laid.

But Kendall wanted more.

He thought it was smart to mess with my head before the fight, make sure I was exhausted, stressed, panicked, distracted. Easier to beat. So he kidnapped Marcela the night before the fight and told me if I didn't win by knockout, she was dead.

I'm not the sit-around-and-worry type.

More like the run-around-hunting-with-a-chainsaw type.

Jairo and I spent the day trying to find Marcela. That's how we ended up forced to fight each other to the death in a cesspool murder pit run by a gang lord named Tezo. Tezo tried to shoot and kill Jairo but hit him in the shoulder, which just made him angry. When we got out I spent a few minutes making Tezo's head look like a Picasso. Found out Kendall told Tezo and the Yakuza to bet everything on Burbank—everybody knew I'd be lucky to survive the first round.

And Kendall was keeping Marcela no matter what.

It was time for Burbank. We hadn't found Marcela, and Kendall was getting his wish. He sent me into the cage flailing and desperate. Funny thing happens when you back something savage into a corner: it kicks Burbank in the face and knocks him out cold.

I knew the only way to keep Marcela alive was to make her a bargaining chip, Kendall's life preserver. When I crushed Burbank, the Yakuza wanted Kendall's soul. Kendall wanted to trade Marcela for Eddie, give them the man they wanted in the first place. I dragged Eddie to a doomsday compound in the Nevada desert built by a madman named Chops.

Kendall and his boys brought Marcela.

Burnt chunks of Kendall are still out there somewhere, spread across the sand by a landmine he ran over after Marcela broke the majority of his important bones.

That's what the Arcoverdes knew. Riding up into the mountains outside of Rio, I wondered if there was a traditional Brazilian welcome for someone who'd got members of the family kidnapped and shot.

Fed to piranhas?

I was just glad they didn't know what had happened after Marcela and the Arcoverde boys flew home.

After Kendall, Eddie owed me. I'd saved his life. He made up for it by showing up seven weeks later with Burch, the ex-SAS soldier, both of them on the run and demanding my help in return for a three-fight contract. For me, that contract was a winning Lotto ticket.

But now the Yakuza didn't just want a piece of the Vegas action. They wanted Warrior. They slipped one of their fighters in under the radar—a catch wrestling terminator named Zombi—and Eddie wanted me to meet him in the cage and send him back to Japan with tail tucked.

That, or he was sacrificing me to the Yakuza gods.

And the Dojin-gumi, the sons of Omori, had gone rogue. They didn't give a shit about the Yakuza mission statement and five-year plan. They wanted blood. I was in Eddie's limo when one of the sons came through the moonroof and tried to strangle him. I held the guy down so Burch could subdue him. Burch stabbed him to death.

So there I was, accessory to murder. Eddie had me via extortion and blackmail. He deserved a Boss of the Year mug, right across the temple. I stayed in Eddie's mansion with him and Burch and Vanessa Brandenberg. Tried to train for Zombi while the Dojin-gumi tried to kill all of us.

Shuko the demon came closest. Back when the Dojin-gumi had Vanessa, Shuko started a tattoo on her back that marked her as his property. Most people like to keep their property nice. Shuko liked to torture his, mangle it for his depraved pleasure until it died, and move on to the next piece.

He snatched Eddie, Burch, and Vanessa into the tunnels below the fight arena while I went to war for three rounds with Zombi, who had me beat until I smashed both our faces into the canvas as hard as I could. My face was used to that kind of thing, his wasn't.

I got my hand raised and followed Shuko down.

Just like he wanted.

What he didn't know: I wanted it too.

When I found them, Eddie, Burch, and Vanessa were all prepped for a marathon torture session. I got them out, left Shuko unconscious and locked in an airtight freezer.

Whatever happened after that, blame science.

Eddie signed the three-fight contract and told me my next match would be in Brazil. When I called Marcela to tell her, she thought I was crying with happiness.

Partially.

After Kendall and Shuko, I knew I didn't deserve her.

It washed over me when we pulled into the Arcoverde estate. The entire family waited in the circular driveway, close to fifty people ranging from infant to elder, everybody wearing white and smiling and waving.

I was so busy plastering the smile on my face and waving back, pretending to be worthy, I didn't notice theirs were fake too.

I didn't realize they were a tribe under siege.

CHAPTER 4

W E GOT OUT OF THE VAN AND I STOOD THERE wanting something in my hands while everybody flooded toward Gil, welcoming him back. Marcela and Jairo dove in too. When it broke up she walked back with her arm around a lean man as tall as my shoulder. He had cropped gray hair and lines on his bronze face like a map of frowning.

Marcela said, "Woody, this is my uncle Antonio, Jairo's father."

The patriarch. The man responsible for this clan of warriors. I shook his hand. It was dry and might have been the prototype for car-crushing machines.

"It's an honor, Mr. Arcoverde."

He turned to the woman standing next to him. "My wife, Cecilia."

"Mrs. Arcoverde."

She nodded and attached herself to Gil, leaving me with Antonio and Marcela.

He said, "You love Marcela?"

I looked to her for help. She was too busy hiding amusement.

"Yes."

"You're going to marry her."

He had a thick Portuguese accent. Maybe I'd heard it wrong.

"I'm going where?"

"Today, in the courtyard. We have the priest and lots of food. You will marry and you will dance and eat."

Jairo had the van keys. I'd have to go through a few women and children to get to him, but they looked durable.

Antonio said, "You know I'm busting your balls."

His charade broke and the frown lines flowed into a smile so big it jumped onto my face. He clapped me on the shoulder, wrapped his arms around mine and squeezed. I outweighed him by fifty pounds and had the sense he could toss me over the roof.

Marcela laughed. "Look at you, more nervous than going into a fight. Don't be scared, Woody. I know you love me."

"We know it too," Antonio said, one arm around my back. "Now come with me. We really do have the food ready in the courtyard."

"No priest?"

"You want one?"

"No," Marcela said. She took my free arm and put it around her shoulders. "I'll say when we need the priest."

Antonio was wise enough to keep quiet.

I followed his lead.

Sometimes the paths of wisdom and confusion lead to the same place.

———

We walked on a flagstone path toward a wide, single-story house with teak floors and trim and white walls. The double front doors led into a sitting room full of long, well-used couches facing each other and piled with pillows. A few children's toys were in the center.

"My home," Antonio said.

Two of the walls had built-in teak shelves, each one filled with books, framed photos, and small chests. Most of the books bristled with yellowed scraps of paper stuck between the pages.

The sitting room opened into a large, airy kitchen with modern surfaces and appliances. Past that a hallway continued into the southern wing of the house.

Marcela and Antonio walked me across the room to a wall made of French doors with sheer white curtains held aside by pewter hooks. The doors led to a courtyard, about fifty yards square. Paths of river rock led left, right, and straight. The edges of the paths were lined with tall plants and bright flowers, everything growing together in a wall of foliage above the rich black soil.

Antonio pointed left. "That is where my sister Christina lives."

A similar house sat at a right angle to Antonio's. He pointed around the square to other houses, naming each resident. Those houses were smaller; two or three together took up the same space as his.

I asked Marcela, "Which one is yours?"

"I stay here, with Uncle Antonio and his family."

Marcela's parents weren't in her life, the same as me. Might have been one of the things we recognized in each other from the first moment, in addition to us being good-looking as long as I crouched behind her and kept my mouth shut.

She touched my face. "Are you hungry?"

I fell in love again. "Very."

They pulled me along the path leading to the center of the courtyard, a small field of soft green grass filled with tables and chairs and blankets. A huge stone grill sat at the corner of a concrete countertop that ran twenty feet along two sides of the field. The flat surface was piled with trays of fruit, vegetables, grilled meat, fresh bread, and desserts I didn't recognize but would greet as best friends.

Gil, Jairo, and the rest of the family followed us into the courtyard. Gil was laughing, wiping tears from his eyes and walking with Javier and Edson, Jairo's younger brothers. They'd been in Vegas for the thing with Kendall and had wanted to rampage through the city looking for Marcela, tipping over slot machines and biting the MGM lions. Jairo made them stay at Gil's gym while we went out. They didn't appreciate it.

Now they hugged me and slapped my shoulders.

Javier said, "Gil is telling us he made you fix the holes we put in his walls."

"All seven," I said.

"Hey, sorry about that, man. But we were upset, you know?"

"Don't worry about it. The fist-sized ones were easy." I rubbed Edson's forehead. "But this makes one helluva hole."

Edson nodded; not the first time he'd heard it. They walked away.

Gil held a hand out to the food, people, land. "Not bad, huh?"

"Was it like this when you were here before?"

"Pretty much."

"It's like a resort. Or the Bellagio."

"Better," Gil said. "This is family."

———

Marcela stuck a plate in my hands and piled it with grilled beef and vegetables.

"What about those chocolate things there?" I said.

"You have a fight this Saturday?"

"Maybe."

"After. But not those, they will be gone because they are so delicious. I will make more for you."

"You cook?"

"I do everything." She put a banana on top of the vegetables. "Dessert."

We mingled. I tried not to talk with my mouth full or spit on anyone—the beef had some kind of spiced glaze and I didn't want to waste a drop of it. The vegetables tasted like meat, the finest compliment they could hope for.

We worked our way to Antonio, sitting in a straight-backed wooden chair, feet spread with his hands on his knees. Gil sat next to him, talking about his wife Angie back in Vegas, the gym, his jiu jitsu students.

Marcela and I pulled over chairs to make a circle. She saw me holding an empty plate and the banana, pushed some beef from her plate onto mine.

"Get that priest," I said.

Antonio touched my knee. "Tell me about Eddie Takanori. I'm not sure we should be in business with him, as a family. Jairo wants to fight, show the world what our name means, but I don't trust any of these Warrior people."

I'd never heard "warrior" used as an insult. "Eddie is a scumbag. He's sneaky, self-serving, and he'd walk over all of us to keep his shoes from getting dirty."

Antonio made a sour face.

"But he keeps his word," I said. "He says something, he means it. Especially if he says he's going to screw you over."

Antonio nodded. "We see how this fight goes. If he treats us with disrespect, we are done with him."

Thinking Eddie would care . . . I wasn't sure if it was ignorance or confidence, but I admired it. I took a bite of the banana.

"Holy shit, what is this?"

Marcela smacked my arm. "Woody!"

"A banana," Antonio said.

"Yeah, but is it some special kind?" I ate the rest in two bites while Antonio looked to Gil for an explanation.

"Woody is a moron," Gil said.

Antonio patted my knee. "You are fighting Aviso."

I nodded and scanned the area for more bananas.

"You know he's very dangerous."

"Mm."

Antonio said, "You have a way to beat him?"

"Punch him in the face until he goes to sleep or the ref saves him."

Antonio said to Gil, "He seems pretty smart to me."

———

Marcela and I walked the stone paths in the courtyard, followed one between two of the houses. We crossed a wooden bridge over a small pond with a few lazy orange and white fish floating in it and she led me to a bench with a view down the mountain. The deep green rolled over ridges and valleys until the city cut it off.

We sat there as close to each other as we could get and kept busy without talking for not nearly long enough.

She broke away and said, "I don't believe you're here."

"I wanted to get out and push the plane, make it go faster."

"You're only here until Sunday."

"Eddie and his crew are leaving late Saturday, right after the fights. Gil and I want to stay a little longer."

"Why not a lot longer?"

"Why don't you come with me?"

"I can't."

"It's safe there, I promise. No more craziness like last time."

"That's not why," she said.

"Eddie's been talking to Gil. I win this fight, I might be slotted for the number-one contender shot. I win that, I'm fighting for the title."

"Sounds like you'll be very busy."

"No, I'm saying I'll be able to buy us a house. Something outside the city if you want, a place like this."

Her eyebrow peaked. "In the desert?"

"Well, not exactly like this. But it would be ours."

"Ours. You want me to come live with you?"

"Yes."

"And not in your apartment?"

"When I packed for this trip, I moved out."

She leaned back. "Where are you going to live? And sleep?"

"The gym. I spend all my time there anyway. Just makes sense."

"I get to stay with Gil and you and all the other fools?"

"Other fools?"

"You know you are."

"Not in the gym."

"I can't."

"If I can't get a house in time I'll find another place."

"Woody, you're not listening. I can't."

"Why not?"

Footsteps on the bridge made us turn. Jairo stood there with a gym bag over his shoulder. "We going to the academy to train a little. Come on, you can see it."

"I'm too full," I said.

"Yes, the banana. I heard. Come on."

He walked away.

Marcela stood and pulled me up.

"Why not?" I said.

She touched my face. "We shouldn't keep them waiting. Let's run to the van, get the food moving."

She took off over the bridge and disappeared along the path. Away from me.

———

I rode in the backseat with Marcela again, Jairo driving and Gil next to him. We went down the mountain and retraced our path from the airport until we cut north before the big patch of trees and nature with my pal the Redeemer in it.

I held Marcela's hand and nodded at the things she pointed out. What I wanted to do was ask her why this wasn't playing out the way it had thousands of times in my head: I ask her to come home with me, she jumps on me and climbs all over and can't wait to start packing. I remind her we don't even have a house yet, she tells me to shut up and stop ruining it.

Ideal.

Instead I sat there and didn't bring it up because of Jairo and Gil, and Marcela worked her ass off trying to distract me from my heavyweight pout. We crossed a bridge and she pointed left. "Down that road is the HSBC Arena, where you're fighting on Saturday."

"Mm."

"We can drive past it on the way home."

"Home?"

"Yes."

"You mean where I'm staying."

"Yes."

"So your home, not ours."

"Okay."

Any other day, that much brattiness would have earned me a smack, maybe a loose choke. All deserved. She just looked out the window with her shoulders slumped.

We broke into the western outskirts of Rio. Jairo sped along narrow roads, the patchwork buildings and graffiti-tagged security walls almost on top of us. When he and I had driven through some of the worst parts of Vegas, he'd been unimpressed. I saw why.

We shot through an intersection. On the corner outside my window I caught a glimpse of red candles arranged in a circle, along with bottles of rum, a few damp cigars, and what might have been a knife.

At the end of the next block I saw another arrangement through the windshield on the left, this one with a meat cleaver stuck in what looked like a dead chicken. I tried to get a better look as we passed, and it still looked like a dead chicken.

"Was that a dead chicken?"

"It was nothing," Marcela said, her tone letting everyone know they'd better agree. It brought me back to the tension between us, momentarily forgotten in the wake of what seemed like a street-side sacrifice. I would not be distracted from my righteous silent treatment again.

She pointed at a tiny blue and white storefront with black iron bars on the windows. "We always used to stop there for lemon drinks, after training. Uncle Antonio said the citrus was good for the blood."

For a moment I pictured her as a little girl, tired from the workout but excited for the treat—

I pushed it away.

I would not be distracted.

We pulled up in front of the Arcoverde Academy and I saw the four guys standing in front of the door, and I got distracted almost to death for the next few days.

CHAPTER 5

THE FOUR MEN LOOKED ROUGH. DARK SKIN STRETCHED tight over sharp bones, hair buzzed or shaved down to the scalp. That kind of toughness can be faked with decoration, but the flat shark eyes had to be earned.

Jairo used his driver's-door buttons to put the windows all the way up.

All seven eyes—one guy sported a Brazilian flag patch over his right eye—drilled into the van. The men carried faded and stained duffel bags made of heavy green canvas designed for combat. My first guess was some kind of convict rehabilitation program. Get out of prison and learn self-control through jiu jitsu. If that was the case, they'd just started. Not one cauliflower ear in the bunch.

Behind them, the front of the two-story academy building was a faded white brick with white steel bars over the windows. Academia de Arcoverde was painted in green letters above a black and white striped awning. The glass door had steel mesh bolted over it, color posters of fighters and events taped to the inside. The whole place was a little more war-zone chic than I'd expected.

I said, "These guys train here?"

"No," Jairo said.

The van was still running, still in drive.

I asked him, "Are we getting out?"

"Wait."

The guy with the eye patch waved, tried to smile. His face wasn't ready for it.

Gil said, "Who are these knuckleheads?"

"Trouble," Jairo said.

He, Gil, and I stared back. I felt Marcela next to me, realized she was tight as a bowstring. She looked straight ahead, no expression, her jaw muscles working.

"You know these guys?"

Five seconds later: "I've seen them before."

"They bothering you?"

"They're nothing."

I checked them again. They hadn't moved.

"Why are they all staring at you?"

"It's what they've been told to do."

"Told?" I said. "By who?"

Eye Patch stepped forward and rapped on my window. "Hey, welcome. Come out and say hello."

His eye was six inches away from mine. It was streaked with yellow and brown clouds. He had a thin black mustache under a crooked nose.

He said, "You American? I need to practice my English. Hi, how are you today? I like soda pop."

"Move back," I said.

"What? I can't hear you through the glass. Maybe I break it so we can talk like regular people. How would that be?"

Gil said, "Jairo, do we need to leave?"

"Probably."

He shut the van off and got out. Eye Patch lost the fake smile and stepped back with his men. I followed Marcela out the driver's side and moved to the back bumper. If these boys came forward again, I'd be between them and her.

Jairo opened the rear doors and handed gear bags out to Gil, held one in front of me.

"I want my hands free," I said.

Marcela took the bag and walked toward the academy. I moved a step ahead of her on the right.

Eye Patch stayed between us and the door.

"Get out of the way," Marcela said.

"I'm here to tell you something."

"I don't care."

Jairo stood on her left. Past him Gil held one of the bags by the strap, like a flail, his breathing deep and even.

Eye Patch scanned us, a pro at risk assessment. His duffel bag was unzipped at his side. He held it open and showed us the combination assault rifle and grenade launcher inside. Six baseball-sized hand grenades were nestled beside it.

"Okay?" he said.

The other three duffels looked heavier than his.

"Easy," Gil said. "Easy."

Eye Patch stared at Marcela. "You want the message or not?"

"Yes."

"Say please."

She took a deep breath. I wanted to crush Eye Patch on his blind side, knock him stiff, and use him like a poleax on the other three.

"Yes please."

"Seu Exu envia o seu amor."

He smiled and walked away. The rest followed, nobody bothering to look back.

I seared all of their faces, silhouettes, movement patterns into memory. "What did he say to you?"

Marcela closed her eyes for a moment, tugged the door open and went into the academy.

I asked Jairo, "What did he say?"

The muscles in Jairo's head rippled. "Your Exu sends his love."

———

The inside of Academia de Arcoverde was a temple. The front room, with its white walls and low ceiling with exposed girders and wiring, took up the entire width of the building. A dozen fans hung between the girders, churning the thick air. The floor was wall-to-wall green mats with a three-foot white border around the perimeter.

Marcela stayed on the white as she cut left inside the door, then right at the corner toward the back of the building.

I followed.

Twenty kids—boys and girls—in white Arcoverde BJJ gis rolled on the green mats, their breathing broken by the occasional grunt when somebody found the right angle on an armlock. The instructor, who wore the dark green gi of a family member, crawled among them on his hands and knees, moving elbows and tilting heads by fractions to get the right results.

He smiled and nodded as we passed but did not take his attention from the students. We turned right again at the back wall and I had to duck left through a wide doorway to keep up with Marcela. Gil and Jairo came in behind me. We were in a small square room with doors on all sides—women's dressing area on the left, men's on the right with an opening next to it showing stairs leading up to the top floor. There was a tiny office with a closed door on the back wall. The office had a window that looked out through the opening behind me to the mats.

Marcela went toward the women's door.

"Wait," I said.

She turned.

"What just happened?"

"Family business," Jairo said. He tugged my arm toward the men's door.

"Those guys are family?"

Jairo scowled. "Those dogs have no family. They are garbage."

I asked Marcela, "Who is Exu?"

She didn't look at me. "Woody, just focus on your fight."

"The fight happens whether I focus on it or not."

"Marcela," Gil said. "You know he won't let it go."

"Tell him to."

"I'm actually with Woody on this. You say it's family business, we like to think we're family. What's going on?"

Jairo shook his head. "There is family, and there is blood. This is blood."

I held my wrists out to him. "How much you need?"

Jairo looked at Marcela. A tear slipped from her eye and fell down her cheek. She slapped it away and nodded.

Jairo pulled in a deep breath and started up the stairway. "Come on. I'll show you."

———

The stairs had one switchback before we emerged on the second floor into the Arcoverde version of an MMA gym: two Thai bags hanging along the back wall and three sections of gray fence angled around a stained canvas. The rest of the space was covered in green mats.

Check out a fighter's gym, you'll see how he thinks he's going to win.

Jairo took us to the corner and opened a white door made of wooden planks, led the way up a tight set of shallow steps. Marcela walked in front of me with her head down. Before I started up I glanced back at Gil to see if he had any clue—he shrugged and looked as confused as I felt.

We came out onto the roof, a rectangle of patched gray tar-paper still soft from the afternoon sun. A disturbing number of electrical wires converged from all angles and formed a dangerous nest on a wooden post at the opposite corner.

The academy was on top of a small rise in the urban sprawl west of downtown Rio. Roofs fell away on each side as the land dipped. To the east, the coastline high-rises were starting to light up.

Jairo asked Marcela, "You want to tell them?"

She shook her head. I put my arm around her and she stepped away, almost to the edge of the roof.

Jairo said, "You know what a favela is?"

"No," I said.

"Yes," Gil said.

I gave him a look—it didn't matter what he knew.

"It's a slum," Marcela said. "A hell."

Jairo waited, making sure she was done. He pointed west at a series of rolling hills. The slopes were clustered with small buildings of every shape and color. From where I stood it looked like they were stacked on top of each other, overlapping into one continuous growth.

"Favela Buraco Quente. And the favelas are more than slums. They are cities within the city. The people inside have nothing but each other. No money, nothing."

"The drug lords who protect them have plenty of money," Marcela said, her back still to us.

Jairo turned. "I thought you weren't talking."

"I won't, you tell them the truth."

Jairo shook his head and pointed south. "Favela Coreia."

The large, dome-shaped hill might have been green once—now it looked like a tumor of crumbling concrete and warped sheet metal bulging out of the landscape.

Southwest, a distant hillside with buildings painted in pastels: "Favela Sumare. Any way you look, you find one."

He pointed southeast, the direction Marcela faced, and let his arm drop like it had grown too heavy. "Favela Axila da Serpente. You can't see it, but it's there. On the far side of the mountain."

Gil frowned, his lips working through the translation. "Armpit of the snake?"

Jairo nodded. "One of the worst."

"Not one of," Marcela said.

Jairo said, "It's run by a drug lord named Carrasco. The Hangman."

I already wanted to get my hands on him. "He hangs people?"

"No," Marcela turned toward us. I expected to see more

tears, but her face was dry and hard. "He was hung. And shot, and stabbed."

"And set on fire," Jairo said, holding a finger up. "At least one time."

Marcela said, "But it was after the hanging, when he came back from the dead, that he got the name Carrasco. Because he believes he came back as Exu, the spirit of Quimbanda."

I put my hands out. "Wait a minute."

She said, "You saw the rings of red candles and cigars and rum at the intersections? The knives? Those were crossroad offerings to the spirits of Quimbanda, requests for Exu to bring harm to someone. Quimbanda is evil. It is black magic. And Carrasco thinks he is the Lord of Quimbanda. His followers believe him, like those dogs on the street, the ones who delivered the message. They kill and steal and burn, all in his name."

I said, "Their message was from him. Your Exu sends his love."

Her knuckles popped as she rolled her hands into fists. "He thinks I am his queen."

———

I had questions.

What the hell was Quimbanda?

Who or what was Exu?

Carrasco?

Most important of all: Was there anyone I could elbow in the neck to make it all better for Marcela?

I didn't get a chance to ask any of them. Jairo's brother Javier stuck his fat head out of the roof access and yelled at us for almost collapsing the ceiling instead of getting ready for Saturday. He waved us inside. Jairo and Gil followed him down.

I touched Marcela's arm at the top of the stairs. "Stay up here and talk to me."

"There's nothing you can do."

"I disagree."

"What, you're going to do what you did in Vegas, take Jairo and go around kicking everyone, shaking your finger in their face and talking tough?"

"Mostly the kicking."

"No, Woody. Not here. Here, you turn the wrong corner and a minute later you are dead, covered in flies. I don't want your help."

"Have you told the police?"

She palmed her forehead. "Of course! So simple! No, no police. Not for Carrasco. Not for a favela. There are some good police, but most would take the money Carrasco would pay them to go away. And they would not go into the Axila da Serpente without an army. You're going to leave this alone. Promise me. I don't want Carrasco to know about you."

"Uh, everybody knows about me."

She fought the smile. "So stupid. If he finds out about you, about how I love you, he will hurt you."

"He'll try."

She pressed her hand against my cheek. "You don't know how bad he is. Just stay here, with me. Stay safe. Do your fight and go home."

"Then what?"

Her hand fell away. "I start missing you again."

CHAPTER 6

WHEN I DROPPED FROM THE NARROW STAIRWAY ONTO the second floor, Marcela was gone.

Jairo rolled through warm-up drills with Javier and Edson, the three of them just starting to sweat. Gil stood along the edge of the mat with Antonio, the patriarch, who had his hands clasped behind his back and a forward-leaning posture, like he was ready to dive in. They pointed at Jairo's technique and grunted at each other, nodding.

I found a tiny bathroom and changed into my training gear, hoping no one paid any attention to me at all. I had some issues to discuss with the Thai bags and didn't want any bullshit critiquing or pressure. My plan was to hit the leather hard and loud enough to send Carrasco a message in Morse code. Maybe cause a landslide that brought the whole Armpit down around him, take care of the problem for good.

When I opened the door, Antonio Arcoverde, master of Brazilian jiu jitsu was there. The laughing, smiling grandfather from the picnic was not.

"Come," he said. "You're going to show me everything Gil has taught you."

Shit.

———

I was on my back, knees bent. The mat was warm under the soles of my feet. Javier knelt beyond them, relaxed.

Jairo was in the same position as me a few yards to my left, with Edson squatting nearby.

Antonio paced between us, hands clasped. "I will use English for Woody. But if I can't explain what I am meaning, someone tell him."

Gil stood to my right and gnawed a thumbnail, eyes flicking between me and Antonio. He took a break from the nail to hold the thumb up for me. "Do well, Woody."

Back to the nail.

All the training Gil had taken me through, all the fights we'd prepped and executed, I'd never seen him nervous.

"Full guard, please," Antonio said.

Javier crawled forward. I wrapped my legs around his sides, crossed my ankles at the small of his back and locked him in. Muscle memory took over and I grabbed both of his wrists to make sure he couldn't pound my face into the floor.

Antonio's bare feet made no sound as he padded all the way around us. He tugged on my ankles, prodded my right elbow with his foot, reached down and nudged my head.

He clucked his tongue. "Why so much tension?"

"I go loose, he'll get out."

"Yes, here." Antonio touched my knee, my head. "Not here.

Relax your throat. Let your neck open."

I puffed my cheeks out. Behind Antonio, Gil closed his eyes.

"What are you doing?" Antonio said.

"I'm not sure."

"Like this," Javier said. He wafted a hand toward his neck, which looked the same as it always had.

"Oh, right." I inhaled a few times to everyone's disappointment.

Antonio jabbed two fingers into my ribs. "Relax here. Sink into the floor."

"What if he punches me?"

"Then you go tense. Not before."

I tried to relax my ribcage. Physiology said: Really?

Antonio said, "Now sweep to mount."

I hooked Javier's left leg with my right so he couldn't stick it out, wrapped his left arm with mine and bridged him up as I rolled right. He went with it, landed on his back with me on top, my knees wedged against his sides.

"Too much muscle," Antonio said.

I thought it was a compliment.

"You want to beat Aviso, yes?"

"Yes."

"Why?"

"Because if I win, Eddie will—"

"No no no. You want to win to prove you are better." He held a hand toward Gil. "To prove what your teacher has given you is better than what Aviso has been given."

I nodded.

Antonio said, "So far, you are proving you will lose."

———

An hour into it, I'd regressed five years in my jiu jitsu training and lost ten pounds of sweat. Marcela hadn't come back and my questions about Carrasco kept bumping into the techniques Antonio called out.

"Mount into arm triangle, from the side."

Techniques I didn't plan on using against Aviso.

"Arm triangle into side control."

Because most of the techniques I planned on using involved knees and elbows to Aviso's skull.

"Side control to Kesa Gatame."

And trying Antonio's commands against a guy with Aviso's skill in Brazilian jiu jitsu would get me strangled.

"Kimura from Kesa Gatame."

And embarrassed.

"Kesa Gatame to full mount."

I fumbled through with help from Javier, little twitches and cues that let me know important things like: This elbow, not that knee.

"Full mount to triangle."

When I was done flopping and yanking my way into it, Antonio stood over me with his hands clasped. He said to Gil, "I thought you taught him the Arcoverde way."

"I did," Gil said. "Well, the parts he needs to know."

Antonio raised an eyebrow.

Gil said, "We have the basics down. Everything else, we've kind of fine-tuned to fit Woody's style. His attributes."

Antonio studied me with no expression. I still had Javier in a loose triangle choke from the top, which felt rude.

Antonio said, "Attributes?"

"Striking," Gil said. "We use the principles of Arcoverde jiu jitsu to keep him out of too much trouble, mostly, and put him in the best position for his striking. Punches, kicks, knees, elbows. Headbutts, before those were illegal."

Antonio looked like he'd swallowed a bug.

Gil said, "We can show you what we've been drilling to get ready for Aviso. Lots of armbar defenses. Some are pretty slick, I think you'll like them."

Antonio sniffed. "Triangle to armbar."

———

When Antonio was done with the technique work—or just tired of my version of it—he moved on to Jairo and Edson to go over the plan against Preston on Saturday. They spoke Portuguese, so the only part I got was "Preston."

I knelt and sat back on my heels, dripping. Javier patted my shoulder on his way to towel off. Poor guy had my panic sweat all over him. Gil wandered close enough to whisper, "Sorry. I didn't know that was going to happen."

"You remember the first time we rolled? When I thought I knew what I was doing?"

"Yeah."

"You made me look like a baby. A fat, slow baby."

"Sounds about right."

"This was worse."

He dropped into a squat. "Don't let it get to you."

"I don't know shit."

"He can have that effect. Makes him a good teacher. A great one."

"Hey, the Wednesday before a fight? I don't want a teacher. I want a punching bag."

"I hear you," Gil said. "Everything else okay? You came down from the roof like you were walking to the cage already."

"I need to find Marcela."

Gil pulled a face.

"Don't start," I said.

"I started when Eddie offered this trip. Bad idea to see her before the fight. You're distracted."

"I'm fine. Well, I was, until I found out I don't know a damn thing about grappling."

"Pretty sure I've been telling you that for a while too."

I didn't laugh.

Gil handed me a water bottle. "You and I, we know what we're doing. We're ready for Aviso. You know it. And come Saturday, you try any of the shit I just saw, I'll jump in the cage and break your arm myself. You know that too."

"Is Marcela downstairs?"

"Last I saw. I don't want to ask, because this has nothing to do with Aviso, but are you two okay?"

I shrugged. Gil made his face again, and we both turned to the stairway. Loud voices were coming up, talking about lighting and acoustics. I saw two guys I didn't know before the blue fauxhawk rose into view, that face below it.

Banzai Eddie.

———

I'll give Eddie credit: he got off his phone long enough to bow to Antonio Arcoverde.

Then he was right back at it, pacing the mats in his thin blue socks and yelling at someone about the banners hanging roof-to-street on the outside of the Rio arena not being big enough.

"Too late now, unless you can make the building shorter. No? So why am I talking to you?"

He dropped the phone in a pocket and said something to the two guys he was with. They were thin and pale and winded from the stairs. Not fighters. They carried black bags with camera brand names embroidered in white on the sides. I recognized one of them—Kevin something—the Warrior producer who'd interviewed me before the Burbank fight. Tried to bait me into taking the fight personally, make a statement on tape about what I was going to do to Burbank in the cage.

And it worked. I said I was going to knock him the fuck out. Which I did.

But that didn't make Kevin less of a weasel. He waved.

I examined the scars on my knuckles. No new ones since the last one.

Eddie pointed the two guys into a corner, turned and held his arms out to me and Gil.

"My guys. You enjoying the culture? Shit, don't get up or anything, say hello. You want to be in the promo we're shooting?"

"Here?" Gil said.

"Yeah, doing a pre-fight bit on the Arcoverdes, the history, all that. I want some shots of you guys training with Antonio and Jairo, show Warrior's roots run deep here, really tap into our respect for the lineage." He sniffed and shook his head at the ceiling. "This lighting is trash. Hey Philip."

The one who wasn't Kevin turned.

Eddie twirled a finger at the room. "You guys can fix this, yeah?"

Philip nodded.

Gil said, "Antonio is okay with this?"

"It's his boy's debut—he gets it. Whether he likes it or not, shit, who can tell?"

"I can," Gil said. He went to Antonio. They leaned their heads together, the words just for them.

Eddie said to me, "Anybody recognize you yet?"

"I haven't been out."

"Don't. These fans, man, they see the guy who's fighting Aviso out on the street, they'll get a few shots in just to help him. Soften you up."

I nodded. After the mess with Burch and Vanessa and Shuko was over, Eddie and I had agreed not to mention it. But it was in the room with us.

"Hey, I got something for you, we get back to Vegas."

"Yeah," I said. "A number-one contender fight."

"Careful. You beat Aviso, we'll talk about that."

"I beat him, there's nothing to talk about. Because you already said it will happen."

Eddie waved that away. "Listen. What I have, it's win or lose. We're almost done with the WarriorDome."

"I thought that name was a joke."

"It's WarriorDome. Or WarriorPlex. I haven't decided."

"I know what a dome is. The hell is a plex?"

"It's short for complex," Eddie said.

"Huh. Like Napoleon."

He took a deep breath. "Anyway. It's not just for fighters. The gyms and equipment will be available to the public. We're gonna have classes. I want you to train there."

I waited for it to make sense.

"You train there for your fights," Eddie said. "People can watch, see how hard you work."

"And what our strategy is."

"Oh, the master plan of getting hit in the face and hitting the other guy in the face? Relax, I'm fucking with you. All the black box shit you and Gil do, keep it behind closed doors at Gil's place, whatever. Okay? Fair enough?"

"I just come there and train?"

"Yeah," Eddie said. "You and a bunch of other fighters. The fans get to shoot video, pictures, buy T-shirts for you to sign."

"It kinda sounds like a zoo."

"It's exactly like a zoo. But gorillas don't give autographs, do they? Oh, and you'll teach classes."

"What classes?"

"The shit you're good at. Some Muay Thai, kickboxing, sub-mission defense—not offense, for chrissake. How to bleed all over the place. Not really, don't fucking bleed during the classes. Seriously, don't."

"And these are fighters taking the classes. Guys who want to compete."

Eddie nodded. "Maybe, yeah."

"Maybe."

"Our marketing is targeting tourists and visiting celebrities, bachelorette parties. That kind of demographic."

"You want me to teach a bunch of soccer moms how to fight?"

He held up a finger, pulled the phone out and made a call. "Hey, start work on pulling the soccer mom demo into the Dome. The Plex, whatever. And look at hockey and football moms too— maybe we can showcase a lower concussion rate. Yeah. Later."

Without breaking stride he said to me, "You don't teach them how to fight. You show them how fun MMA is. Get a good sweat going, make them feel like they're real Warriors."

"With a capital W."

He grinned. "Always."

"I'll pass."

"You can't. Your contract stipulates mandatory participation in promotional activities, to be determined at the discretion of Warrior, Inc. That's a direct quote, by the way. And this is a promotional activity, as determined by me."

I thought about the guy on the street with the eye patch and grenade launcher. Carrasco's man. Eddie could give him lessons on how to say "Go fuck yourself" with a smile.

"And there's no swearing in the WarriorDome. Everybody will have a camera going, we don't want that shit all over the internet. So when you're in there teaching or training, keep it clean."

"Eddie, I even swear when I'm stretching."

"Not in the WarriorDome. Plex. Which one sounds better?"

"The one that doesn't include me."

"You'll be great. Hey, we'll get some shots of a bunch of cute party girls choking you out, put them up on the strip." He pulled the phone out again, had it pressed to his ear and said over his shoulder, "And good luck on Saturday. I talked to Aviso before I came here. He's ready."

CHAPTER 7

EDDIE AND HIS GUYS LEFT, SATISFIED THEY'D BE ABLE TO get what they needed when they came back to shoot the next day. Antonio and Gil were tinkering with the angle of Jairo's elbow when he applied a guillotine choke from the mount. Edson was calm, flat on his back and trying to breathe through clenched teeth while Jairo stretched his neck.

I stood behind them for a while before offering, "Why don't you release the choke and put that elbow in his eye socket?"

They all looked at me.

"Smash him a few times, maybe open his face up. He hates life and rolls over, now you have his back. Easier to choke him from there, you still want to."

Nobody said anything.

"Not you, Edson. On Saturday, against Preston."

Gil said, "He's getting the choke easily, Woody."

"So what's the problem?"

"We're refining it."

Antonio shook his head and turned back to Jairo. I took my

hint with me into the bathroom and dried off as much as possible, changed into jeans and a T-shirt and went downstairs.

Marcela was teaching a class of little kids how to fall and roll, tumble around and get back to their feet. She was flushed and laughing, crawling around to help them tuck their heads and slap the green mats. A few parents beamed from the white perimeter.

Marcela saw me. Her smile grew and she glanced at the clock: quarter to nine. She said, "Fifteen minutes," then growled when one of the kids jumped on her back and tried to get a tiny arm around her neck for a rear naked choke. She shook twice to get him off, tapped even though he was choking her shoulder.

I made my way around the edge while she got them lined up at one end and demonstrated how to shrimp across the floor. Five seconds in, they were kicking each other in the back and cackling. Marcela darted around straightening some of them out before they shrimped out of the room.

Give me this class over Antonio's any day.

I slipped through the front door to get a breeze on my face. It was fully dark outside, one orange streetlight buzzing over the narrow road. People walked on both sides, heads up and smiling, nobody in a hurry. Some waved to each other and stopped to chat, sharing food and drink.

I smelled something frying and heard tinny music playing somewhere close. A man hooted and whistled. In Vegas I wouldn't have noticed any of it, but the smells were sharper, the air heavier, the music faster, all of it alien and preventing me from relaxing.

And I needed to relax.

I put my earbuds in and listened to a series of phrases and mantras I'd added to my playlist before the flight to Rio. Male and female voices saying things I wanted to understand. The voices repeated them, as if they knew I needed extra guidance.

The words skimmed across the surface tension but couldn't sink in. I was wound up about Antonio, Eddie, Aviso, Carrasco. I couldn't see how to get Marcela to come home with me. Standing there staring at my reflection in the van's windows, I figured my best plan was to whip Aviso on Saturday night without using a scrap of Arcoverde jiu jitsu, wink at Antonio, stuff Marcela in my suitcase and tell Eddie I'd be at the WarriorDome on Monday to teach a class called Stubborn Victories: The Best Kind.

As for Carrasco and his followers, they could burn candles and eat all the sacrificed chicken they wanted—they weren't getting my queen. Not if she was in Vegas with me.

I just had to get her there.

I was bashing my head against the relaxation wall so hard I almost missed the movement behind me in the reflection.

Eye Patch stepped out from the shadows with his hand inside the duffel bag.

———

"I'm alone," Eye Patch said. He grinned but his hand stayed inside the bag.

"So what?"

"I just want you to know, I'm like you. Out here all alone, no trouble."

"Your English is better than before."

He nodded. "Thank you, I been working on it."

"You still have a machine gun in that bag?"

"What's a machine gun?"

"The English comes and goes, huh?"

"I guess so."

We stood a few yards apart, people walking past but not between. I said, "What do you want?"

"To see if you gonna try something."

"Like what?"

He shrugged. "Something stupid."

"Oh, that's guaranteed. But you'll only see the first part. The rest, they'll tell you about at the hospital."

That really made him smile. "You think so?"

"How'd you lose that eye?"

"Bullet."

"Shame. A little to the left, I'd be having a much better time right now. You take it for Carrasco?"

"Yes."

"He's worth getting shot in the face?"

His grin dropped. "You don't get it—he is the one who shot me. Right before, he told me I would not die. And he was right."

"You let him shoot you. In the head."

"It was what Exu wanted."

"Can I try?"

He smiled again. "Exu does not want that. Exu wants the woman."

"You say Exu, you mean Carrasco?"

"He goes by many names."

"Well, all of them will stay away from Marcela. Get it?"

"I told him about you."

"Good."

"He wants you to come see him."

"Not interested," I said.

Eye Patch shrugged, looked at the academy entrance. "Okay.

So one night, maybe now, I walk past the door and open it up."

He lifted his hand out of the bag, a fat grenade in his palm.

"I toss this inside and close the door, keep walking. Exu gets the woman on the other side of death, where you can't help her, huh?"

He waited for me to try something stupid.

I fought it, barely won.

He said, "I think you leave here and come to the bottom of the Axila da Serpente instead."

"Just me?"

"Bring whoever you want. It's a party, man."

He turned and walked away.

———

I knew the Axila da Serpente was east. If I hit salt water, I'd gone too far.

I also knew asking directions to the Armpit of the Snake would get me unwelcome attention, considering Eddie's warning about the citizens of Rio being ready and willing to start my fight against Aviso a few days early.

Taxis were all around, but I knew how that could go too. Years back I ran close security for a guy from Chicago who flew into Vegas a few times a year to sit across tables from people, work things out. The last time he made the trip, he skipped the security detail and told an airport cabbie to take him to a corner in the northeast part of the city.

Problem was, the cabbie knew who owned that corner, a Chechen named Lugo, and his cousin's boyfriend was at war with the guy. So he drove Mr. Chicago to the boyfriend's and they made a ransom call to Lugo, who said something along the lines of "Fuck Mr. Chicago and the two of you," and they composted Mr. Chicago in a pit in the desert.

No taxis for me.

That's why I pulled Jairo aside in the small room at the bottom of the stairs, enough racket on the green mats to cover our conversation. I told him about Eye Patch's threat and invitation. The veins on his head pulsed accordingly.

"I just need you to get me there," I said.

"Why, so we can never see or hear from you again? Man, it's not happening."

"Then keep the front door locked at all times. Put two armed guards on the sidewalk and one on the roof. And replace the windows with concrete blocks."

He shook his head. "They know better. Everybody knows better. You don't come after my family. You don't come after the Arcoverdes. Maybe you talk about it, but you don't do it."

"Okay, so Carrasco's men know better. That's why four of them stood between us and the academy door with bags of guns."

"You go see him, what are you going to say?"

"'Find another queen.' Marcela is coming to Vegas with me."

He took a step back. "She is? When?"

"Sunday, the day after the fight."

"She didn't say this to us."

"Well, she's still figuring things out."

"What things?"

"Just about all of them. She hasn't agreed to come with me yet."

He ran a huge hand over his scalp. "Of course not, why would she leave here? She has us, she has this." He flung the hand at the training room.

Marcela knelt in front of the kids, all of them sitting back on their little feet. She bowed and they mimicked, glancing at each other to make sure they were doing it right. When she dismissed them they sprang and rolled into chaos, tugging Marcela's gi for goodbye hugs and running to their parents.

"She doesn't have me," I said. "And I don't have her. And some lunatic who thinks he's a god is sending men with grenades to scare her into being with him. I need to see this guy, Jairo. I need to see if he's a real threat. Because if he is, and she won't come home with me . . . I don't know what I'll do."

Jairo watched Marcela, nodded. "Maybe I need to see him too. No, maybe he needs to see me. See why no one comes after the Arcoverdes."

"Hey, just take me there. That's all I need."

He put a finger under my chin. "I don't care what you need. Come or don't. Carrasco wants to talk about Marcela, he can talk to me."

"That's nice of you," she said.

Jairo and I turned. She stood there with her gi top folded over her arm, wearing a skin-tight rash guard soaked with sweat. She stepped into the room, took her time examining both of us.

"You are going to see him?"

"I am," I said.

"We are," Jairo said.

She wiped her face with the sleeve of her gi. She seemed to be working very hard to remain patient. "Why?"

I said, "One of his men was outside. Carrasco wants to talk."

"About me?"

"Yes."

"Don't worry about it," Jairo said. "I'm going, I'll straighten him out. You don't have to go to Vegas to be safe."

Marcela's eyes flashed onto me. "So this is what happens when you speak for me."

"No, I—"

"I let you two fools go to Carrasco, suddenly I'm married to him and have to live in a garbage pile. What's worse, that or Las Vegas? Tell me."

Jairo put a hand on her shoulder. "It's okay, we—"

She knocked the hand away and shoved me with both hands, knocking me back a few feet. "Nobody speaks for me. And nobody goes to see Carrasco. He wants to talk, let him talk to the spirits."

Jairo said, "We don't go and they put a grenade through the door, what then?"

Marcela frowned. "What grenade?"

I didn't want to tell her. I knew what her response would be.

She squared up with me. "Woody. Just like nobody speaks for me, nobody controls what comes into my ears."

"The guy with the eye patch. He said if I don't talk to Carrasco, maybe he tosses a grenade in here while you're teaching a class."

"Of the children?"

"That was the feeling I got."

From the moment we'd met, I'd had a talent for getting her frustrated, riled up. This was a level of fury I'd never seen, let alone caused. For one thing, she couldn't talk. She turned and pushed through the door to the women's locker room.

Jairo looked like he'd been startled awake. "Oh man. She's being silly."

"She is? I just asked you for a ride. Now look."

"Yes, now we all go. Maybe you won't be killed."

I shook my head. "Arcoverdes."

His chest puffed.

Five minutes later Marcela came out in jeans and a light jacket, her dark hair shiny from the shower. "Let's go."

———

The van ride to the Axila da Serpente was quiet. I sat in the back with Marcela, my hand on her knee. She wouldn't look at me, but she didn't break any of my fingers either.

Small victories.

We'd told Gil and Antonio we were going to check out the arena, maybe drive along the coast and walk on the beach.

Gil had thought about it. "I don't think you can get into any trouble doing that. But I'll probably look back on that statement and laugh, laugh, laugh."

The roads near the academy were crowded with people and lit by random streetlights and hundreds of personal ones, strings of colored lanterns and halogen work lights rigged on roof corners that made intersections seem like the ends of tunnels.

Rings of red candles burned at some of the crossroads. Nobody mentioned them, even when we started passing through intersections with offerings at all four corners.

At night the favelas were easy to spot. Dense lights on steep hillsides, fires as big as cars sending sparks into the sky. Maybe they were cars. Colored strobes whipped across crumbling, spray-painted facades, advertising places to go and get what you needed to forget where you were.

Or celebrate, if it was your kingdom.

I focused on a set of white and orange strobes that had no pattern, flashing sporadically halfway up a slope a hundred yards apart and getting closer with each burst. I realized it was gunfire and looked away. We bent south and dark mountains bit into the sky outside the passenger windows. The black shapes amid the city lights looked alien, as if they'd plopped down instead of risen.

Below the mountains along the road there was a giant billboard for Aviso's cologne. Or his shirts. Maybe both. It was mostly black and white, his big stubbled face with some female model, her head wedged under his square jaw. They both stared out over Rio, her eyes bright blue. His were golden. They seemed amused and followed the van as we passed.

We curled around the fringe of the range and Jairo pointed to a vein of clustered buildings creeping up the side of one of the smaller mountains. "Axila da Serpente."

It started at the base and spread up a steep, narrow valley all the way to the peak. The valley twisted between high ridges, almost doubling back on itself in a couple spots. All in all, it looked like a burning, glowing snake climbing up the mountain.

I dipped and torqued to get a better look. "All right. Things start to get hairy, we don't hang around. We pack up and head for the van. Sound good?"

Jairo shook his head. "If they going to make trouble, they will probably steal it."

"Or just blow it up," Marcela said.

"So where do we go?"

They spoke to each other in Portuguese. Marcela said, "We go in the direction that has the fewest men and figure out what to do once we get through them. Maybe run into the jungle."

"That's a terrible plan."

"Hey, this was your idea."

"No, it was my idea to go alone. I don't want you anywhere

near him."

"Woody, he knows where I am. He sent four men today, he could send a hundred tomorrow. If he wants to take me, he can. Any time."

Jairo growled something into the steering wheel.

I said, "Why hasn't he?"

She shrugged. "Ask him. But now they threaten our students? This, I will not tolerate."

"Just drop me off. I'll talk to him, call you when I need a ride."

"Would you do that for me? Drop me off and let me handle it, even though you would worry to death?"

"No way."

She put a hand on my cheek. "Then shut up."

———

The road along the base of the mountain was tight and dark. The slope loomed on our right, black and overgrown and concealing a million things. On the left, abandoned two-story buildings stared with empty windows, gasped with doorless entries.

Ahead, the entrance to the Axila da Serpente was the only light we could see.

We rolled past the one road leading up the slope. It was narrow with four Dumpsters lined across the entrance. They were piled above the rim with blocks of concrete bristling with rebar.

"I don't think we're driving up," Jairo said.

A small pickup truck shot out of an alley and stopped in front of us. Two men in the bed pointed assault rifles at us. They didn't bother to aim—at that range, they couldn't miss.

I looked out the back window. Another truck, lights off with dark lumps in the bed, rolled out to block that path.

A man stepped out of a doorway on our left and strolled to Jairo's window. He peeked in and scanned up with his one eye.

"Hey, you all came. Now it's really a party." He put his hand out. "Keys."

Jairo paused, shut the van off, and dropped the keys into Eye Patch's palm.

"Oh, no tip for the valet? Maybe I put a grenade under your seat, huh? I'm just kidding. Come with me."

I opened the door and asked Marcela, "You okay?"

"No. Let me close his other stupid eye, maybe then."

We followed Eye Patch single-file between two Dumpsters. The men in the trucks stayed there. If anyone else was around, I couldn't see them. The dirt road went up the slope a hundred yards at a twenty-degree angle before it cut left in a switchback. As soon as we started climbing, the rickety shacks and cracked concrete buildings teetered in from both sides. An odor of warm shit rolled down the mountain into our faces.

Fifty yards up the street Eye Patch took us left toward a two-story building that might have been painted white once. The windows and doorway were black.

"Hold up," I said.

He turned.

"What's in there?"

"Come on, you'll see."

"Just so you know, I usually react to surprises by kicking people in the face."

"Man, you're fun to be around." He stepped up to the dark entrance and pushed through the black wooden door. It swung open into the building, which was bright with red candles burning

on the floor along every wall. The light from it spilled into the
street and made Eye Patch a silhouette.

"Surprise."

———

The room was square and empty except for the candles and some
white chicken feathers on the concrete floor, which had a random
display of dark stains. They were not the same kind of stains that
were on the ceiling, streaks and clouds of black soot from the red
candles, whose flames sounded like an endless sigh. The windows
were covered with plywood and scraps of metal. The air was hot
and thick and heavy with incense.

A concrete stairway with no railing hugged the wall on the
left. Red candles drooped from each step. Eye Patch started up,
peering back at us with his left eye like he couldn't wait to get
our reactions. I went up first, Marcela behind me, with Jairo last.
His eyes were wide and jumpy.

"You all right?"

"I don't like this place," he said, crossing himself.

Marcela did the same.

I rolled my neck and flexed my hands.

The second floor was much larger, lined with even more red
candles. The side walls were made of particle board and sheet
metal. They angled into the space and funneled us toward a wide
opening where the wall in front of us had been knocked out so
the room could expand into the structure next door. The building
we'd first entered had a low, flat ceiling. The one connected with
planks and odd pieces of steel had a high, vaulted one, which gave
the impression of a small cathedral as we crossed the threshold.

The far wall had two closed doors on either side of a high-backed leather chair. They were both painted with a faded and flaking light blue color.

A withered man in large sunglasses sat in the chair. He wore white linen pants and a long-sleeved white shirt. His hair was thick and black, except for a large swath above his left ear where the hair was missing, exposing a scalp rippled with pearlescent scars and dents that squirmed in the flickering candlelight.

He sat with his hands folded in his lap. A lazy smile pulled the lower half of his face to the right.

Eye Patch flapped his hands at us until we stood in a line facing the chair. He knelt in front of the man's feet and spoke in Portuguese.

I asked Marcela, "That's Carrasco?"

She nodded.

I considered ending the whole drama by walking over and blowing on him—the guy was on the brink of collapsing into dust—but we seemed to be in some kind of temple, and I wasn't sure of the etiquette.

Carrasco nodded at Eye Patch, who stepped to the left of the chair and faced us.

Carrasco took a deep, ragged breath. "Hello, Pomba Gira."

Marcela rolled her eyes.

"I have been missing you." Each word sounded like it had to climb out of a gravel pit. A deep, dark groove was carved beneath his jawline, curling up toward each ear. Whatever they'd try to hang him with had been thin and strong.

Marcela said, "I am not Pomba Gira."

"Who's Pomba Gira?" I said.

Carrasco's smile twitched. His sunglasses shifted toward me.

"A better question, I think, is who are you?"

"I'm with her."

"Ah, yet you don't know she is Pomba Gira. Is she not insatiable in her lust?"

"Watch it."

"And her wrath. Enough to make you bow, beg for forgiveness, yes?"

I left that one alone.

Carrasco said, "So you know she is Pomba Gira too, you just don't know her name. I do." He shrugged, just sharing facts. "And I know she is mine."

"I am my own," Marcela said. "I am with whoever I want to be with, and I am with Woody."

His mouth twisted. "Who is Woody?"

"Me," I said. "Seems like a god ought to know this kind of stuff."

"I do know," Carrasco said. "I wanted to see if you would come forward, be a man. And you did. So congratulations, you are a man. But you are right, I am Exu. And Exu gets what is his."

"What's his, or what he has coming?"

Carrasco frowned. "There is a difference?"

"Some. Because I don't give a shit what you think is yours. What you have coming is I walk over there and tear Exu into little pieces."

Eye Patch straightened up and glared.

"Save it," I said. "You don't have your bag of toys."

"Woody," Marcela said.

I was rolling. "I put you down, we don't have to worry about grenades coming through the door, or you bothering the Arcoverdes in any way."

It didn't feel great threatening a guy in such bad shape, but he wasn't getting the message.

Eye Patch said, "You speak of harming Exu, you will anger Malhar."

"Go ahead, light some candles and summon Malhar. I'll wait."

Eye Patch yelled, "Malhar."

The door on the right behind Carrasco opened and a muscle shaped like a man squeezed through.

———

Malhar was about five-foot-six, didn't stand much taller than the back of Carrasco's chair. When the muscles on his shaved head rippled he might have broken six feet. He looked like an angry kid's forced drawing of a pit bull walking upright and unhappy about it.

He had a rib bone jutting out of the corner of his mouth like a toothpick and shiny grease around his lips. Hanging from his belt was a massive framing hammer, thirty-two ounces of stainless steel and a smooth hickory handle with finger grooves worn into the shaft.

"Malhar doesn't know English," Carrasco said. "So he does not know you threatened Exu. Should I tell him?"

Malhar crunched the bone and sucked at the marrow. His eyes flicked from me to Jairo, back and forth. Jairo crossed himself again. Beads of sweat had blossomed on his head. He hadn't been this nervous—no, scared—when he and I got tossed into the cesspit to kill each other.

Marcela put a hand on my arm. "No. We are here to talk."

Carrasco said, "I will listen to anything you say, my Pomba Gira."

She pulled me down and whispered, "Remember where we are."

Right. The blocked road, gunmen, blacked-out buildings that could have hundreds more waiting inside. I wouldn't smile at Carrasco, but I quit staring him down.

Marcela said, "Your man threatened our students."

"Which man?"

"That one."

Eye Patch grinned.

Carrasco glanced at him. "Ah, he was only trying to help."

Marcela said, "Those people come to us to be healthy and safe. You can't take that away. They already see your men standing around, watching, and it makes them nervous."

"If they came to Exu, they would not be nervous anymore. Just like you would not be scared anymore."

Marcela closed her eyes, took a breath. "I'm asking you to leave our students alone. Leave the academy alone."

"Is that where you will be?"

She paused. "Yes."

"Then I will be there too. Until you are with me. It is the way it should be, Pomba Gira."

Marcela looked at the floor, worked her hands out of the fists she'd made. I put my hand on her back, felt her shaking.

Carrasco crossed his legs, two shriveled sticks inside his white pants. "But you don't need to be afraid. Exu will never do you harm. And Exu will never bring you here, lock you up. Exu will wait for you to know, to realize, this is where you should be. Then you will come willingly, sure."

Jairo finally spoke up. "Why do you think she is Pomba Gira?"

It sounded more curious than challenging.

Carrasco turned to him. "You share her blood. You are welcome here too, my warrior friend. How does Exu know? Because it is the truth. Some of these students you protect, they need more to be safe. Sometimes they come here."

"For drugs?" Marcela said.

"For truth, in whatever form they seek it. And when they stand before Exu, they share things with him. They make offerings, say they know a family with much money. The Arcoverdes."

Marcela let out a sharp grunt, like she'd been gut punched.

Carrasco said, "I go to see the place they talk about, your academy. And I see a goddess inside. She is full of life and fire, desire, beauty. She is my Pomba Gira, sure. It is why the students came to Exu. So Exu could find their teacher, Pomba Gira."

"I am not that," Marcela said.

"You are. And Exu wanted to see this man who enjoys you, yet does not know what you truly are. Does not understand." Carrasco turned to me. "Do you understand now?"

"I've always known what she is."

He uncrossed his spindly legs and leaned forward. "Yes?"

"The best thing that's ever happened to me."

"Pomba Gira is this to everyone."

"And much, much too good for me."

"Yes, sure."

"But she is not your Pomba Gira. She is my Marcela."

His mouth twitched as he sat back. His dark sunglasses hid what he was looking at, but I felt his eyes on me. "Is too bad. I thought you might get it, but no. On your way here, you saw the candles along the road. The blades, the offerings."

I nodded.

"You know those are for Exu, for me. I am the crossroads, the choice between this and that. You had a choice to come here, or not come here. You came, and for that Exu was happy."

Was happy.

I didn't like the sound of that.

"Now you get another choice," Carrasco said. "This or that, sure. But now Exu is not so happy. I don't think you're going to want either one."

———

Malhar walked toward me, stopped with his chest pressing against my right arm. He crunched the rib bone again. Something dripped off the end of it onto my shoulder. It might have been his breath.

I eyeballed him. "Step back."

He didn't.

Carrasco said, "He's there to make sure you listen good. Make sure you hear the choices."

"I heard you fine when he wasn't chomping in my ear."

Carrasco said something in Portuguese. Malhar spit the bone onto the floor between my feet. When he smiled he had gristle between his sharp, crooked teeth.

"I could straighten those for you."

"Woody," Marcela said.

"They'd be on the floor, but they'd be straight."

Carrasco said, "You know what Malhar means? Hammer."

"Hey, I was gonna guess that."

Carrasco ignored me. "Look, he even has the shiny head. But I haven't swung him at you, not yet. I do that, man, you'll know it, sure. Now you have to choose."

"No I don't. I don't believe in Exu or Pomba Gira. Your stupid candles."

Jairo said, "Woody, stop."

I told Carrasco, "Far as I'm concerned, this is a really shitty play I can't wait to walk out of. So save your choices—here's the only one: Leave Marcela and her family alone. That's it."

"Oh, okay."

The candles flickered. A breeze pushed against my back, impossible in the enclosed space. Jairo started praying in Portuguese. I turned toward Malhar just in time to see the particle board and sheet metal walls in the room behind us swing shut and close us in. Damn things were doors. Somebody threw a bolt on the other side.

Malhar kept on grinning.

"Now you ready to listen?" Carrasco said. He held his left hand out toward the door behind him, brought it back to his lap. Did the same with his right and the door on that side. "Two choices. You going to pick one, man. From there the spirits will decide what happens."

"What spirits?"

"All of them." He tilted his head to the door on the right. The one Malhar had come through. "First choice. You say goodbye to Brazil, to the Arcoverdes, to my Pomba Gira. You never come back. You never talk to her again. You choose this, Exu forgets about you. Like you never happened."

"Keep this shit up, I'm pretty sure you aren't going to forget me."

"Oh, you think you want the second choice?"

I just waited for him to get to it. Even without the Aviso fight on Saturday, the first one wasn't an option.

Carrasco said, "The second choice is the Coluna da Cobra."

"No," Marcela said. "He chooses number one."

"You can't choose for him, Pomba Gira."

She turned to me. "Take number one."

"No."

"Woody, you don't even know what he's saying."

"I don't care."

Marcela yelled at Carrasco, "This is bullshit."

He shrugged. "It is what Exu wants."

"No," she said. "Give me some choices, I will pick instead."

I said, "Marcela."

She told me to shut up.

Carrasco said, "You have had your choices for a long while now, Pomba Gira. This or that. You chose this."

She blinked hard, slamming the tears of rage down. "Okay. I will go with him. We will both leave Brazil and not come back."

"No no, Pomba Gira." The scars on his scalp writhed in the candlelight when he shook his head. "This is your home, here in Brazil. Here with Exu. If you go, Exu will be angry. I think your family will suffer, sure."

"I will do it," Jairo said. He was panting, his voice shaking. "She is my family, I will do this for her."

Carrasco leaned back, impressed. "I can feel your fear, blood of Pomba Gira. It is strong of you to make this offering to Exu. But Exu does not accept. It must be him."

Jairo's jaw muscles boiled. He wiped the sweat out of his eyes. "She is my cousin, he is my brother. I will do it for both of them."

"Exu already refused."

Jairo paused, wavered, spat. "I don't care. I am doing it."

Carrasco took a deep breath, let his head tip forward, droop until his chin was on his chest. He mumbled in a language that wasn't Portuguese, full of clicks and growls.

The candle flames danced, just once.

Carrasco lifted his head and faced Jairo. "I am sorry, my friend. But it was Exu's wish."

Jairo blinked. "What was?"

Carrasco just smiled.

"I choose the second one," I said. "The Coluna . . . whatever." I needed to speak up before Marcela and Jairo offered up kidneys and lungs to cover my ass.

"Coluna da Cobra," Carrasco said. "Exu is happy with this."

From the way Malhar was panting against my arm, he was too.

"You going to tell me what it is?"

Carrasco's face pulled to the side in a smile. It slid to a grimace as he pushed to his feet. "We walk through the door together, man. Then I show you."

———

Eye Patch pulled a straight black cane from behind the chair and handed it to Carrasco. He braced it next to his right leg and took his time getting to the door. Malhar stood behind me, Marcela, and Jairo and grunted while he breathed, tapping his fingers against the wooden handle of his hammer.

We followed Carrasco through the door.

This room was much smaller, fifteen feet square. The window on the left was boarded from the inside and a single bare light bulb hung from a cord in the center of the drooping ceiling. Someone had painted a mural of the mountainside on the wall across from the door. It showed the narrow road snaking up through the trees, some of the buildings in splashes of white and color in the dark green. It even showed the Dumpsters at the bottom, blobs of rusty blue. No sign of the pickups full of gunmen.

Eye Patch stood in the corner with his arms crossed. Malhar filled the doorway behind us. All told, the room set a record for the most Brazilians per square inch.

"My Axila da Serpente," Carrasco said. He spent a full minute leaning on his cane, staring at the mural.

Marcela and Jairo said he'd been shot, stabbed, hung, and set on fire. It all showed. I suspected he'd been run over a few times as well, but I didn't ask about it.

Carrasco drew a ragged breath. "See it, Pomba Gira. This is all mine. It could be ours. Maybe it does not look like much to you, but there are great things here. Some on the surface, some underneath."

"You're talking to me now," I said.

He pointed the blank sunglasses at me for a while. "The Coluna da Cobra. You know what it means?"

"No."

"Spine of the Snake."

"Do I have to eat it?"

He coughed a laugh. "More like it eats you, sure. Anyone who wants to follow Exu—to kill and die for him, to enjoy his victories—runs the Coluna da Cobra."

He tapped the Dumpsters with the tip of his cane.

"They start here."

He traced the road through its twists, turns, switchbacks, all the way to the top. A large black house with red windows arranged like a skull squatted at the peak. Carrasco underlined it with his cane.

"They try to get here. If they don't make it, maybe it's because they died, or got hurt too bad to keep going."

"Died how?" I said.

"Oh, from Exu's soldiers hunting them, finding them, beating them. Sometimes stabbing, but only when Exu knows they are not worthy. Never shooting—Exu's people live here. He protects them. And if the runners don't get to the top but Exu knows they tried very hard, sometimes they get to steal for him, or beg on the streets. Or cook. But if they make it, man, they are Exu's soldiers. Like Malhar. Like Nuncio."

"Who is Nuncio?"

Eye Patch frowned. "I am."

"Huh. I'm gonna call you Eye Patch." I turned to Carrasco. "And I don't want to be your soldier. Why would I do the Coluna?"

"No, you don't see it. You run the Coluna da Cobra so Exu gives you what you really want. Those who run it to become Exu's soldiers, it is what they want, so badly. But you, you want Exu's Pomba Gira. So you gonna run the Coluna da Cobra and see if Exu will give her to you."

"No," Marcela said.

"It's the only way, Pomba Gira. Otherwise, like I say, Exu will be angry."

"You're going to kill him."

Carrasco shrugged. "Many have survived the Coluna."

"Because you let them." She grabbed my hands. "This is just a way for him to murder you."

Carrasco put a hand on his caved-in chest. "Pomba Gira, you hurt my heart."

I asked him, "No shooting?"

"Please, there are children. Only the police shoot here, until we kill them."

Marcela said, "Woody, no."

"I make it all the way to the top and you leave Marcela and her family alone. Forever."

"Yes, sure," he said.

"Okay."

Marcela fell against Jairo. He put his arm around her and stared at me, his eyes frantic.

Carrasco's face twitched with a smile. He cocked his head, listening.

"Hmm."

He considered the mural.

"Exu knows this is something different. You don't want to be his soldier. You want to be away from him, to have Exu out of your life."

"Damn right."

He touched a finger to the skull house, black with red windows. "So you will begin here, at the top. Not at the bottom. You will run the Coluna da Cobra head to tail."

I rolled my neck and shook my hands out. My breathing was picking up.

"Okay. Let's do it."

Carrasco frowned. "No, it happens when Exu wishes."

I stopped in mid-arm circle. "When is that?"

He shrugged. "Only Exu knows."

CHAPTER 8

THE PICKUP TRUCKS WERE GONE WHEN EYE PATCH walked us to the Dumpsters and said goodbye. Empty black windows leered down at us from both sides of the silent street.

I opened the van's side door for Marcela. She got in the front passenger seat and closed her own door. I sat by myself in the middle row, hands out on the worn leather bench to keep from tipping over. Jairo got us rolling and nobody said anything until we were under streetlights and surrounded by other moving cars.

Marcela turned in her seat. "What the hell is wrong with you?"

"Me? What the hell is wrong with Jairo? He stood there like a statue the whole time, didn't say a damn thing."

Jairo shook his head. "That is a bad place. We should not have gone there."

"See?" I said. "He's all spooked out."

"So am I!" Marcela said. "And you should be too, but you're too stupid to know it."

"What, because of the candles? Exu? Come on, the guy's a

thug. I've gone through gang initiations before. Only thing I'm worried about is breaking a hand on that Malhar thing's head. Shit, or getting cut. I'm banged up, the doc won't let me fight Aviso on Saturday."

Marcela covered her face, growled some Portuguese into her hands. She pulled them down and turned on me again. "They aren't going to bang you up, they're going to kill you. You can't go. I'm telling you no."

"If it gets him to leave you alone, I'm going."

"You can't go back there," Jairo said. He stared through the windshield and sounded like he was talking in his sleep. "You go back, you never come out. I won't let you go. Gil won't let you."

"Gil doesn't know about this."

"I will tell him," Jairo said.

Marcela nodded. "We will. Maybe he puts you on a plane first thing in the morning."

"With you sitting next to me?"

She didn't answer.

"I'm not leaving. I have a fight. Two of them, now. And you're in danger."

"You're suicidal," she said.

"Nah. Carrasco is."

I thought it was a good line until Jairo said, "He has already died. I smelled it on him."

He shuddered, and I felt the van shake.

———

Jairo parked the van in front of Antonio's house, got his bag and walked off along a trail without a word. Marcela and I watched

him go. I tried to think of something smart to say. She helped
me by walking away.

She turned back. "You don't leave this house. You stay inside
until it is time for you to leave."

"Marcela, I have a fight on Saturday. I have to train tomorrow
at the academy for Eddie's stupid video. Then the weigh-ins and
all that nonsense on Friday."

"Okay, so flip it. What if someone was coming for me, who
knows when, to take me away and kill me? What would you do?"

"I'd ask you to come live with me in Vegas. Wait, I already did
that. I guess I'd find the people coming for you and put myself
between them and you. Shit, I did that too."

"I won't let you go with them."

I reached for her hand. She didn't pull it away.

"I think they're all talk," I said. "I don't think they're ever
going to come."

"They will come," she said.

———

Antonio and Gil were the only ones awake inside. They sat at a
large wooden table near the windows overlooking the courtyard.
Scrapbooks were stacked up and spread everywhere. They both
looked like they'd been crying in a good way.

"See some good stuff?" Gil said.

"Oh yes," Marcela said. To me: "Anything you want to
tell them?"

"Rio is lovely at night."

"That's it?"

"They don't need to know anything else."

Antonio and Gil frowned at us. Gil lifted a huge white mug to his face, sipped some of the Brazilian coffee he hadn't shut up about for weeks leading up to the trip. He smacked his lips and waited. "Hold on. Did you two really get engaged?"

Marcela laughed. A chuckle would have sufficed, but she looked me in the eye and brayed it out. She turned to the table with a tight smile. "We went to see Carrasco tonight."

Antonio stood up.

"What's Carrasco?" Gil said. "A band?"

Marcela said, "I'm done talking about it."

She pointed down the hall along the south wing of the long house.

"Your room is that way. Good night."

She turned and went down the hallway to the north.

Antonio and Gil stared at me.

"You got any more of that coffee?"

———

I told them about Eye Patch and his grenades. The visit to the Axila da Serpente. Carrasco and Malhar. Exu and Pomba Gira. The Coluna da Cobra.

Gil put his head in his hands. He kept it there and made sounds like someone was letting the air out of him.

Antonio's expression didn't change through any of it, but he seemed to be vibrating. Bristling.

When I finished he said, "You took Jairo into that place?"

"Yeah. Like I said, he didn't do much."

"Days before his first fight for Warrior, when he shows the world what the Arcoverdes do, you take him to a favela to be shot, stabbed, killed, cursed."

"None of that happened."

"None? You are sure?"

"We all made it back. Nobody's bleeding."

"Ah," he said. "You all made it back. Did you bring anything with you, I wonder."

"I have my gear bag . . ."

Gil popped up. "He's talking about a curse, jackass. This Exu thing. You said it had Jairo spooked, so now he's thinking about that instead of fighting Preston on Saturday."

"Got it."

"And you're supposed to be sleeping and dreaming about shit-stomping Aviso, but instead you're challenging entire slums to a battle to the death."

"I didn't challenge them."

Gil looked into his coffee cup. If there had been any left, I would have worn it. "Warrior fights aside, you took Marcela and Jairo into a place where you all could have been killed. Are you out of your mind?"

"They both wanted to go. Demanded to."

"Not until you arrived," Antonio said. He sat with his back straight and his hands on his thighs, elbows flared. Like an emperor.

Gil asked him, "Will you please call the police about this?"

"There are men I can talk to. What Marcela told him is correct, though. It may do no good."

"But it can't hurt," Gil said.

Antonio gave a slow blink of acknowledgement.

Gil turned to me. "You don't leave my sight until we land in Vegas on Sunday. You hear me?"

"Hey, they come for me and I don't go, they—"

He grabbed my forearm. Though short and stocky, he had hands that could palm manhole covers. When he squeezed, I paid attention.

"You don't go anywhere. You don't fight anybody except Aviso. You don't nod your thick fucking head right now, you're going to fight me."

"And me," Antonio said.

I nodded.

And I lied.

———

My room was small and square. White walls with teak trim and a sliding glass door to the courtyard. The bed was narrow with soft clean sheets.

I considered sneaking to Marcela's room but figured everybody needed a good night's sleep. That, and I'd probably end up fighting the whole house.

I got my head down and listened for her footsteps or her knock on the glass door.

Or Carrasco's.

Neither one came, and I dreamt of waiting at an intersection while a giant snake filled the cross street in front of me, its sides pulsing as it squeezed between the buildings. I could hear Marcela calling for me from inside its belly and see her little hands pressing against the scales from within.

CHAPTER 9

IT WAS STILL DARK OUTSIDE WHEN JAIRO WOKE ME UP WITH a glass of fresh juice made from blended oranges, limes, butter, and coffee beans. I squinted at him as I chugged it to see if I'd fallen for some Arcoverde hazing ritual, but he was already heading for the door.

"Put your running shoes on," he said.

Good news: The drink wasn't hazing.

Bad news: The running was.

We walked to the end of the driveway, leaving the estate's dim yellow landscape lights behind. There were no streetlights on the mountain road and no other houses that I could see. The sky was just starting to bruise in the east. The stars faded one by one, sidling away from what was about to happen.

The road went uphill to the right, down to the left.

Jairo faced right and lifted one knee to his chest, tugged it, then the other.

I wiggled my hands and said, "Hey, about Carrasco."

"We're not talking about it. Fighting only."

"I am talking about fighting."

"Warrior fights," Jairo said. "Preston. Aviso. That's it. Ready? Go."

The bastard started running uphill. I jammed my earbuds in, hit Play, and kept up with him until I lost the juice five minutes in.

Jairo slapped my back and laughed. "You don't get the nutrients like that."

He took off again.

The road varied between long uphill stretches and short uphill ramps. My calves sucked all the blood from my face and turned it into cement. The calm phrases in my ears made me furious with their lack of panting.

Jairo turned around a few times and ran backward to hit his quads. I followed suit, mostly so he wouldn't see me drooling. My quads said: Fuck your ego, turn back around.

I'd done hill sprints before. The two key words there are hill and sprints.

This was turning into a 5K up a mountain.

And it worked.

I forgot about Carrasco and Exu, Pomba Gira and snakes. It was one foot in front of the other and intense concentration on not shitting my shorts.

Jairo slowed his pace until he was next to me. "Aviso runs a mountain like this every day."

I yanked the earbuds out, let them dangle, and formed an exhale into a word: "Liar."

"It's true. He says it keeps him in shape for his modeling, and his fighting. He doesn't lift weights. He does jiu jitsu, and he runs up a mountain. Sometimes with sandbags or a heavy pack."

I risked a deep breath. "How can you talk so much right now?"

"I don't want you to think he's going to lie down easy. Or break in his mind. If he runs up a mountain like this every day—no, bigger than this—what is fifteen minutes of fighting? It's nothing."

"Won't go three rounds." I gasped like a man coming up from a deep-sea free dive.

"I think it will if he wants it to."

"Don't care what he wants."

"He wants to not get hit, and to break your arm. It's what he's done to everyone he's fought already."

"Not everyone."

"Close enough," Jairo said.

I let the lolling of my head turn into a nod. "That's it. Right there. Close enough. He grabs my arm, he's close enough to hit."

"You won't have the time, man. The way he works, he calls it trap-snap-tap. You see?"

"Yeah."

"He takes hold, he breaks your arm, then you tap out. Because he's so fast."

"I get it."

"And he runs his mountain so he won't get tired."

We were on a long stretch that seemed almost flat compared to the rest. It curved to the right up ahead, and I could see part of what came after, a tight switchback that headed for the top. It looked like it should have had rungs.

I said, "What's your point?"

"Don't look past him. Don't think about nothing else but him."

"Nothing else, like Carrasco?"

"Not even that name. Aviso. Only Aviso."

"What about Marcela?"

He ran a few dozen steps without saying anything. "No man,

not her either. Better to start now."

He took off up the switchback and left me gasping and choking, grinding my way to the top and wondering what the hell that meant.

———

I thought downhill would be better.

It was, in the way getting stabbed is better than getting shot. I never got close enough to Jairo again to talk about Marcela, and when I walked into the house there were people everywhere.

Javier and Edson were chopping up fruit. Cecilia had a carafe of coffee for anyone with a cup. Gil took all of it.

Antonio sat at the table reading a newspaper, but his eyes followed me while I walked on wet noodles toward the hall to my room.

He said, "Jairo came through here."

I turned, wobbled to the table and put a hand on it. "Yeah?"

"He said you ran the mountain."

"That's right."

"What did you think?"

"I think I used to like this mountain."

He smiled. "You did good. You didn't quit."

"Is Marcela awake?"

"Awake? She is already at the academia. She teaches the morning class on Thursday."

I rapped the table with two knuckles, maybe a bit harder than I'd wanted. Antonio's coffee cup jumped. Aviso got slapped out of my head, replaced by Carrasco and Malhar, the stained framing hammer, Eye Patch and his bag of grenades.

All of them staring at me, nudging each other: See, he tried to forget.

I said, "She's by herself?"

"No, with the students."

"Enjoy your breakfast."

I ran into Gil on my way through the kitchen. "So you did the mountain."

"When are we leaving for the academy?"

He checked the clock. "Eddie wanted to start filming with Antonio and Jairo around ten, so—"

"We leave now."

"There's plenty of time."

I stepped close, just me and him. "Marcela is there alone."

"Okay, easy. I'm sure she's fine. She does this all the time."

"That was before last night."

"You kind of stink."

"I'll shower there."

"You're not going anywhere alone. Not with those favela guys thinking they can grab you off the street."

"Then you better get ready."

Gil nodded. "I can see you're a bit intense about this. I'll get the van."

I was already moving.

———

I drove. Gil braced himself against the dashboard and the door and gave directions between bursts of profanity. A lesser man would have worn his coffee, but he coddled the mug like a newborn.

When the academy was in sight I scanned the road for smoke,

shattered glass, little bloody gis hanging from the power lines. When I didn't see that, I looked for Carrasco or his men, ready to take me for the Coluna.

A man stood outside the front door. He was waiting for us. I can count on a closed fist how many times I've been happy to see Eddie, and that was one of them. His media crew were swarming in and out of the door, hauling cords and lights and cameras.

He looked up from his phone long enough to nod at us. "One of you stinks."

"It's me."

"Well, take a damn shower before we start shooting, yeah? I don't need anybody gagging on my promo. Hey, you tell Gil about the WarriorDome?"

"No."

"I thought that name was a joke," Gil said.

"You two talk about it." I went through the door. Marcela was on the mats with a group of teenage girls, showing them how to make sure they were choking off blood to the brain and not air to the lungs.

She looked up and smiled, then must have remembered she was mad at me. Her eyes and mouth squinted down. I didn't care—she was safe. My stomach unrolled itself and let my diaphragm work again.

I carried my bag into the men's room and took a fast, hot shower. When I came out Jairo was at the base of the stairs in his forest green Arcoverde Academy gi. His head was extra shiny.

"How your legs feeling?" he said.

"Like they got run over. How are yours?"

"Fine. Why wouldn't they be?"

"You're an asshole."

He slapped an arm around my shoulders. "Come on, they want to start."

I stayed put, watching Marcela work with the young women, looking them each in the eye while she spoke in Portuguese.

"What's she saying?"

Jairo echoed her words: "You are never powerless. People will treat you the way you allow them to. A boy approaches you with disrespect, or another woman? It is your choice to allow it or not. Me, I never do. Never. You don't treat me with respect, good-bye. I tell you good-bye and you don't leave? That gets us to the next lesson: armlocks."

My girl.

In English, she said, "We need a volunteer. Woody, hello. Come here please."

She was smiling ear to ear now, very happy with herself.

Shit.

Eddie poked his head around the stairway landing. "Hey dicks, you're wasting my time. Let's go."

Twice in the same hour I was glad to see him. This was getting unhealthy.

"I gotta go film."

"Of course you do," she said. Then something in Portuguese to the girls that made them all look at me and laugh.

Jairo said, "She told them—"

"Yeah, I got it."

I winked at Marcela. She fought a smile and lost.

I went up the stairs, grinning like a fool and happy for the first time since I'd sat on the bench with her looking down the mountain, thinking she was coming home with me. We felt like us again.

The feeling lasted until I got to the second floor and saw what Eddie had done.

———

Bright lights on tripods cooked the room. The monastic walls of the Academia de Arcoverde were draped with Warrior banners made to look like alleyway graffiti—neon colors shouting words like DOMINATION and NO MERCY, all of it covered in a fine mist of blood splatter.

Antonio stood in the far corner in his faded Arcoverde gi with his hands behind his back, as if he was afraid to touch anything. His red belt and the black and white stripes around it were frayed. By the look on his face, the thing he wanted to touch most was Eddie's exposed heart.

I'd never seen a red belt before, let alone one with degrees. It hit me again what this man was: a grandmaster. Gil's sixth-degree black belt was the highest jiu jitsu rank in Vegas unless Jairo was in town. The two of them were talking with Eddie in the middle of the green mats. The green mats that were covered by a Warrior canvas crammed with more gaudy sponsor logos than a stock car.

"This is my promo," Eddie told them. "You don't want to be in it, that's fine. We'll use the whole time on Preston, show this all-American kid and his big right hand going up against the royal fucking Brazilians who were too good to talk to our cameras. You want that, let's do it. It'll play real well in the flyover states."

Jairo said, "You told us you wanted to show the tradition of the Arcoverdes. The pride, the honor."

"Yeah. The new tradition. The new pride and honor. Nobody gives a shit about what you can do on a jiu jitsu mat. It's what you can do inside the cage. That's what I'm here to show, but you don't even have a cage. You have a goddam fence. Gil, you know I'm right."

"That's entirely untrue."

Eddie held his hands up, let them drop. "What we're trying to do here is link your heritage with the Warrior name. The Arcoverde style is what fighting used to be. Warrior is what fighting is now. We serve each other, see? MMA is built upon what you did, and now MMA is lifting you up to what it's become."

Jairo shared a look with Antonio. Antonio nodded a fraction—he was leaving it up to his son.

Eddie smelled blood. "Get left behind if you want. But this is your debut. Your one chance to make a first impression. Are you going to make fans around the world say, 'Holy shit, I need to get an Arcoverde Warrior shirt'? Or are you going to make them say, 'Who the hell is Arcoverde? Whoever he is, I hope he fucking loses'?"

I'd seen Eddie yank the puppet strings before, over the phone or on his staff during fight nights. A few times with Burch. When he did it to me, it was hard to look up and see them when he had the contract down on the table. Only after I signed it could I see the filaments trailing back to his middle fingers.

But with Jairo, I was watching Eddie manipulate my friend, my brother, into taking the first step along the path of selling his soul. Antonio, Jairo, and Gil all had emotional attachments to what Eddie was pissing on.

I did not.

Eddie turned to me. "Woody, tell them what's up. This is how it goes."

I told them, "This is how it goes," and started tearing the

banners down.

———

Eddie tried to stop me. He grabbed my arm with one hand, two. He let go when his feet came off the floor.

Kevin the producer stepped between me and the next banner. "Hold up, Woody."

I reached over his shoulder and pulled it down on top of him. From inside his shroud he said, "Nice. Real mature."

I lifted one corner of the Warrior canvas. "Pardon me, gentlemen."

Jairo and Gil bit down on their grins and stepped off. I gathered the canvas in a heap and threw it down the stairs. The green mats felt much better underfoot. Less oily.

Eddie asked Antonio, "You going to let him do this?"

"I think he is done."

"Almost," I said. "Eddie, you want to show the world what a real warrior is? And that's lowercase, the true version. Not whatever you're selling. Just turn the cameras on and leave. There's more honor in Antonio Arcoverde walking across the mats than anything you clowns could slap together."

"You mean like your promo?" Eddie said. "Oh wait, your promo just got scrapped, along with my banners. It's going to be all about Aviso, baby. Now get off the set. Your stupid face isn't showing up anywhere in this."

"Jairo, you good?"

He gave a thumbs-up. "I am good, my friend."

I kicked the banners into a pile and scooped them up to make sure Eddie didn't slime them back onto the walls. The bundle came up to my chin. I felt my way to the stairs and started down.

"Hey, watch it."

I swiveled in the narrow space and caught a glimpse of Marcela's head below me. She had the canvas in her arms. We looked like two sumo wrestlers trying to shake hands.

"This was on the landing," she said.

"Here, set it on top of mine. Where's the trash?"

"It is out back, but just drop it at the bottom, I'll take care of it."

There was something in her voice. Not apologetic, but . . . sorry. I moved again, trying to see her face. "Is your class done? Let's go get some lunch, just you and me. I feel like we haven't had any time for just, you know. You and me."

Words. We didn't get along.

"No, we can't."

"What's wrong?"

"Woody, there's a policeman here for you."

———

Before I met Gil and got into serious professional fighting—and got my shit somewhat together—whenever someone told me, "The police are here for you," I would say, "What for?"

Reason being, there was a list of possibilities.

This time I asked because I had no idea.

Marcela said, "He wouldn't tell me."

She and I stood in the small area between the locker rooms, watching the Brazilian policeman. He looked about fifty, tired of everything, short with a little belly poking through the flaps of his brown blazer. He was talking in Portuguese to the class of young women.

"What's he saying?"

Marcela whispered, "He's telling them not to be prostitutes. Get him out of here."

I walked the white fringe to the door. "You're here for me?"

He feigned surprise, leaned back with his fists up as he looked me over. "Hey, big boy. You are Aaron Wallace?"

"That's right."

He stuck his hand out. "I am City Detective Rubin. Your security."

"Security for what?"

"You are here to fight Aviso, yes?"

"Yeah."

"Security for that. Have you had any trouble?"

"Nope."

Marcela did a poor job of casual eavesdropping long enough to hear that much. She resumed her class. Rubin had a solid grip. Up close, there were small white lines in his eyebrows and the bags under his eyes became old, swollen scar tissue.

"You used to box," I said.

"Ah, hundreds of years ago, before they invented defense. So you haven't run into anybody who wants to make your time here in beautiful Rio anything less than spectacular?"

"I've only talked to the Arcoverdes."

"Oh, such a great family, eh? They are a national treasure to us. Jairo is going to win his fight on Saturday, yes?"

"Anything can happen, but I wouldn't want to be Preston."

Rubin laughed. "For sure, for sure. I see the rental vehicles outside—Mr. Takanori is here now?"

"You can call him Eddie. He's upstairs shooting a promo with Jairo."

"I won't disturb him." Rubin waved a hand at his ear. "These girls are getting loud. Let's step outside, eh?"

I didn't know how it worked in Brazil, but when a cop asked you to step outside in the States it usually led to ducking into the back of a squad car. I also didn't know if they could shoot you for running away, so I got ready to take a ride.

Rubin put his hands in his pants pockets and smelled the air on the street. "You like it?"

I shrugged.

"You didn't even try. Come on, with me."

We both took in a deep breath.

"See?" Rubin said. "That is Rio, my friend. The food, the earth, the smell of happy people enjoying life. I love it. Are you having a good time here?"

"Sure."

"You are ready for your fight with Aviso?"

"Yes."

"You are used to speaking with policemen, eh? Yes. No. You want your lawyer here to chat with me? I ask him if his client is having a good time. He whispers to you, then says to me very seriously, 'No comment.'"

"Nah."

Rubin nudged me with an elbow. "Come on man, loosen up. You going to be a pain in my ass the whole time?"

"No comment."

"Ah, there we go. I'm going to keep an eye on you during the press conference and weigh-ins tomorrow. I'll have some officers with me too, and we'll be with you the whole time. We'll drop you off—wait, where are you staying?"

"You said you're a detective?"

"Shit man, I liked you better when you didn't talk."

"I'm at the Arcoverde estate."

Rubin clutched his heart. "Way the fuck up there? Now we have a budget crises, paying for gasoline to babysit you. Okay, damn. So we take you halfway around the world, pick you up before the fights on Saturday, and we take you home after."

"You sure this is necessary?"

"Once you see the crowds and hear the chants about how you should die, you'll believe it."

"I guess. But I don't see how this falls on a detective's desk."

"Because this detective has seniority, and he likes the fights. Even more when he is paid to go watch them."

"Got it."

"Now Sunday, we'll come get you and take you to the airport, but only if you beat Aviso."

The look on my face made him explain.

"Aviso wins, nobody gives a shit about you anymore. You got your whipping already. But if you beat him, some people will want to avenge him, avenge Brazil."

"Sounds about right. Plan on making that trip on Sunday."

He looked into the street. "Eh, I'm not filing the request for officers until Sunday. No offense."

"You rooting for Aviso?"

"Of course. I wish he would learn to box, but hey, maybe he doesn't need to."

"You ever seen my fights?"

Rubin shrugged, scanning the traffic and the people flowing past. "They show the highlights whenever they talk about Aviso."

"You want to cheer for a boxer, come on over."

"That's not boxing, big boy. What you do, I don't know.

I've seen better technique in street fights. You ever been in a street fight?"

He still wasn't looking at me.

I didn't say anything.

He nodded. "No comment."

———

Marcela met me on the white border and attached herself to my hip while we cut into the space between the locker rooms.

She pivoted in front of me and grabbed my hands, made sure I had both eyes on her. "He is here to protect you?"

"Yeah, his name's Rubin. Warrior set it up."

"But he will protect you from all things, not just crazy Aviso fans."

"You mean Carrasco."

"I mean yourself. He will make sure you don't do anything stupid when I am not close."

"No mortal can accomplish that."

"Be serious. When is he coming back?"

"He'll meet us at your place before the weigh-ins on Friday."

"And he will be with you for that? And for the fight on Saturday."

"That's what he said. Him and some policemen."

She frowned. "So I have to worry all day today. We will go from here back to my home. We will stay there until he comes tomorrow, and I will tell him not to leave until you are on the plane."

"If Carrasco comes to the house—"

"You will do nothing. You told my uncle you would not. And now you will tell me."

I stayed quiet.

"So you lied to him."

"I told him what he wanted to hear. And if Carrasco never shows his scrawny face again, I'm the guy who shooed him away."

"And when he does show his face? Because he will, Woody."

I looked into her tan eyes and didn't say anything. Watched the hurt cloud them over, the anger roll in.

She pulled her hands loose and walked away.

——

Eddie waited at the top of the stairs like I was late for his dirty look.

"You really throw my banners away?"

"They're down there somewhere."

Kevin and Philip were moving cameras and lights around. Antonio stood with his hands behind his back, staring at the marks being made on his green mats. Jairo, Javier, and Edson were halfway through their warm-up.

Eddie said, "That cost is coming out of your fight purse."

"I did you a favor. You want to connect Warrior with the tradition here, you have to show the tradition. Not some vinyl you got printed this morning."

"I'll let you make it up to me. I need ambient gym noise. Like there's a shitload of people here training while we shoot Jairo."

"You want the class from downstairs?"

"The girls?" Eddie said. "Yeah, let's have giggling and squealing while my new prospect for the heavyweight belt makes his debut."

I wanted to make sure I heard that right. "Your what?"

"Hey man, I don't bring a fighter on unless I think he has a chance to wear the strap. Especially a heavyweight, and especially a guy who's almost thirty. This is rare air you guys are breathing. Jairo does well on Saturday, he might get fast-tracked to a shot. A Brazilian champ would bring in millions of eyeballs down here and overseas. The look on your face, I bet you're thinking, Where's that leave me?"

I didn't say anything.

"That leaves you in a spot where you shouldn't have torn my banners down. And you better show me something amazing against Aviso, you want that number-one contender tag. Now get with Gil and do some pad work and rolling in the background so I can wrap this up and get out of here."

I ground my teeth together so they wouldn't sink into his face.

"And no swearing," Eddie said. "It'll be good practice for your gig at the WarriorDome."

"Hey. You might want a Rubin of your own around full-time, make sure I don't throw you out on top of the banners."

Eddie frowned. "Who the hell's Rubin?"

"We're ready over here," Kevin said.

Eddie pointed at me while he walked away. "Don't fuck this up more than you already have."

Gil stepped up with my training gloves and the focus mitts. "Was Eddie's face on any of those banners?"

I took the gloves. "No, why?"

"Figured we could cut it out, tape it to one of the mitts for you."

He held up the mitt on his right hand.

"Eddie."

The left.

"Aviso."

"Switch 'em."

"My my. Eddie gets the left hook today?"

"Aviso will get it enough on Saturday."

I got to work. Carrasco's face wasn't on either of the mitts.

Add it to my list of mistakes.

———

We went through jab, jab-cross, jab-cross-hook, threw in some slipping and bobbing. When I was warm we added low kicks and knees, focusing on speed and accuracy.

Gil made sure the cameras weren't on us—no reason Aviso's camp should get a free preview. He ditched the mitts and took a stance similar to the Brazilian's. Left leg out in front, body leaning back with his hands low, just above his waistline.

When Aviso did it, he looked like a statue of a Greek god.

Gil's version was closer to a drunk gorilla.

He recited the mantra he'd developed for this fight: "Do not attack the head."

"But it's right there, man."

Didn't matter how many times he said it or made me pay for ignoring it. My instincts and muscle memory howled to go after that pumpkin, seemingly unprotected.

"You know what happens," Gil said.

"Yeah yeah."

"Alright, let's skip right to the part where you ignore me and do something stupid. I'd like to think we don't need to address it, but let's be honest."

I didn't have an argument, so I leaned forward and took a slow swipe at his face, floating there like an exposed balloon begging to get popped.

At half-speed he ducked underneath and wrapped me in a neat

double-leg, hooked an ankle and planted me on my back. He dug a knee into my belly—unnecessary, but noted—slid it off and settled into a full mount, his thighs clamped against my ribcage and the crown of his head wedged under my chin.

He ground his head against mine while he moved his knees into my armpits, straightened up and planted his heels against my hip bones.

Again, his face was right there, begging to get smacked. Aviso was taller and his face would be farther away, but I doubted that would diminish my desire to cave it in.

"If this happens," Gil said, "the laws of physics and the history of all things from the beginning of time dictate Aviso will armbar you. It's just a matter of time. And if he armbars you, he will break your arm."

I tried to squirm out the back door, toward his heels. No good.

I bridged and bucked and tried to roll him off without using my arms, but he was too high up on my chest.

"Worst case," he said, and started slapping me in the face.

I chomped my mouthguard. I hated this part.

Not the slapping—I barely felt that.

What came next.

I covered my face with my forearms, as if Aviso was raining down the punches and I couldn't take it.

Gil didn't waste any time. He hooked his left arm through my right so the insides of our elbows were touching, pulled my arm straight and clamped it against his ribs. His left foot landed next to my right ear and that knee compressed my head against the mat.

His right foot came into my left armpit. His left foot stepped over my face and met his right. He kept my arm pinched between his thighs and my thumb pointed toward the ceiling as he fell back, lifted his hips and pulled my arm down toward his chest like a slot machine lever.

I tapped.

Gil released the pressure but kept my arm. "Faster, Woody."

He didn't mean the drill.

"He gets your arm and starts to fall back, you tap. Don't wait for his hips to rise, and if he pulls your arm down it's too late. Snap. You're in a cast for two months."

"I don't like it."

"I know you don't, and I don't care. I've let you get away with a lot of dumb shit, getting your face blasted apart too many times to count, but I won't budge on this. He gets your arm, you tap. Say it."

I growled something that would have made Philip vomit if his mic had picked it up.

"Woody," Gil said.

"He gets my arm, I tap."

"Good." He let go of my arm and rolled to his feet, pulled me up. "Let's go through Plan A: Don't get taken down in the first place, because you listened to your trainer and did not attack the head."

"That's a terrible name."

"I came up with a short version. Plan A: Unlikely, but I can hope."

"Accurate."

Gil checked the cameras again and lowered his voice. "Then we'll do Plan B: Woody didn't listen, now what?"

"I keep telling you, we should just skip to that one."

"Plan A," Gil said. "Go."

———

We ran through it a dozen times and took a break to stand behind the cameras while Jairo sparred with Edson. Antonio wove around them like a matador, calling out encouragement and small adjustments.

That's what I thought he was doing, anyway.

Jairo dropped into a low stance, his fingertips brushing the mat as he circled Edson, who seemed to be attempting an impersonation of Tim Preston by puffing his chest out. Jairo moved like a panther sliding through the brush. Antonio said something in Portuguese and Jairo leapt up, threw a front kick at Edson's face and shot in for a perfect single-leg takedown.

From there he flowed into side-mount and dropped his full weight onto Edson's ribcage. He froze, waiting for Antonio to step around so he could see what was happening.

I shared a frown with Gil.

Antonio crouched near Jairo's head, his eyes darting over the situation. He issued a command.

Jairo patted Edson's face with a few hammerfists and locked in a kimura that earned an immediate tap. Jairo released the arm and hauled Edson to his feet, everybody smiling.

"Good," Eddie said.

Kevin stopped filming. He joined Eddie at a laptop and they watched what they'd just shot. Javier and Edson trotted downstairs.

I asked Gil, "Are they putting this out as misinformation?"

He winced. "I don't think so."

Jairo saw our faces. "What's wrong?"

Antonio was already scowling. I didn't know the rules about

second-guessing a grandmaster's plan in his dojo, but I was likely about to break a few.

"Is that how you're going to fight on Saturday?"

"Yes," Jairo said. "I am going to make him scared to engage, then I am going to take him down and submit him. Most likely by choking, but arm, leg, whatever he gives up, I will take."

I could have left it there and slept fine. "What about the coaching part?"

"Coaching?"

"Yeah, with Antonio."

The patriarch's chin lifted an inch. He waited for me to continue dancing through the minefield.

I said, "Are you going to wait for him to tell you what to do during the fight?"

"He knows what to do, all times. You listen to Gil when you fight."

"Eh," Gil said.

I nodded. "But I don't stop and listen. For one thing, you aren't going to be able to hear anything. And if you freeze up and wait, Preston will demolish you. He throws that right hand as a reflex."

Antonio exhaled through his nose. It took about an hour.

Jairo said, "We know what we are doing."

"That's just it. You absolutely know what you're doing—you don't need to wait for instructions. Just fight, man."

Antonio finally spoke. "He should not listen to me?"

"I didn't say that. He shouldn't hesitate so he can listen to you. And if you want him to listen, you better make sure he doesn't have to wait for it."

His eyes widened. "You are telling me how to fight? You are

telling Jairo how to fight?"

"I'm trying to—"

"The Arcoverdes have won hundreds of tournaments."

"Right. Jiu jitsu tournaments."

He waited for me to make my point, which I already had. I didn't want to pull Gil into it. This was my grave, and I'd dig myself out. Eddie, Kevin, and Philip were all watching now, Eddie grinning like a hyena.

I told Antonio, "This is going to be much different than your tournaments."

"Yes. Our opponent knows nothing about Arcoverde jiu jitsu. He has no idea what is waiting for him."

Eddie nudged Kevin and whispered something. They both waited, arms crossed, eager to find out if I was as stupid as they thought.

I said, "Jairo may be your son, but he's my brother. I can't let you send him out there to get killed."

"You're going to let me?" Antonio's hands came from behind his back and pressed together in front of his stomach. "It is up to you?"

"It should be. I know a helluva lot more about it than you do."

Gil said, "Okay, time to go."

He grabbed my arm and tried to tug me around.

I stayed. "We can't let them go into the cage with this plan."

Gil stepped close and spoke through his teeth. "We are going to leave and get some fresh air, maybe some food, because you have obviously lost your goddam mind."

"I'm the crazy one? Antonio wants Jairo to call time-out so he can check the fight like a chessboard. Meanwhile, Jairo's face is getting pushed through the back of his head by Preston's right.

That's if he doesn't get knocked out with one shot."

"From what I saw yesterday," Antonio said, "what you call jiu jitsu, you should not be telling anyone a single thing about fighting."

Gil said, "I trained him to use jiu jitsu for MMA. It's different."

"It's disgraceful."

I'd seen Gil take some serious shots over the years. Most of them from me. This one hit him square in the chest and knocked the soul right out of him. Now in addition to sending my brother to the gallows, Antonio had slapped my chosen father across the face.

Grandmaster or not, he'd pay for it.

I stepped forward.

Antonio knew what it was. He smiled and dropped into a rigid stance.

Jairo tried to get between us.

Antonio barked something that made him jump back.

"Woody," Gil said. "Don't do this."

I took a deep breath. Let my hands drop.

Antonio's mouth twisted in disdain. "You are not good enough for Marcela."

My hands came up again on their own.

"Shit this is good," Eddie said.

I glanced over, realized Kevin had the camera running the whole time on the tripod. I was in profile on the laptop screen, squaring up with Antonio Arcoverde. Behind me, Gil had his hands pressed to his temples.

I stepped back.

Antonio looked me up and down. He spat something in Portuguese at Jairo.

My brother told me, "You find somewhere else to sleep tonight."

CHAPTER 10

I'D BEEN IN BRAZIL LESS THAN TWENTY-FOUR HOURS, AND already I'd infuriated the woman I loved, accepted a challenge to fight an entire slum of drug-fueled murderous zealots, and insulted the grandmaster of Brazilian jiu jitsu in his dojo.

I was beginning to suspect some of it was my fault.

Marcela was taking a shower when I came downstairs, so she didn't get to see my thundercloud face when I stomped across the first-floor mats. I stood on the sidewalk outside the Arcoverde Academy, the debris of my actions churning in my wake, and dreaded what I had to do next.

Ask Eddie for help.

He came out behind Philip and Kevin, carrying his phone like a tray of champagne while they waddled with cases and bags of equipment.

Eddie's cheeks were flushed, eyes bright. "That was intense, brah."

"It was a disaster."

"Oh, absolutely."

"Don't be happy about it."

"Hey, my juices are flowing. Thought it was gonna go down right there. Then they kick you out, man. That's rough."

He shook his head and watched his guys load the rental SUV. He was going to make me ask.

"I need a place to stay," I said. "Gil too."

He sucked air in through his teeth. "Might be tough. We had to book the rooms for the other fighters months ago, before we announced the event. We knew everything was going to fill up fast. You remember me asking if you needed a room?"

"Yeah."

"You said no."

"That's changed."

"I'm not sure the world cares, buddy."

I said, "You remember what happened right before you asked me?"

He dropped the crooked grin. Maybe he'd flashed back to the room deep below the Golden Pantheon arena where Shuko had made his nest. Where he'd drugged Eddie, Burch, and Vanessa and prepped them for a marathon torture session before I showed up. I hadn't walked into that room, Eddie would have been flayed and turned into bone-in steaks.

"I'm just teasing you," Eddie said. "You don't have to go full asshole about it. I got extra rooms at the Promenade, about fifteen minutes from the arena. Where you should have stayed to begin with, by the way. You guys can have one."

"Thank you." I needed something to replace the bitter after-taste. Fruit juice, gum, gasoline.

He said, "Hey, least I can do after the footage you just gave me."

"Eddie, I'm not in the mood."

"I'm not teasing anymore."

He climbed onto the backseat of the suv before I could tell if he was joking.

I forgot about him as soon as the vehicle pulled away.

I was looking across the road at Eye Patch and his duffel bag.

———

I don't remember looking both ways before crossing the street. But I did check the sidewalk for more guys with bags, or Malhar, or Carrasco with his scars and cane.

Eye Patch was alone.

I got close enough to smell his face.

He tried to step back but hit the cinderblock wall behind him. "Hello, American friend."

"Is it time?"

"Time for what?"

"Are we going? Let's go. You picked a great time."

"Is time for you to step back, is what I think."

I stuck my hand into the duffel bag. Whatever I grabbed was going into his mouth. Gun barrel or grenade, I wasn't picky.

I pulled out an orange.

We both looked at it.

Eye Patch said, "You want half?"

I dropped it into the bag and ripped the flaps open. He had assorted produce and a sack of coffee beans.

"Are you robbing me?"

"What are you doing here?"

"Shopping for food." His head tilted toward the bag. "See?"

"Bullshit. Who are you watching, me or her? And there is a

wrong answer."

"We just want to make sure you still around, you know? We getting ready, would be a shame for you to run away before."

I debated what to say next. If Carrasco knew I wasn't at the Arcoverde estate anymore, maybe he wouldn't go there to snatch me or cause trouble. But he would also know I wasn't there to protect Marcela. His Pomba Gira.

"Woody."

I turned. She was outside the academy. She wore a tight yellow sundress and white sandals, her hair tucked under a white cotton hat with a short brim. She had her hands on her hips.

"What are you doing?"

I held up a finger and turned back to Eye Patch. He was still staring past my shoulder at Marcela. The look on his face said he couldn't wait to offer her up to his Exu. He licked his lips. That decided it.

I gave him a short, hard shot to the liver with my left and kept him from crumpling to the ground with my right. To anybody walking past we looked like two guys having a heart-to-heart. Which we were. Kinda.

I told him, "Listen up. Stop wheezing. Look at me. I'm staying at the Promenade. You know it? Answer or nod."

He nodded, his one eye blinking sporadically.

"You don't come here again. When it's time, you find me there. Got it?"

He nodded again and took a ragged breath. "We going to kill you, man. Is going to be fun."

I left him slumped against the wall.

Marcela waited for me. The good news was I didn't have to tell her Antonio had kicked me out of the house.

From the look on her face, someone already had.

———

As I crossed the street Marcela divided her fury between me and Eye Patch.

"Is he here for the Coluna? To try and take you?"

"No, he's just shopping."

"Shopping? Then why did you hit him?"

"You look very pretty."

"Don't try to distract me with obvious things I already know. What did he want?"

"To scare me. But that was dumb, because when I get scared, I hit."

Her eyes broke away from whatever Eye Patch was doing. She brushed at nothing on the front of my shirt and her voice softened. "Gil told me what happened upstairs. Are you okay?"

"Other than insulting your entire family, not too bad."

She hooked my arm and pulled me into a stroll away from the academy. I checked for Eye Patch. He was gone. We came to an intersection bathed in sunlight from the cross street.

Marcela turned her face into it, eyes closed. "Uncle Antonio can be too sensitive sometimes. And stubbornness is a big part of Arcoverde jiu jitsu."

"Explains how you got your black belt so young."

"Yes, it does."

We kept walking.

She said, "Gil told me you were only trying to help Jairo with his fight."

"Marcela, he'll get destroyed if he follows that strategy. You and

Jairo have both seen my fights. Jairo was cage-side for Burbank. How has it gone this far without someone stomping the brakes?"

"Imagine telling your father almost everything he knows is wrong."

"Gil is the closest thing I have to a father. I tell him he's wrong all the time."

"It is different with Jairo. To go against what Antonio is telling him would be a slap in the face."

"So why didn't you say something?"

"I owe my uncle everything. I could not disrespect him like that."

"But you're okay with Jairo getting locked in a cage and torn to pieces."

"No, I knew it would come up."

I stopped walking. "Hold on. You mean you knew I wouldn't be able to keep my mouth shut."

The little bump on her nose wrinkled. "And you didn't. Thank you."

She kissed me and I forgot to be offended.

———

We got some grilled chicken and vegetables from a street vendor. The food had been rolled in some kind of sauce and spices that made the tin foil edible.

"I will come stay with you," Marcela said.

"In Vegas?"

"Nice try. At the hotel."

"I'm sharing a room with Gil."

"Hm." She shrugged. "So we will not be intimate. Is not good before a fight, anyway."

"That's a myth."

"Says who?"

"The guy who hasn't seen you in over six months."

She leaned her head against my arm. "I know. I don't like it either."

"So come to Vegas."

"Woody, we don't even know if we can survive in the same hotel room. So we try that first, okay?"

"Promise me something."

She peeled her head off my chest to squint at me. "What?"

"What I say next won't affect the chances of you coming to live with me." I didn't know what those chances were, but I couldn't afford to take a chunk out.

Marcela frowned, stared along the street for a few steps. "No. I won't promise. Now say it."

So much for that.

I said, "You can't stay with me at the hotel."

"Can't?"

"As much as I want you to, as much as I want to spend every possible second with you, you're safer at home. Your whole family is there, it's private. And I'm not going to tell Detective Rubin I'm not there anymore—I want him and his guys with you and your family. They'll escort you in for the fights, if you still want to come."

She squeezed my hand, maybe too overwhelmed to say thank you. She kept squeezing.

"Careful, I have to punch people with that later."

She tried to pull my arm off, yanked me around to face her. "Listen, stupid. You aren't here to protect me. I am keeping you safe. So don't be such a hero and send your security to watch over me. They are with you, all the time. We just saw Carrasco's man across the street from the academy. This whole time, I'm watching the street for them to come for you."

"Yeah, me too."

"Oh? What are you watching for?"

"You know." I scanned the narrow road and sidewalks, people walking in small groups and alone, carrying lunch, boxes, sacks. They smiled as they passed us, enjoying the show. "Vans. Gangs. Maybe a pickup truck with guys in the back."

"A pickup truck."

"Like the ones we saw at the Axila."

She nodded. "If they come for you here, they will block both ends of the street with buses and garbage trucks. They will move in from all directions, dozens of them, and spray you with gasoline. They will hold up lighters and tell you to come with them. Have you been watching for that?"

"No."

"I have. Don't you dare tell me I cannot be near you and keep you safe. And I will tell Rubin where you are staying. If he wants to sleep in the bed with you, I will let him. He takes you to the fight, and after that to the airport."

"Yeah? Then what?"

"You fly home, away from Carrasco and his men. You are safe."

"And where are you?"

She hooked my arm again, started walking. "Come on. Let's get to the hotel before Gil. We are together now, and we are still missing each other. No more, okay? While you are here, just be with me."

I felt the sun on my face and the heat coming off her, the smell of her clean hair, and allowed myself to bask in it all, knowing it would be a moment I'd take out and look at, forever, thinking: See how perfect it can be?

———

We took a cab to the Promenade Barra First Hotel. The outside looked nice as we sprinted past it—some palm trees, classy bricks. Probably windows.

Eddie had my name on a room but check-in took too long, the woman behind the counter asking all kinds of pointless questions.

How are you?

Are you enjoying Brazil?

Finally she gave me the damn keycard and Marcela and I stepped into the slowest elevator in the western hemisphere. It made me wonder if gravity was stronger below the equator.

The room had walls and a floor and a door that locked behind us.

The bed put up a valiant effort and the headboard used to be attached to the wall. If anyone was on the other side, they kept quiet and probably hid in the bathtub until the hotel quit shaking.

———

We showered and tried to make the white sheets and blanket on my bed look normal for when Gil showed up. Compared to his bed, which looked like an ice rink—still tight and flat from the housekeeping professionals—mine looked like an abused ski slope.

"Good enough. I'll tell him I took a nap."

Marcela smiled. "I like your naps."

Now that I had the time and focus to look around, the room was impressive. Soft tan walls, real wood floors the color of honey, and a view down onto a pool sparkling in the sunshine.

It pissed me off—one more thing for Eddie to smirk about.

Marcela slipped under my arm and wrapped me up, her face against my chest. "I have to go back to the academy. I have a class to teach."

"I'll come with."

"No, I don't think Uncle Antonio is ready to see you yet. I will talk to him. You stay here. Relax, get ready for your fight. Anybody else would think that sounds silly, but you don't get nervous, do you?"

"Nah. What's the point?"

She tilted her head so I could kiss her.

"I will come here for dinner," she said. "Maybe I bring my uncle, if he stops being a mule. If he comes, will you apologize to him?"

"For trying to save his son's life?"

"For yelling at him in his own academy."

"Right. That. Yeah, I'll apologize."

"Such a grown-up."

I walked her out. The elevator went too fast on the way down, confirming my Brazilian gravity theory. The lobby was mostly deserted, save for a few MMA trainers I recognized checking in and a man reading a magazine in one of the plush chairs against the wall near an elaborate water fountain. He stood up as we passed.

It was Detective Rubin.

I stopped, looked at Marcela. "When did you have time to call him?"

Her eyes were wide. "I didn't."

Marcela's cab puttered away, tilting on ruined suspension.

Rubin stood next to me at the curb. He wore a cream-colored fedora with a tight brim that didn't shield his eyes from the sun, but he didn't seem to mind squinting. He nodded at the hotel grounds. Now that I had the time and interest to look around, I saw the hotel was part of a huge campus of pools, landscaped paths, and towers of rooms and condos.

"Very nice here," Rubin said.

"Did Eddie tell you I was relocating?"

"Hm, no."

"So you're following me? I thought the security didn't start until tomorrow, the weigh-ins."

"That's right."

He turned in a tight circle, his boxing footwork still there, and pulled at his chin. The hotel had an outdoor café along the side of the building, red umbrellas over black tables. Rubin pretended to notice it for the first time. He pointed at it, hand still near his chin.

"Let's get some coffee, eh? My treat."

"What for?"

"So we can talk."

"About what?"

He pulled his chin some more, finally put his eyes on my face. "Carrasco."

Rubin sipped his espresso and grunted, smacked his lips. "Man, they do it right. I hope I didn't break up your date with Marcela."

"She was leaving anyway."

"Good, good. I also hope you didn't, you know. Have too much fun. It's bad right before a fight."

"That's a myth. And I thought you were rooting for Aviso."

"You know, you're right. I'll call some ladies I've arrested, they'll wear you out." He used his index finger to spin the tiny cup on the saucer. "I wasn't going to talk to you about Carrasco, but when you came here, checked in, I knew I wouldn't be able to keep a good eye on you all the time. Not like at the Arcoverde estate. And I need to keep a good eye on you, buddy."

I had an iced tea with a slice of fresh lemon, plucked that morning off a tree on the property according to the server. It was trying to be sweet, but the bitterness ruled. "Who told you? Marcela? Antonio?"

"No no, I am a detective, remember?"

The way he looked at me, sly and playful, made me ask: "What department are you in?"

He shrugged, took his time sipping the espresso. "Batalhão de Operações Policiais Especiais."

"The hell does that mean?"

"For you, it means Special Police Operations Battalion."

"That sounds military."

He lifted the empty cup so the server could see it. "I deal with the favelas."

"From what I saw at Carrasco's place, you aren't doing very well."

"Eh, some people think rules are a good idea for this work. Like you go into your fighting cage, they tell you not to take a chainsaw."

"Nobody has to tell me that."

"But you get the idea," Rubin said. "The way they want to do it, I go in with my team and we arrest the mean people, or shoot them if we really, really have to—but try not to, guys—then we leave it all nice and cozy for the Unidade de Polícia Pacificadora, the Pacifying Police Unit. They swarm into the favelas after we are done and teach the lifelong criminals, these murderous traffickers of drugs and people, how to get a job, wear shoes, contribute to the growth of Brazil. My way, we drop napalm at the top of the Axila da Serpente and watch it roll all the way down. Beautiful. When it's done, we have our mountain back. That, my friend, is pacification."

"Don't people live there? Civilians?"

He leaned back and waved a hand at my point, shooed it away. "If they are there, they are with Carrasco. Or Exu, take your pick."

That floated above the table for a while, waiting for me to chase it.

I said, "You know about Exu?"

"The people who talk to me, they say don't bother bringing my guns and armored vehicles to the Axila again. Their Exu can't be killed. You've seen him?"

"Yeah."

"So you know. Maybe they are right. One of those scars is from me. I shot him point-blank, closer than you and me, sitting here. This was three years ago, when we first tried going into the Axila da Serpente. Everything is so close there, right on top of everything else. Some rooms no bigger than a bathtub, alleys tighter than a phone booth. I turned a corner and there he was. I shot him."

"Was he going to shoot you?"

"How would I know? I wasn't going to wait and see. He fell backward and that monster he keeps, Malhar, dragged him through a doorway. Then we are being shot at from everywhere, every window. We had to retreat."

Rubin stared at his fresh espresso, seeing something else in the steam. "So that was the first time. I've gone in thirteen more."

"And he's still there."

"Taking what he wants, doing what he wants. Killing who he wants. Now I hear he wants your lady. Marcela. For his Pomba Gira?"

I nodded.

"And you think you're gonna run the Coluna da Cobra to keep her."

"That's right."

Rubin gave a low whistle. "This is serious stuff, man."

"Yeah. And it's why you should be protecting her, not me."

"That's not how it works. Carrasco can't just take her. He's a god to his people, he is Exu. He needs them to believe it is Exu's will that Marcela becomes his Pomba Gira. If he just grabs her, it's a man taking a woman. Nothing special. But if it is fate," Rubin twiddled his fingers up toward the umbrella, "it again proves he is Exu."

"Or disproves, after I make it through the Coluna."

Rubin's eyes popped. "Well, since we are talking about the lands of make-believe, we can talk about this. You're right, he's put himself into a little corner, up on his little hill. If he says Exu wants a thing, and Exu doesn't get that thing, what then? I don't think it's happened yet. But now you are here, invited to run the Coluna da Cobra, and stupid enough to think you will survive."

"It's an initiation ritual for the gang. If no one survived, there would be no gang."

He shook his head. "The ones Carrasco wants with him, he lets live. The others, he uses for practice. Or to send a message. A man owes him money, won't pay, Carrasco convinces the man's son he should join Exu's army. The son runs the Coluna and gets cut to pieces. You see? It is Exu's will. If the man had paid, he'd still have his son. Now, if Carrasco does that to an innocent boy over money, what will he do to you for his queen?"

He had that look again. I flashed on him putting me in a jail cell until the Aviso fight, driving me from the arena to the airport afterward to make sure I didn't meddle in his jurisdiction. Telling me it was for my own good while I chewed the bars, knowing Marcela was out here without me.

Rubin said, "So I'm sorry, you not gonna run the Coluna for your lady, for Marcela. You gonna run it for me."

———

I said, "Wait, you want me to go up against Carrasco?"

"Let's not say I want you to. That would be, what's the word . . . unethical? Is that a word?"

"But you aren't going to stop me."

"That sounds better."

"I gotta tell you, this throws up some red flags."

He raised his eyebrows.

I said, "It makes me think you want me to run the Coluna so I can get shot, blown up, an American tourist killed in a Rio favela, so you'll have an excuse to go scorched-earth on Carrasco."

"No no, they won't shoot you. The Coluna is all about beating people to death. Cutting them up."

"Still, red flags."

"I understand your concern."

I waited. "And?"

"And I want to tell you, in the most sincere way, I hope you don't get beaten to death."

"I'm not planning on it."

He studied me. "You really think you can survive this."

I didn't say anything. No reason to repeat the truth.

Rubin said, "Why did you put yourself here? In this position?"

"Marcela is in trouble. My position is between her and it. I didn't put myself there. It's where I belong."

He narrowed his eyes and nodded. "I gotta tell you man, I am in awe of your ignorance and stupidity. It is beyond my understanding. But I will do all I can to make sure you live to tell people how stupid you are, and how smart and brave City Detective Rubin is."

"Yeah? How's that?"

Rubin put his elbows on the table and lowered his voice. "We never know when a Coluna is going to happen. We only see the aftermath, when the gutters at the base of the Axila da Serpente are full of blood. This time, with you, we know. Carrasco wants his Pomba Gira. As soon as they grab you, the Coluna begins."

"I'm still waiting for the part where you help me not get killed."

"All of Carrasco's men will be armed with fists, chains, pipes, clubs, ready to smash your bones."

"You could have skipped that, but go on."

"My team and I will be armed with rifles and shotguns and grenades." He pulled the salt shaker away from the center of the table. It became Carrasco's mountain, the Axila da Serpente. Rubin pointed at the base. "And we will be positioned right behind you, as close as we can get to his territory without alerting him. When you begin the Coluna, we sweep in and catch up to you going up the mountain. You just take cover, sit tight, and we will come to you. Then we go past, and we kill—or arrest, whatever—all of Carrasco's people. When we find Carrasco and Malhar, I have a feeling they won't want to be arrested. This is for the best. If he really is Exu, he belongs in the spirit world anyway."

He tipped the salt shaker over.

"The Axila da Serpente is no more. You and Marcela are safe."

He sat back, ready for admiration.

"I'm starting at the top," I said.

"You're what?"

I set the shaker upright, tapped the lid. "Carrasco wants me to start here. Symbolic, he said, of me trying to escape Exu rather than join him."

Rubin frowned at the salt for half a minute. "This is even better."

"I guess I'm still stupid, because I'm not seeing 'better.'"

"We will come up behind them. All of Carrasco's men will be focused uphill. We will take them by complete surprise. Can you survive until we get to you?"

"I'm going to survive way past that. Whether you get to me or not."

He slapped the table. "Is it confidence or idiocy? I can't tell!"

"Just don't shoot me by accident."

"I make no promises."

Rubin stuck his hand out.

I shook it.

His trigger finger was calloused.

CHAPTER 11

I T WAS NEARLY DARK BY THE TIME GIL SHOWED UP AT THE hotel. I was sprawled on the bed watching a show about fútbol stadium construction. If Gil noticed the multiple used towels and lingering Marcela echoes, he didn't mention it.

He dropped his duffel on the structurally intact bed. "Well, that was a fun day."

"Is Antonio still mad?"

"Mad isn't the right word. Boiling? Maybe seething." Gil stepped to the window to check the view. "He said he isn't going to talk to the police about the Carrasco thing. Doesn't want to ask any favors on your behalf. But you have that detective guy looking after you for the Aviso fight, so we're set there. And you're done with that favela bullshit anyway. Right?"

"Right."

He wasn't looking at me and my wince of shame didn't seep into the tone.

Gil said, "I thought he'd forgotten about it, as offended as he is over what you said to him."

"Ah, man. I'm sorry."

He turned and pointed at me. "Hey. You can't be right and sorry unless you're married. And you're right about the plan they have for Jairo, so no more apologizing." He dropped onto the bed and pulled his shoes off. "I just wish we'd come down here a month ago, hell, a week. Enough time to do something about it."

"We don't need time. All Jairo has to do is fight instead of listen."

"No, what he has to do is ignore everything his Arcoverde jiu jitsu grandmaster father told him leading up to his international MMA debut, in his home city, with the mystique and legendary status of his family on the line. Usually takes more than two days."

"Is he pissed?"

"He's . . . confused. Almost timid. It's weird. I've never seen him like this."

We watched a giant crane swing a block of concrete into place and set it down like a baby.

I said, "Are we welcome at the estate?"

"I am."

"So why are you here?"

"Woody, you're my fighter."

"Yeah, and Antonio is your mentor."

He nodded, hands on his thighs. "The day always comes when the student challenges the teacher. I guess that's today. I had a choice. Keep my mouth shut and let him be wrong, or speak up and let him be offended. Jairo deserves the latter. And Antonio needs it."

"Will he get over it?"

Gil shrugged.

I said, "So when will the day come when I challenge you, teacher?"

He stood up. "You challenge me every goddam day. It's a miracle I haven't thrown you off the Hoover Dam yet."

He walked past the foot of the bed on the way to the bathroom and tossed one of his shoes onto my chest. The odor rolled over my face. I wretched and slapped the shoe into the far corner.

"Jesus, that smells like stale buttered popcorn and expensive cheese."

He started the shower. Before he shut the door he said, "And this room smells like athletic sex. Next time Marcela comes here, open a window."

———

I called Marcela while Gil cleaned up.

"I miss you."

She laughed. "You just saw me. A lot of me."

"Not enough. Are you at the academy?"

"Yes, we are about to leave."

"I need to talk to Jairo. Face to face."

"Mm, Uncle Antonio won't like that."

"I figured. That's why I'm calling you."

"Oh, how nice."

"One of the reasons I'm calling you. Can you get Jairo out of the house, meet me for dinner?"

"No," she said. "The family is getting together tonight."

"Again?"

"I mean the rest of the family."

"There are more?" I said.

"Why do you want to meet with Jairo?"

"I need to talk to him about his fight with Preston."

"Didn't you already do that? It's why my uncle's jaw is shut like a clam."

"What about breakfast tomorrow?"

She paused. "I have an early class to teach. I can bring him with me and drop him off with you."

"I don't want you to get on your uncle's bad side."

"That will never happen. He will know you talked me into it, and he will hate you more."

"Sounds about right."

"I have to go now."

"Be safe."

"Dream about me," she said.

"Always."

———

I did dream about her. Sort of.

I was at the base of a mountain of red candles, some of them lit. Marcela was at the top. She crouched and turned in a circle, getting ready to fight something I couldn't see. I climbed, the candles shifting and swallowing my hands and feet.

Aviso was there, watching me and shaking his head. "Come on. Let's fight."

"I have to do this first."

"Why?"

I ignored him and kept climbing.

Marcela yelled at me, "Don't! You're going to ruin it!"

If I kept going, I'd erode the platform she was on and she'd tumble down.

I could get to her first.

My next burst up the slope brought the whole thing down. Red candles slid past me like lava, heavy wax clunking together.

Marcela said, "Now it won."

She tipped into the avalanche and disappeared.

More candles caught fire. The wax dripped and pooled, formed a hard shell across the face of the mountain, sealing her in. I tore myself awake, blinking at a lingering image of my hands caked in red from trying to dig her out.

———

I left the room and Gil's snoring and found the hotel gym. The only other person in it at seven a.m. was a lightweight fighter named Kuthe. He was walking on a treadmill wearing a knit cap and a silver sauna suit that looked like a trash bag. He saw me and nodded.

I said, "How much weight you cutting?"

"Twelve more pounds, last time I checked." He nodded at the swath of sweat glistening on the treadmill runner. "Might be down to ten by now."

"You got plenty of time."

The press conference and weigh-ins weren't until two in the afternoon.

"That's the idea," Kuthe said. "Don't want to pass out on the scale like last time."

"Or you could fight at one-seventy. Stop trying to kill yourself."

"And start over at the back of the line? No thanks. I win this one, I'm in the top three."

"Eddie tell you that?"

He shrugged. "It's my best shot at a belt."

I slapped his shoulder and left him alone. He was miserable enough without me jabbering at him. I grabbed a treadmill three over, stuck my earbuds in and started running.

Outside would have been better—maybe barefoot on the beach, see if these Brazilian fighters knew something we didn't—but I wanted to keep my blinders on and just get some work done, blood flowing. As soon as I stepped out the door I'd be checking for Rubin, Carrasco, Eye Patch. Rabid Aviso fans who wanted to drag me into the surf and hold me under.

I pushed all of it to the side and concentrated on Aviso, the serious black and white billboard face. I shadowboxed with it. Gave it a black eye, a split lip. A nice swollen gash through the eyebrow.

Much better.

My imaginary Aviso kept zeroing in on my arm, trying to clamp on and wrench it around. Every time I smacked him with a fist, shin, elbow. Kept him off me and within the range I liked— the one where people get hurt.

I put the face back on the billboard. The female model cringed and sidled off the canvas.

Kuthe the lightweight dropped off his treadmill and shuffled toward the sauna. I checked the clock, which said I'd been running for an hour and fifteen minutes. The mantras in my ears had cycled through without notice. I felt good.

Gil was awake and dressed when I got back to the room. He said, "I checked with Eddie. He knows we can't really go back to the academy, said we can use the arena for our training today— not the cage, one of the prep rooms—but we'll still get our time in the cage to feel it out."

"What a guy. I'm gonna have breakfast with Jairo. Maybe he

and I can work it out, get us off Antonio's shit list."

Gil said, "My guess? You meddle more with his son, you'll get us bumped up to the top slot on that list. No one's been able to displace Diego Maradona for twenty-nine years."

"Who?"

"Argentinean soccer player who had a rivalry with Antonio's favorite player, Pele. He cheated in the '86 FIFA World Cup, drove Antonio crazy."

"Man, that guy can hold a grudge."

"He issued a challenge to Maradona to a fight to the death." Gil blinked a few times. "I don't think Maradona accepted. My point is, don't make it worse."

"Who, me?"

Gil didn't bother acknowledging it. "I'm going to find coffee. Let's meet up at the arena at eleven, keep your technique sharp. And I mean it. Don't make things harder on Jairo than they already are. Don't make him choose between us and his father."

"I want him to choose between winning and losing."

Gil considered it, shook his head. "Nope. I need coffee before I can deal with this. Good luck."

———

I grabbed the same table Rubin and I had used, where I could see the street through the ornamental palms and the lobby on the other side of giant windows.

The academy van swerved into the horseshoe-shaped drive-way before I could ask the server if they had whey protein. The passenger door flopped open and Jairo dropped out, took a few steps to keep his balance because the van was still rolling. Marcela leaned across his empty spot to wave at me, smiling and yelling something, her seat so far forward the steering wheel was in her lap. She took off fast enough to thump the door shut, teetering the van to the exit and rolling into traffic.

I never saw a brake light.

Jairo sat down with a tight smile and dark circles under his eyes. The rest of his skin looked waxy. His bald head, typically gleaming like polished bronze, had no luster.

"Marcela's driving," I asked, "or do you have the flu?"

"I'm fine."

The server appeared. I ordered six eggs, a pile of bacon, and pineapple juice. Jairo asked for a hot tea, no lemon.

"You should get more than that," I said.

He shook his head.

"At least get the lemon. It's really good here."

"What do you want to talk about?"

All right, straight to business.

"Does Antonio know you're talking to me?"

"No. And he won't find out."

"It's such a scandal, why did you come?"

"Because you stepped up to help Marcela, even though it was a stupid thing to do, agreeing to fight . . . them. And you are my brother. But don't ask me to disrespect my father. You do that, we are no longer anything. We are nothing."

"Okay, take it easy. Is that why you're all stressed out? What I said yesterday about your game plan?"

"No. A little. It has made me think about things I did not want to think about."

"What things?"

"It's bad enough to think them. To say them, even worse."

"What could be worse that what we've been through?"

He wiped his beaded forehead with a napkin and stared at the table. Maybe flashing back to the cesspit we got thrown into. Nothing creates a stronger alliance than giving two warriors a common enemy. What we had to do to get out of that hole would haunt us forever. And it would bind us.

"The other night," Jairo said. "At that place."

"The Axila?"

"That . . . man."

"Carrasco."

He winced, nodded. If I wasn't absolutely sure it was Jairo Arcoverde sitting across from me, I would have thought he might cry.

Jairo said, "I think he cursed me."

———

"Since we drove away from that place," Jairo said, "I have felt heavy. Like I am under water. Moving too slow."

"You were moving fine when you made me run up that damn mountain yesterday."

"You think I was pushing you, huh? Good, it's what I wanted you to think. But I was trying to outrun whatever he did to me. What he put on me. It did not work. Even though it was dark."

"I don't understand."

"There are rumors about the kind of magic he does."

"You can say his name. Carrasco. Hangman. Exu. Asshole."

"Please, no more." Jairo crossed himself. "One of the curses, you ask the spirits to cling to a man's shadow. One by one, the spirits gather. They fill your shadow, making you heavy, so heavy you can't move. You don't get out of bed. The shadow of your arm is so heavy you can't feed yourself. So you grow thin, but you weigh too much to breathe."

"And you think Carrasco put this curse on you."

"I am dragging myself around, man. I pick my foot up, it wants to crash back to the floor. I spar with Edson and Javier, I throw a punch at their face, you know what I hit? Their stomach." He let his fist fall in an arc, shoulder to lap. It stayed there, a limp collection of fingers. "So I tried running in the dark, with no shadow. And it didn't work."

"Jairo, you aren't cursed. You're nervous. Your first Warrior fight is tomorrow night."

"No. I don't get nervous for tournaments. Never have."

"This ain't a tournament, buddy. This is you locked in a cage with a large man seeking to destroy you. And you have a shitty game plan—which might actually be a curse—and you know it. Every muscle in your body is telling you you're walking into a disaster. Listen to them."

He wasn't convinced.

"Come with me," I said.

———

We jumped in a cab and looped around a small body of water to get to the HSBC Arena. I checked for any sign of Rubin and his men, Carrasco and his soldiers. If any of them were around, they were better at being sneaky than I was at being perceptive.

The exterior of the arena was bright white and sparkling glass and looked like a high-end airplane hangar. It had some architectural flair: windows set at an angle to make it seem like the walls were either sinking into the ground or getting sucked toward the wide entrance doors.

The only people going in and out were arena employees, getting the place ready for the press conferences, weigh-ins, and the big show on Saturday. The lobby was plastered with Warrior banners for the event, scowling faces staring at each other across Eddie's logo.

Jairo pointed at one and gave a tired smile. It was at least forty feet long and twenty high. On the left end was my face, looking like it was a day past evolving from cave life, giving the stink eye to Aviso on the right. His cut jaw and perfect stubble were bathed in warm light. Instead of glowering back at me he looked into the camera with a raised eyebrow and a smirk, asking everyone who passed, Can you believe this guy?

Right below it was another banner, just as big, shouting something in Portuguese. My face was on that one too. And my name.

I asked Jairo, "What does that say?"

He was still smiling. "Come to Las Vegas and train with the nasty American fighter Aaron 'Woodshed' Wallace at the all-new WarriorDome! Choke him! Punch him! Let your children jump on his back!"

"It does not."

He shrugged and started toward the inner sanctum of the arena. I stared at the banner, judging if I could jump high enough to rip it down, and finally caught up to Jairo in mild defeat.

The workers smiled and waved at him, pumped fists and hollered things that sounded encouraging. When they noticed me something pulled their fists and faces down. One guy waxing the floor stopped what he was doing, glared at me, and spit on the patch he'd just finished. He blew a kiss at Jairo and went back to work, whistling something festive.

I held my fighter ID by the thick black lanyard and showed it to any security guard who looked at me twice. It would have been easier to just hang it around my neck, but I felt like there wasn't any room what with all the clamped hands—Carrasco, Rubin, Eddie—I think I even felt a finger or two from Antonio, checking my pulse.

As we went deeper into the cinderblock hallways lined with production equipment and sponsor stockpiles, the arena began to feel like a sanctuary. The hype banners fell away, replaced by framed evacuation diagrams and pieces of paper taped next to bright red prep room doors, fighter names written in black Sharpie. The rooms were big enough for multiple fighters to get ready but each paper held only two names.

This was where my work started.

I wasn't dumb enough to think we couldn't be followed. Rubin and his men could flash badges. Carrasco's could produce something even more effective—cash. I didn't care. The whole point of agreeing to the Coluna was to keep Eye Patch and the others away from Marcela, so if they wanted to try to keep up with me, fine.

We found my door first. The sheet of paper had three names written on it. The first name was Wallace. Below that Arcoverde had been scribbled out and replaced with Preston.

Jairo's opponent.

"What the hell?" I said.

Jairo didn't seem surprised. "My father must have called them."

"No. You and I are in the same room."

"He will not allow it."

"Hold on." I stalked past the other doors, found Jairo's name on the last one, as far away from me as Antonio could get him.

The other name on the sheet was Aviso.

"You're shitting me."

Jairo didn't say anything.

"I don't want to seem dramatic here, but do you think your father would talk to Aviso and his trainers, let them know my game plan?"

Jairo paused, gave the question a furrowed brow. "I think, if he believes you will benefit from learning a lesson, he will do what he thinks is necessary for you to learn it."

So Antonio's fingers weren't checking my pulse.

They were looking for pressure points.

Weak spots.

And they were pushing.

———

I found some poor guy with a marker and made him redo the names. He kept looking at Jairo for confirmation that I wasn't trying to get him fired.

Inside our prep room, Jairo said, "He will move me again."

"That's up to you, not him. No matter what, you're stepping into that cage with a new strategy."

"Woody. I can't fill my head with new things the day before the fight." He shook spread fingers around his shaved scalp, still waxy under the fluorescents. "It's already crazy in here, everything scattered and bouncing around."

"I know, brother."

The room was a forty-by-forty square of painted concrete with thin carpet and exposed steel beams twenty feet above our heads. The front left and back right corners were set up like conversation pits with short black leather couches arranged in a square around tables covered in water bottles and fruit. An open doorway in the back left corner led to a three-stall bathroom with two showers.

The floor along opposite walls was lined with a double run of sparring mats, plenty of room for both fighters to get warm and work on strategies, use the wall to simulate the cage. That left a swath of no-man's-land about twenty feet wide down the middle, more than enough for the pacing, celebrations, and consolations when the show was over.

Tables along the back wall were stocked with sponsor equipment—shorts, shirts, gloves, headgear—for fight teams to take home.

I found the right sizes for Jairo and shoved them into his arms, told him, "You've taught me so much about grappling, jiu jitsu, submissions, escapes. Worked with Gil to make sure I didn't do anything too stupid, and told me how to survive when I did. Saved my ass against Burbank and Zombi. I've tried to repay you by helping with your striking. The right distance. How to use your knees, elbows."

He nodded.

"Now I'm going to teach you the most important aspect of my fighting. The thing that gets my hand raised while the other guy's gets tapped for an IV."

He looked worried. "What?"

"How to forget all that shit and just fight."

"I am Preston," I announced.

We were on the mats along the left wall, both of us suited up in the sponsor gear and clothing like we were filming a how-to video on selling out. I threw a slow right jab and shot in, wrapped my arms behind Jairo's knees and got ready to drive him backward for a double-leg takedown.

"Now what?" I said.

Jairo sprawled, dropped his hips onto my shoulder and shimmied to his left, got his back against the wall and stopped. I still had his legs and was staring at the mats, waiting.

Nothing happened.

"What's going on up there?"

Jairo said, "This is the plan. You saw it at the academy."

"Yeah, and I still don't know what you're doing."

"If Preston goes for a takedown, I get my back against the cage and stay upright. I wait to hear what my father is saying."

I swore into my headgear. "And what's he going to say?"

"I don't know. It changes."

"It changes?" I let go and stood up. "What's that mean?"

Jairo wouldn't look at me. "He wants to spend the first round watching how Preston is trying to fight me. The second round, we will try different things, see how he responds. The third round is for picking one strategy we think will work and executing it."

I took a deep breath. "I've seen Preston fight. The first round, his way of fighting you will be trying his damnedest to knock you stiff with that right hand. That fails, he'll dump you on your ass and pound your face into the canvas. Rounds two and three, rinse and repeat."

"I won't let him do that."

"How?"

He spent way too long adjusting his gloves. "That is for my father to decide."

"Jesus, I'm starting to get depressed. This is like watching a lion at the zoo—every fiber of his body wanting to stalk, chase, tackle, devour—but the handler keeps saying, no, you just lie there. I'll tell you when you can eat."

Jairo didn't respond.

"Then another lion comes into the cage and attacks. The handler says, wait, let's see if he uses his teeth or his claws. Jairo, I've never seen you get in a bad position. No matter what random shit happens, you always end up in a spot where you know what you should do. You get side mount, work to get a knee on his chest. From there you get the mount. Then a submission. You did it to me hundreds of times when you came to Vegas. Hell, I knew it was coming and still couldn't do a damn thing."

He nodded.

"So why, all of a sudden, should it change?"

"Because this is different than jiu jitsu. You said it yourself."

"No, I said this isn't a jiu jitsu tournament. This is fighting. You don't worry about points or progressing to the next match. You pack yourself like a cannon and fire into your opponent's face. I've seen what you can do when you're pacing yourself for a long day of training. What happens when you know you only have fifteen minutes to live or die?"

"Okay."

"No, scratch that. Not fifteen minutes. Preston doesn't deserve three rounds with you. He's a lamb in a lion's cage. He gets one round. Five minutes. How much damage can you do in five minutes?"

Jairo smiled. "A lot."

"Says who? Your father?"

"Says me."

"Well let's see it."

We stepped away from the wall and I shot in for another takedown.

The ceiling looked very interesting as it passed.

———

Gil stood in the doorway to the prep room, looking between his phone and me and Jairo sprawled on the couches in the front left corner.

He chucked the giant duffel with our gear into the room. "Huh. The text you sent me says, 'At the arena. See you before presser.'"

I emptied my sixth water bottle and cracked another, tossed one to Jairo.

Gil said, "I don't see anything here about you and Jairo beating the shit out of each other. What's that on your forehead?"

"Wall burn."

He accepted this. "Either of you seriously hurt? Anything that'll make the doc pull you from the fights?"

Jairo and I looked at each other. He had a little goose egg under one eye from a stray elbow and was rubbing one of his knuckles, which had found the top of my head in a scramble. I had my forehead patch and tired arms from slapping the mats to absorb takedown impacts. All in all, a damn fine day.

"We're good," I said.

"You're idiots. You think Antonio was pissed before, you should see him now."

Jairo stopped massaging his hand. "You spoke to him?"

"I listened. He's not interested in conversation right now." Gil pulled a smaller bag from the duffel and tossed it at Jairo. "You'd better get cleaned up. The press is starting to roll in, and Eddie has half the room set up for you."

Jairo rose from the couch and stood over me. He held his fist out. I bumped it with mine. He carried the bag into the bathrooms. A shower kicked on.

I said, "Where'd you get that bag for him?"

"Told you. I talked to Antonio."

"You went to the academy?"

"Somebody has to try to make peace, Woody."

"You see Marcela?"

"She's fine. And no, I was not able to make peace, in case you're interested."

I shrugged against the leather couch. "If he wants to apologize, I'll accept."

"He does not feel the same way."

"I'm not sorry for trying to help Jairo. He and I made a lot of progress in here, but I can't say we undid all the damage. Antonio fucked his head up, man."

"Yeah, well, Antonio says he was fine before you showed up."

"He wasn't. He just didn't know how to tell his father he was doing it wrong."

Gil hesitated.

"What?" I said.

"He also told me Jairo was fine before you took him to that place. The Axila da Serpente."

"Are you serious? He's still talking about curses?"

"Whatever it is—doubt, fear, a damn curse—he's different. You can't deny that."

"The past few hours, in this room, the Jairo we know came back. It was like when he was in Vegas, strutting down the Strip and blowing the walls out of the gym. Untouchable. Antonio should have been here watching instead of bitching to you."

"If he was here, I don't think it would have happened. He told me he switched rooms." Gil stepped into the hallway and checked the names next to the door, came back in massaging his temples, mumbling to himself. "Well, that's going to be interesting."

"No way am I sharing space with Preston," I said. "And if Antonio wants to whisper in Aviso's ear, he can walk his ass down the hall to do it."

"Careful," Gil said. "Things are dicey right now, but that's still Jairo's father. My mentor."

"He's acting like a spoiled brat."

"No, he's acting like a man who has spent decades earning respect and the right to do things the way he sees fit."

"Jairo's earned that right too. So have you."

"It's not that simple."

"Sure it is."

Gil cocked his head, leaned into the hallway again. "Fuck, here he comes."

I stood up in case of attack.

Antonio stopped in the doorway. He wore black pants and a white button-down shirt, crisp lines head to toe, and carried a small white canvas bag that might have been green when it was made during one of the World Wars.

He nodded at Gil, took his time staring to the left, where the sheet with our names was.

One eyebrow twitched.

Without looking at me, he said, "You are no longer allowed

to see Marcela. I will tell her good-bye for you."

He walked away.

Simple.

CHAPTER 12

I TRIED CALLING MARCELA TWELVE TIMES AFTER SHOWERING and before getting dressed for the press conference. Each time it went to voicemail.

I texted her: Call now.

When five seconds passed and she didn't call, I told myself it was because she was teaching a class.

Not obeying her uncle and on her way to forgetting about me.

Not stuffed into the trunk of a car and on her way to Carrasco.

Teaching a class.

I paced the prep room and started sweating again.

Gil watched me from the couch, his head turning like an oscillating fan. "Take it all and put it toward Aviso. That's all you care about over the next twenty-four hours."

"Easy for you to say."

"I find the truth easy to say. And your fight is the only thing you can control, so why waste energy on anything else?"

"Antonio wants me to lose this fight."

"Maybe. Take it out on Aviso."

"Telling me I can't see Marcela."

"Hey, maybe so Aviso can date her."

I stopped pacing. "Did he say that?"

"No, but did it work?"

I thought about it. "Yes."

"Good! Picture that—the two of them, laughing about you. Your jiu jitsu, your gross scars."

"Gross?"

"You ever write her love letters, anything really sappy?"

"They aren't sappy."

"Sure." Gil tugged at his chin. "Okay, they're laughing about the way you kiss."

"Jesus."

"And they're laughing about it while they're kissing."

"I'm starting to get miserable here."

"You fight better when you're miserable. You're a beast. Hey, you think Aviso would put Marcela up on the billboards with him?"

"You're gonna get this guy killed."

Gil checked his watch. "Time for the press conference. You get close enough to Aviso, maybe you can smell her."

It worked.

I forgot about Antonio, Rubin, Carrasco.

Until I saw all three of them about five minutes later.

———

I stalked out of the prep room and followed the waving arms of men in red blazers through a door that led to the backstage side of a giant black curtain.

The noise from a large crowd buzzed on the other side.

A short woman wearing a headset and Warrior Staff shirt grabbed my arm. Her laminated photo ID badge told me her name was Carol. She pulled me into the line of fighters waiting to go onstage, arranged according to where we would sit.

I was in front of Preston and behind a Japanese kid named Okari, who was challenging a water bug Brazilian named Leandro for the featherweight title. Aviso was somewhere in front of all of us. I caught a glimpse of him talking to Jairo, rubbing my brother's shaved head.

Preston nudged me. "Hey, no hard feelings when I put it on your boy tomorrow, huh?"

He was three inches taller than me and built like a power-lifter—thick torso, slaughterhouse slabs of lats and traps. He had deep-set eyes and little cauliflowered ears stuck onto his flat-topped head like an afterthought.

"Not now," I said.

Carol pulled the curtain aside and let us out. We filed onto the platform below a dizzying, floor-to-ceiling Warrior backdrop. There was a pit of reporters and cameramen in folding chairs in front of the stage. Behind them, stadium seating rose into the darkness below the roof, at least four stories high.

The crowd roared and jumped right into Portuguese chants. Eddie waited at the podium, centered between two long tables. All the Brazilian fighters were seated on his left, foreigners on his right. So it was Okari, Eddie, and Leandro between me and Aviso. I could trip over the bantams on my way and Eddie might get stuck in my teeth, but that wouldn't stop me.

I leaned forward and back to get a good look at Aviso. He smiled and waved at the crowd, slapped the Brazilian guys on the shoulders and posed for photos. He was loose, having a good time.

The balls on this guy, yukking it up when he was about to get locked in a cage with me. I turned away before my feet carried my fists across the dais. The curtain was still pulled aside and I locked eyes with Antonio Arcoverde, standing at the edge of the shadows, hands clasped behind his back. His expression was flat, dead.

Behind him, Gil was talking to Detective Rubin. Three men stood off to the side in civilian clothes, watching everything. Rubin glanced at me. He didn't smile or wave.

Shit. He'd said he'd be around during the pre-fight circus, but why was he talking to Gil? And what was he telling him? If Rubin told him I'd been lying, that not only was I still planning to run the Coluna but that I was also working with Rubin to bring Carrasco down, I'd know it when Gil's hands clamped around my neck.

Eddie leaned into the microphone and started rolling hype. "All right guys, take a seat. How you doing, Rio?"

The response ruffled my shirt. Each fighter had a wired earpiece for the various interpreters and a pair of water bottles. You could tell who was still cutting weight—they shoved their water aside or under the table so they wouldn't stare at it.

I checked Gil and Rubin again. Rubin was explaining something, his hands pressing and squeezing the air. The other three guys were gone.

Eddie said, "Whoa, you're gonna blow the color out of my hair. This crowd knows what's up."

They cheered louder, stomping and singing and waving giant Brazilian flags that slapped five rows of people who didn't seem to care. My eyes were drawn to a gap in the frenzy, in the first row of seats above the reporters' pit. Two seats in that row held the only people in the crowd sitting down.

One was Malhar.

The other was Carrasco.

—

Carrasco lifted a hand and nodded when he noticed me staring. He wore a brand-new baseball hat—Brazilian green with the flag on the front—a white linen suit and had his walking stick between his feet. His black sunglasses were in deep shadow under the brim of the hat, hiding whatever was behind them.

Malhar was squeezed into a gray suit, a sheen of grease on his face and bald head. He glared at me and leaned to his right so his massive left shoulder wouldn't invade Carrasco's space.

The poor kid who'd paid for the seat next to Malhar stood and leaned against the railing. He wasn't cheering or chanting. Both hands gripped the rail with white knuckles. He glanced back and shuffled to his right, pressing into the guy next to him to get away from Malhar, who looked like a grumpy, sweaty shark.

I checked on Jairo. From his smile and relaxed shoulders, he hadn't seen them yet.

Eddie said, "Okay, let's get it started. We brought some amazing fights to Brazil for you guys, the best fight fans in the world."

The crowd rose to a boil. Eddie worked from the ends of the tables toward the center, introducing the matchups of preliminary fighters, the undercard, then the main event.

When he got to Jairo, Eddie said, "Now this is how lucky you guys are. For the first time in history, we have three fights that could be on top of the card. The first one—you might know this gentleman—features Jairo Arcoverde in his Warrior debut against the very formidable Tim Preston."

He was shouting by the end of it. The fans drowned him out with chants of "Ar-co-ver-de! Ar-co-ver-de!" until Jairo stood and bowed, waved them down.

Eddie said, "You all know what Jairo can do in jiu jitsu. We all can't wait to see what happens when he gets in the cage, and we don't think there's anybody better suited to giving him a tough-as-hell fight than big ol' Timmy Preston. Preston won two wrestling titles at Iowa—"

Eddie's amplified voice was lost under the crowd's singing. He quit talking and looked at Preston, who shrugged and held up his right fist, about the size of a four-door compact.

The interpreter spoke through my earpiece: "They are singing 'Eu Sou Brasileiro,' which means 'I am Brazilian.' It's a popular song at fútbol matches."

After all the horror stories about the Brazilian fans screaming for our blood, this wasn't so bad—just a bunch of people passionate about their country and their fighters.

Eddie shouted, "Moving along. He's on billboards and inside every fashion magazine and every woman's fantasies, but we love him for what he does inside the cage. Rio de Janeiro, it's your very own Rafa de Jaguaribe, but we all call him Aviso!"

The cheers and stomping shook our table and knocked some of the water bottles over. I kept my eyes forward, not looking at Aviso or Malhar and Carrasco. The biggest compliment I could give any of them was an indication I cared, so I acted like I didn't.

Aviso wasn't going to allow that.

He stood up and vaulted over the table, stood with his fists raised over his head and bellowed at the crowd. Cameras flashed from the pit and the stadium seats. It got to the point where if I kept looking away, it would be obvious I was looking away, which was worse than looking. So I got my first good view of the man I was going to fight in about twenty-four hours.

Aviso was tall and lean with the bone and muscle structure of an Olympic swimmer. His wide shoulders made an inverted triangle down to a narrow waist. His arms and legs were long, ending in large hands and feet.

He did a cartwheel into a back flip, landed on his feet in front of my chair and faced me with his hands on his hips. He tilted his head back and aimed his squared jaw and sharp cheekbones at me, pointed a finger.

"This is new," Eddie said, "here's Aviso helping me introduce his opponent."

The crowd started chanting something else. It sounded like "buy more air."

Eddie said, "He's from the back alleys of Las Vegas and has more scars on his face than a dog has fleas—everybody give him a warm welcome—Aaron 'Woodshed' Wallace!"

The interpreter said, "The fans are chanting '*Vai morrer*,' which means 'You are going to die.'"

I nodded. Slightly more harsh than "I am Brazilian."

Aviso whirled to the crowd and started dancing, some blend of salsa and capoeira that had the reporters locked in and the fans foaming at the mouth. Malhar and Carrasco were motionless in the sea of madness, Malhar's pig eyes and Carrasco's dark lenses on me.

Aviso took a deep bow, rose into a handstand, walked on his hands around the end of the table and sat down.

"Amazing athleticism," Eddie said. "Just spectacular. Ladies and gentlemen, this is going to be one helluva fight!"

He introduced the main event. Okari earned a chant that

sounded like "Oh-lay, oh-lay oh-lay oh-lay, oh-lay, oh-lay."

The interpreter said, "They are chanting 'Olé, olé-olé-olé, olé, olé.' It means nothing."

Okari patted my shoulder.

Eddie said, "Those are your fighters, Brazil. Man, I wish it was going down tonight! I hope you're all coming to the weigh-ins after this, because who knows, the way some of these guys look right now, the first round might start a day early. Look at Woodshed down there—he's ready to chew through the table."

The crowd answered. "*Vai morrer! Vai morrer!*"

Eddie said, "Let's do some questions now. We'll start with reporters' row down here, then you fans can have a chance to ask your favorite fighters anything you want."

Malhar finally moved, standing and waving at the Warrior usher who carried the wireless microphone.

———

The first reporter was a blonde woman from Sports Illustrated. She asked Jairo, "How much pressure is on you to represent and uphold the Arcoverde name in this fight?"

Jairo didn't hesitate. "I feel no pressure. Our name is strong no matter what happens."

"Does that mean you're prepared to lose?"

"No, I will not lose. But the Arcoverde name is bigger than this fight."

The reporter glanced at Eddie. "Bigger than Warrior Inc.?"

"To me, yes," Jairo said.

She said, "Eddie, what is your response to that?"

Eddie leaned into his microphone. "My response is: stop

causing trouble. And Jairo has obviously been hit in the head a lot getting ready for this fight. Next question."

In the crowd, the body language and expression of the usher with the wireless mic showed he was carefully trying to explain to Malhar it wasn't time for audience questions yet. Malhar snatched the microphone out of his hand and squeezed it in a gnarled fist, turned and handed it to Carrasco. He sat down and glared at the usher, who crouched on one of the aisle steps, defeated.

Carrasco held the mic in his lap and crossed his spindly legs, a tight smile tugging his mouth to the right.

Gil and Antonio stood shoulder to shoulder backstage. I couldn't tell if they were listening with severe concentration or royally pissed. Maybe both. Rubin was gone.

A reporter from Fox Sports asked Jairo, "Do you feel there are any issues of loyalty when it comes to your country and your friendship with Aaron Wallace?"

"No," Jairo said.

"But aren't you helping him get ready to fight a fellow Brazilian?"

"He is my brother. There is no problem."

Some of the crowd booed.

The reporter said, "A source told me that you and Tim Preston had switched prep rooms, so you were with Aviso and Preston was with Woody. But I checked the names on the rooms, and you're with Woody. Any comment on that?"

"No," Jairo said.

"So there's no trouble between you two?"

"None."

The reporter said, "Woody, anything to add?"

"No."

"Man, it's like a mob trial up there. Preston, what do you think?"

"It don't matter which room I'm in, or who's brothers with who. I'll beat anyone Eddie puts in front of me."

The reporter waited for the crowd's hatred to subside. "Aviso?"

Aviso gave a lazy shrug. "Maybe they having trouble now, but they really gonna have it after the fight. Because I'm gonna carry Brazil with me into that cage, and I'm gonna carry his broken arm out when I leave."

The fans started singing again.

Aviso shouted, "So Jairo, I'm sorry man, but your brother over there is gonna ask you, 'Why was Aviso so mean to me, why he break my arm, what I do now with my arm so useless?' When he ask you these things, you just tell him, 'Hey, Aviso warned you.'"

The singing and chanting lasted longer than my patience. Aviso basked in it. Malhar and Carrasco were statues. I didn't see Rubin or any of his men lurking near the exits or aisles.

A reporter was asking me something.

"—think you will be intimidated by Aviso's handsomeness and godlike movement?"

"Huh?"

The reporter, a Brazilian man, grinned. "I guess I am asking if you will be too worried about hitting Aviso's face. It is very important to him, and to all of us. The world, really."

"I'll be worried if I don't hit it. But that won't happen, so no, I'm not worried."

Aviso chimed in. "Not so fast, dog face."

Dog face?

He said, "You not gonna hit my face, you not gonna hit my body. You not gonna hit anything man, because I'm so fast. I make you look stupid, and slow, and ridiculous."

"We'll see."

"Yeah, we will. Look at my face, man. Look at it." Aviso stood and leaned over the table, turned his jaw left and right so everyone could see. His grin spread wide. "No scars, man. Not even a broken nose, ever. Why is this? Because I don't get hit."

"Yeah, I heard that about you."

"Now you gonna see it."

"What I heard is, you can't take it. You get smacked once and give up."

"No, that's wrong."

I frowned, tried to look confused. It came a little too easily. "But isn't it true you fire sparring partners who manage to hit you in the face?"

Aviso shook his head. The grin slipped a bit. "You dreaming, man. Your brain is mushy. Who tole you that?"

"Hey, maybe I'm wrong. I guess we'll find out tomorrow when I smash your nose flat, bust your eyebrows open and knock that jaw crooked. Remember, though, you can't fire me."

Eddie couldn't resist sticking his needle in the balloon. "I can. But hell, the way you two are pumping this fight, why would I?"

Aviso said, "I didn't want to say it out of respect for the Arcoverdes, but maybe he don't know what he is saying because Antonio kicked him out of the Academia. And his home."

The hush started on the dais and flowed through the reporters, washed over the crowd once the interpreter was done.

Eddie turned and waited for a response from me. It didn't matter who told Aviso—Eddie, Antonio, hell, maybe even Rubin—I couldn't let it turn into a distraction for me or Jairo.

I smiled. "See? I haven't even put leather on his face yet, he's already running and changing the subject."

Eddie was smart enough to see what could happen. If this

turned into America vs. the Arcoverdes—or worse for him, Warrior Inc. vs. the Arcoverdes—he might not be welcome in Brazil again.

He yelled over the buzz, which was building into an angry hum like a shaken hornet's nest. "You reporters done? I'll come back to you—let's hear what the fans have to say. You guys have something to say, right? Hell yeah! We got a few mics running around out there, who has it first?"

———

Carrasco turned the microphone in his thin fingers, flicked a switch on the bottom and tapped the black foam. The speakers thumped.

"Hello, how are you? I have a question for the American fighter, ah, Mr. Wallace. You seem so serious about this fight, so much like a businessman. But you are in lovely Brazil, a place of joy and fun. Are you doing anything while you are here to enjoy yourself?"

Past the podium, Jairo's hands had turned to fists on the table. He glared at Carrasco, his chest rising and falling like he'd just finished another run up the mountain. I had no interest in whatever Carrasco was pulling. I would have grabbed Jairo and walked out if my stupid pride didn't make me stare into his black lenses and open my mouth.

"I enjoy fighting."

"Yes, we all know you are very tough, sure. But you must have other things to do while you are here."

"Nope."

Carrasco's grin twitched. "This is too bad. Maybe I help you find something to do. Are you busy tonight?"

I glanced at Eddie. His face was pursed, like he didn't know what the hell was going on and didn't appreciate it. He said, "Let's keep the questions focused on Warrior topics, thanks."

"Sorry, sure," Carrasco said. He asked me, "If you are no longer welcome in the Arcoverde home, who is watching my Pomba Gira?"

Jairo cursed and pounded the table. I resisted the urge to whip my phone out and try her again. Gil and Antonio had vanished from offstage.

Relax. They left to get Marcela to a safe place.

The reporters smelled something, murmured to each other to see who knew what this guy in the white suit was talking about. When no one did, hands popped up. The crowd started bubbling again.

Eddie said, "Thank you for coming, sir. Next question."

"I have another one."

"No, you're done. Usher, who's next?"

The usher gestured for Carrasco to toss the microphone. He didn't want to get within Malhar's reach.

Carrasco's lenses stayed on me. "See you soon, sure."

He let the microphone fall to the floor and pushed himself up on his walking stick. Malhar led the way to the aisle. They disappeared into an exit tunnel.

I waited for gunshots, Rubin yelling for everyone to get on the ground, the sound of someone hitting Malhar with a truck.

Nothing.

Eddie looked down at me from his podium. "You got some weird groupies, man. Who's next?"

I walked off the stage, chased by camera flashes and a resurgence of "*Vai morrer! Vai morrer!*"

———

Gil was in the prep room, jamming gear into his coffin-sized bag. I had my phone stuck to my ear.

Gil didn't look up. "Antonio just talked to her. She's fine. She's at the academy with Javier and Edson."

"They need to bring her here."

"Why?"

"So I can keep an eye on her, make sure she's safe."

"Well, that won't work. Because we aren't going to be here."

"Fine, I don't give a shit about the rooms anymore. Antonio wins that one. She can even stay with him and Jairo, as long as she's close by."

Gil zipped the bag shut and straightened, looked at me for the first time since I'd come in. His cheeks were wet. "No, Woody, we aren't going to be in Brazil. We're flying home. Now."

"Whoa. Hold on. What?"

"That was Carrasco in the crowd, right? The fucking Hangman?"

"Gil, just—"

"Shut up. Antonio knew it was him. And that cop, Rubin, said he was here to protect you from the fans, but I heard him tell his men to get ready in case you left with Carrasco. Not got grabbed by him, not attacked. Just walked out of the arena with him. Why would that happen, Woody?"

"Okay. Here's what happened."

"You lied to me. That's what happened. I was so excited for you to come down here and be with Marcela, meet her family. The family who took me in and treated me like a son. Bad enough you insult them, but at least your intentions were good. I can mend that. But you lied. And for what?"

"To protect you. I didn't want you to worry."

"No," Gil said. The tears were flowing down his face, dripping onto his chest. "You didn't want me to stop you. And I would have, because Woody—now I want you to listen very closely to this—you are going to get murdered."

"No, I—"

"Stop it! Just stop. How fucking selfish of you. Look around at everything we've worked for, what people have done for you, how much they love you. I love you, Woody. Antonio loves you, otherwise he wouldn't care enough to be as furious as he is."

Gil carried the duffel to the door and dropped it.

"Jairo loves you like a brother. Marcela loves you more than anything in the world. And what you're doing will make her miserable for the rest of her life. Because you will die thinking you're protecting her, when really, it's for nothing. Nothing. So I'm putting your ass on a plane and we're going home before you can commit suicide down here."

"Gil, I have a fight tomorrow."

"Fuck the fight. Eddie will get over it, or he won't. I don't care. What matters is you live long enough for us to sit around drinking whiskey and laughing about how goddam stupid this is. And that's going to be a very, very long time from now."

He lifted the gear bag, clamped a hand on my upper arm and hauled me toward the door. I was so stunned from the whole outburst I didn't resist. We turned left in the hallway. It was quiet, everyone still at the press conference or moving to the weigh-ins adjacent to the mini stadium.

Gil took two steps and stopped.

Malhar and Carrasco waited at the end of the hallway with

four lean, hard-eyed men.

Gil spun me around and started the other way.

Eye Patch stood from his crouch against the wall. The green bag slung over his shoulder was familiar. So were the three guys with him—they'd been outside the academy on my first visit.

Carrasco's voice carried down the concrete tunnel: "Exu wants to talk to you."

———

"Come with us," Carrasco said. "We not gonna hurt you. Not now, sure."

I knew Gil wouldn't let them take me. And if they were determined to do so, they'd kill him or hurt him badly enough he'd crumple out of the way.

I also knew if they laid a hand on him, they'd have to shoot me to make me stop ripping them all to pieces.

"I can hear you fine," I said.

"No, come closer."

Eye Patch and his crew moved toward us.

Gil was breathing hard. "Security!"

"They busy," Carrasco said. His walking stick was planted between his feet. He leaned on it with both hands, relaxed. "Come here."

I walked. Gil still had a vice grip on my arm—he was either going to let go or go for a ride. He dropped his hand but stayed next to me. We stopped ten feet from Carrasco, Malhar, and the other four. Eye Patch stayed an equal distance behind us, fencing us in. Malhar hissed through his teeth, the veins on his head rippling.

"What?" I said.

"You never answered my question. Who is watching my Pomba Gira if you are in exile?"

"Still me. And her cousins and uncle. The entire Arcoverde clan and every student who walks through the academy door. Hundreds of people."

Carrasco nodded. "And Detective Rubin, too?"

I didn't say anything.

"We see him hanging around you, talking to you. This makes Exu unhappy."

"So light a candle."

Gil said, "Rubin is our security. Protection from the fans."

"Oh, they crazy, sure. Their blood gets so hot when they wave the flag and scream their chants. You should know, many of them have left the red candles and knives at Exu's crossroads, asking for Aviso to hurt you bad."

"He needs all the help he can get."

Carrasco's face twitched into a smile. "If Exu finds out you are working with Rubin and his corrupt police, it will be very bad for you. Exu will make sure you regret this. He will take my Pomba Gira, and her family will suffer. All she loves will be turned to ash because of you."

Gil's breathing changed, shifting from the edge of panic into a deep, controlled rhythm of building fury. It was nice to have some company. It hit me how desperate and scared he must have been if he was ready to pull me out of the Aviso fight and run back to Vegas. Gil doesn't run from anything. He stands like a granite wall and lets the bullshit—all the immaturity and drama and ego nonsense of professional fighters, sponsors, promoters—bounce off him.

And I'd finally worn him down.

My willingness to risk my life—a life he'd saved, dragged out of a steep downward spiral and done his best to keep clean and safe—had swept his foundation out from under him.

The hardest punch wasn't that I'd made him desperate and scared.

It was that he was right.

I told Carrasco, "I'm going back to Vegas. No more Coluna. You leave the Arcoverdes and their academy alone. And if Marcela chooses to be your Pomba Gira, so be it. But it has to be her choice, because Exu wills it. Right?"

Eye Patch and the other men from the Axila da Serpente grew still, waiting. I'd backed him into his spiritual corner. Now to wall him in.

"That is right," Carrasco said. "Exu stands at the crossroads, this or that. And she can choose, sure. But Exu already gave you your choice, remember?"

He held his left hand out to his side.

"This door, to leave and never come back."

Brought his left back to the walking stick and floated his right hand out.

"That door. To run the Coluna da Cobra and see if you are worthy. Which one did you choose? Yes, I'm afraid so. You don't get to go back and choose the other. If you do, the spirits will be angered. Exu will seek justice."

He took his hat off and handed it to Malhar. The scarred flesh above his left ear was rippled and waxy under the bright hallway lights. Carrasco's head tipped forward. He pulled the black sunglasses off and dropped them in the hat. Lifted his head.

His left eye was filled with blood. It bulged beyond his eyelid like a red jellyfish, the fluid swirling and busy. A pitch-black iris floated in the center, flicking left and right, independent of what the other eye did. His eyelid slid down, and the red sac slurped beneath it like a shy tongue.

Carrasco said, "All of it. Everything. To ashes."

He put his glasses and hat on. Turned and limped away.

Malhar and Carrasco's men followed without looking back.

———

Gil shuffled the gear bag back into the prep room, set it down on one of the couches like it was full of the good crystal. He scrubbed his hands over his face and head, asked me, "Are you working with Rubin?"

Gil was ready to give up everything to keep me safe. The least I owed him was the truth.

"Yes."

"Beyond him keeping you safe from fans."

"Yes."

He crossed his arms, waiting.

I said, "When Carrasco takes me for the Coluna, Rubin and his paramilitaries are going to stack up at the bottom of the Axila. I find a hole to hide in. While Carrasco's men are hunting me, Rubin sweeps up the hill and takes them all down."

"All of them?"

I nodded.

"Whose idea was this, yours or his?"

"His."

"And you agreed to it."

"Yup."

"So who's crazier, the first guy off the cliff or the one who follows him?"

"Hey, I don't know what's going to happen between me and Marcela. So far she isn't coming home with me. If Rubin gives Carrasco the scorched-earth treatment, at least I'll know he can't go after her. Or the rest of her family."

Gil blinked. "You asked her to come to Vegas?"

"Yeah."

"For good?"

"Forever. Then pick a time when her judgment is compromised and ask her to marry me. House, yard. What else? Bird feeder? Is that typical?"

Gil wrapped his arms around mine, crushed me in a bear hug. Stepped back, tears in his eyes again—happy and sparkly this time—and said, "Okay. So now we really gotta get you home safe. Both of you."

"Like I said, she's not quite on board yet."

"I'll talk to her."

"Good, because I can't, remember?"

Gil scoffed. "Antonio forbidding you two from seeing each other is the best thing that could happen. Now you're irresistible."

"And you're okay with me helping Rubin, running the Coluna."

"Fuck no. But now I see you're not just being a moron. You're being a moron for a good reason. Kinda. If we can find another way out of this, we're taking it. Deal?"

A skinny guy wearing a Warrior shirt and carrying a walkie-talkie stuck his head in the door, panting. He let out a grunt of irritation, told the radio, "I found him." To us: "We need you back on stage for the weigh-ins. Now."

Gil asked me, "You're okay going against Aviso, all this shit going on?"

"Okay? I can't wait. He can't shoot me or stab me or blow me up with a grenade."

Gil shrugged. "Right, he just wants to break your arm in half."

"Kid stuff."

We turned to the gofer, who shook his head. "Fighters."

———

The podium, tables, and chairs were gone, replaced by an intricate scale and officials from Warrior, the Brazilian MMA Athletic Commission, and the International Mixed Martial Arts Federation. It seemed like a lot of guys to make sure none of the fighters were too fat.

Aviso was just stepping off the scale in his black high-cut briefs when I walked onstage. He flexed for the giddy crowd and made his billboard face, eyes half closed and lips somewhere between a pout and smirk. I imagined them split open and swollen, which made me happier than the crowd.

Eddie slithered next to me while I kicked my shoes off.

"Where the hell did you go?"

"I needed to cut a little more weight."

"Bullshit. You're nowhere near two sixty-five."

"Then I needed to add a little more weight."

Eddie nodded. "Keep it up, keep embarrassing me, you'll be teaching MMA Pilates at the WarriorDome. Now get your ass on the scale."

I kept my clothes on and came in at 242. The chants of "*Vai morrer! Vai morrer!*" made it difficult to hear the weighmaster—he had to yell twice to make sure it was recorded correctly.

I stepped off the scale and faced Aviso, Eddie between us and back a step for the pre-fight stare-down. Aviso moved in close enough to put one of his feet behind mine.

"I gonna break your arm, man. Take it home with me."

"Why, so it can keep smacking you around after I'm done?"

"The counting starts right now. They close the cage, I let you know how much time you got left with two arms. I tell you right now, it won't be much."

"You should be nicer to me. I'm giving you a career opportunity—official spokesmodel for poseurs, huge mistakes, and plastic surgeons."

He drove his forehead into mine and started cursing me in Portuguese.

Eddie and a few Warrior security guards separated us. Gil and I walked across the stage, the chants louder than ever. The crowd had taken up a dance as well, slapping right hands against left elbows with each syllable.

"Vai-mor-rer!"

Slap-slap-slap!

Letting me know which arm Aviso was going to break. I stopped and smiled to keep them going—their hands and elbows would be red and swollen for the fight the next day.

Gil said, "Hey," and nodded backstage.

Rubin waited for us. We stepped out of the lights, which didn't diminish the crowd's fervor.

"I just talked to Carrasco," I said.

"Yes, I know."

"With eight of his guys standing around. Fifteen if you count Malhar."

Rubin said, "You seem upset."

"Where the hell were you?"

"Waiting, of course. To see if they were going to take you. My shooters are on high alert, they can assemble like this." He snapped his fingers.

"Who else knows about what you and I talked about?"

He glanced left and right, eyeballed Gil and leaned close. "You mean . . . the big plan?"

"Yes. And Gil knows."

"Man, you got a big mouth. I don't tell nobody. Not even the men who are here with me, or the shooters. I make the call, they gear up, I tell them where we are going."

"They don't need a plan?" Gil said. "Some sort of strategy?"

Rubin winked. "My friend, we have a plan for the Axila already. We practice it all the time. My boys can walk through it in their sleep."

I said, "Carrasco knows you're around. I told him you're keeping me safe from the fans."

"Which I am, no? I must tell you though, I didn't think they would hate you this much."

"Can you guarantee Carrasco won't know about this until it's too late? Until it's happening?"

Rubin sucked air through his teeth. "Guarantee is a strong word. I can assure you I am doing all I can. How is that?"

"No help at all."

"Well, we hope for the best."

"We can do more than that. I want your men with Marcela, starting now. And her family."

"Ah, I did not put in a request for this. If you were with her, okay. But to have men all over the place . . . and at least one woman, because Marcela must use the ladies' facilities, I assume?

Is too much."

"It's just right, if you want to get Carrasco."

"Man, now I get why the fans don't like you. But I told you before, he won't go after her. It will make Exu look weak."

"Not if he finds out I'm working with you to burn his temple down."

"He said this?"

"He said Exu will want justice."

"Huh." Rubin put his fists on his belt, stretched his back. "Okay, I will send some people to look after the honorable Arcoverde family. Maybe we got some tips about foreign fans who don't like them so much. Good? Happy?"

"I'm smiling on the inside."

"And you are done with all this bravata now, we can go?"

Gil said, "Straight to the hotel. Dinner and relaxing, then sleep."

Rubin frowned. "Oh no, we need him out in the public, where Carrasco can find him. He didn't tell you when you had your chat?"

"Tell us what?"

"My sources tell me the Coluna da Cobra is happening tonight."

CHAPTER 13

GIL AND I TOOK A CAB BACK TO THE HOTEL, RUBIN AND his men somewhere behind us. Allegedly.

"This is bullshit," Gil said.

"I know."

A dark blue van passed on the left and cut us off. Our driver hit the brakes and the horn equally hard. He wore earbuds, the fast and jangly music loud enough for us to bob our heads to it. I watched the rear doors on the van, waited for them to burst open so Carrasco's fire ants could pour out, snatch me from the backseat.

The van swerved right and exited the street.

Gil said, "This thing happens tonight, even if you don't get a scratch—which I highly doubt—you'll be exhausted for Aviso."

"I'll sleep all day tomorrow. Just wake me up on the way to the cage."

Some kind of truck rode up to our rear bumper and put its headlights on the back of my neck. I squinted into them, couldn't tell if it was one of the barricades from the Axila or just a shitty driver. I kept my breathing even and moved my head and eyes to avoid tunnel vision—didn't want to waste an adrenaline dump on road rage.

Gil was antsy, picking at a seam on the gear bag across our laps. "I don't know, man. I've been trying to imagine how I'd feel if you were doing this back home, helping Vegas cops shut down some gang, joining one of their stings."

"And?"

"I think I'd hate it just as much. Maybe a little less, because I don't trust Rubin. And who knows what kind of cowboys he has working for him."

"The kind who want to get rid of Carrasco even more than I do."

"And probably don't care who else they shoot in the process."

"I'll stay low."

Gil said, "You find a cast iron bathtub, or a steel tank, or a bank vault, and get your ass inside it. Don't come out until the ambulances leave."

"A bank vault?"

A white stretch limousine floated next to us on the right. It was the same color as Carrasco's linen suit. One of the windows facing me slipped down and a young male stuck his head out and stared at me with slight panic. I didn't recognize him, but I hadn't memorized all the faces in the arena hallway.

His head tipped forward and he vomited down the outside of the door, looked at me again with spittle on his mouth and hooted. Someone pulled him into the limo and the window slid up.

Gil said, "You know what Roth does after he makes weight?"

Roth was the Australian fighter who trained at Gil's gym and had sprayed all my gear with Aviso's cologne. His nickname was

"Cut Snake," from the Aussie expression "mad as a cut snake."

"Not much," I said.

"Right. He sits on the couch and eats Fritos and hot sauce. Plays video games. You make yourself into bait for a military-scale police raid against a Brazilian drug lord who thinks he's a god."

"I wouldn't put it that way."

"No? How would you put it?"

"I'm doing what is necessary to keep the people I love safe."

Gil looked out the window for a bit. "Yeah, that does sound better."

———

Rubin wanted us sitting outside. We took a table at the hotel's outdoor restaurant, ordered dinner and tried to keep our shoulders from hunching, waiting for the ambush. Gil ate like a robot. I don't remember what I ordered or how it tasted.

The only part I remember clear as day is a hand falling onto my shoulder. I turned, ready for Eye Patch and a sweaty ride to the Axila.

It was Marcela.

I knocked my chair over standing up to hug her. She said hello to Gil from somewhere in my chest. We sat down much too soon and she ate something off my plate.

I said, "Did you get my messages?"

"Yes, but I knew you were busy, I didn't want to bother you."

"You could never bother me."

She scrunched her nose and asked Gil, "Why are his eyes funny?"

"He's very happy to see you."

I said, "Does Antonio know you're here?"

"No, why should he?"

"You haven't talked to him lately?"

"About what? Is he okay?" She looked back and forth at us. "Wait, is it Jairo?"

I glanced at Gil. He shrugged. "I'm not surprised he didn't tell her."

Marcela picked up a steak knife. "Tell me what?"

I said, "Antonio forbid me from seeing you anymore."

She kept the knife. "Forbid?"

"Yeah."

"Why did he do this?"

"Woody's general disrespect," Gil said. "Lack of etiquette. The way his behavior represents his personality."

"That'll do," I said.

We ducked and covered when Marcela threw the knife onto the table. "Of course. And why would he bother telling me, I'm just a girl, right? It's not up to me who I am with."

Gil said, "From Antonio's point of view, it's on Woody to be honorable and respect his wishes."

Marcela laughed. "Wishes? He is commanding. Ordering."

"I didn't know he hadn't told you," I said.

She turned to me. "Wait, is that why your eyes are so funny? You thought he told me to stay away from you, and I listened to him?"

"Well, I wasn't sure—"

She punched me in the arm hard enough to turn heads three tables away and called me something in Portuguese that made a busboy gasp.

"Your head is made of bone." She grabbed my ears and pulled

me to an inch from her face. "Even if you told me to stay away,
I would not listen."

"That's a little scary."

"You should be scared. Love like this comes once a lifetime. I
am terrified to lose it, and so are you."

She kissed me, her hands wrapped behind my neck, warm
and small. I would have stayed there forever.

She let go and sat back. "It is why I got so mad when you
wanted to go with Carrasco, run the Coluna and get yourself
killed. Like taking my heart out and stomping on it. But that is
over. You are here with me, safe."

Gil froze, lips clamped shut.

I held Marcela's hand and nodded.

———

We were the only table left. Marcela and I split a fruit sorbet
and watched the servers stack chairs upside down on the tables
around us. I was torn between getting Marcela home safe, away
from me, and spending every possible moment with her until
Carrasco's men came.

Gil savored the last coffee of the day and tried to keep the
conversation light. "Remember, if Aviso gets hold of your wrist,
you need to smash his face apart."

"I know."

"The only way he'll let go is if his face is in danger."

"I got it."

"Tell me Plan A again."

Marcela pointed her spoon at him. "No more fight talk. It is
time for bed. Come on, I'll tuck you both in."

I couldn't help glancing around. No sign of Rubin or Carrasco. "I want to stay up late and sleep in. Keeps me from getting worked up too soon on fight day. In fact, I believe you mentioned something about going dancing."

Her eyes popped. "You want to go dancing?"

Gil said, "You know what dancing is?"

Marcela sprang out of her chair. "I will get a taxi."

When she was out of earshot Gil said, "The hell you doing? Rubin wants us to stay put."

"No, he wants me out in public."

"But with Marcela? Not safe, man."

I was working the keypad on my phone. "I'm telling Rubin, they see any of Carrasco's men, let me know. We'll pack it up and fly back here. I kiss Marcela goodnight and send her home with a police escort, wait here for the Axila boys to catch up."

"This sounds incredibly stupid."

"And you stay here just in case they come around. Tell 'em I'll be back soon."

"Woody, these aren't vacuum salesmen. They think killing you will make their god happy."

"I've never danced with her, Gil."

He sat back. Finally realizing, I think, that I needed a thin coat of delusion to keep from falling into the rusted pocks and holes spreading around my feet.

"Tomorrow, I might be on a plane back to Vegas and never see her again. I might be banned by her entire family from talking to her. I might be dead. And I've never danced with her. I think I ought to, at least once. Before it all goes to hell."

———

I tried to keep track of where we were. The closest I could come was most likely in Brazil, maybe somewhere in downtown Rio. I hoped Rubin and his men had taken tactical driving courses—otherwise they had no hope of keeping up.

Marcela saw what she was looking for and was out of the cab before it stopped moving, shoved some cash at the driver and dragged me across a busy road to a row of blacked-out windows throbbing with bass. The club was between a twenty-four-hour liquor store and a twenty-four-hour Laundromat. I appreciated the convenience of executing a legendary night out without leaving the block.

There was a short line of young women in tight colorful dresses and men in tight black shirts. Marcela went straight to the beefy doorman, who smiled and hugged her. They exchanged words in Portuguese and she pulled me through the door.

On my way past I asked the doorman, "Does she come here a lot?"

He smiled and slapped my shoulder.

Inside, the subwoofers compressed my ribcage, but just a little. Mirrors, flashing lights, and drifting fog made the walls hard to find. We skipped the bar lined four people deep and threaded our way to the dance floor, fifty square feet of wooden tiles that must have been crucifixes in a former life to get this job.

At the far end of the dance floor, a raised stage ran the width of the back wall of the club. At least fifteen people were up there, playing drums, horns, keyboards, banjos, and some kind of board with springs attached to it. They played a fast, festive song over the thumping beat provided by a bobbing DJ in the center of the stage, one ear covered by a thick headphone.

Nobody wore an Aviso shirt.

Everybody was smiling.

Marcela found two feet of dance floor and turned into me. Her body dropped and flowed and twisted to the beat, hands on my chest, shoulders, hair.

I found her ear. "I don't know how to do this."

"I don't care."

Her head tilted back, eyes closed, lips parted. It was the happiest I'd seen her since . . . ever. She let everything go.

Three songs later—or one very long song—we were both slick with sweat and laughing, singing words I didn't understand. A cackling guy with a ponytail bumped into me and spilled his drink down the front of his embroidered shirt. He never stopped laughing, just grabbed me and jumped up and down a few times, long lost brothers, and faded into the crowd.

I buried my face in Marcela's hair and breathed her in. She jumped and wrapped her legs around my waist, pulling guard in the middle of the club, let go with one arm and twirled it around above her head like a lasso.

I turned in a circle, looking up at her and trying to understand how I could be so lucky.

I set her down. She turned her back against my chest, wriggled against me with promises for the next time we were alone. We found the same rhythm, pressing and sliding, everything and everyone around us forgotten until I caught a glimpse of a Brazilian flag eye patch in the crowd.

———

I pulled Marcela around and tossed her over my left shoulder, bounced a few people out of the way before a path opened in the crowd. They cheered and clapped for us, two lovers overcome by the passion of dance and music until we couldn't take it anymore, had to rush out and find a dark corner.

Marcela let me carry her, laughing and touching outstretched hands as she passed. I scanned the faces for anyone putting hard eyes on me. They were all joyous, ecstatic, reveling.

Except for one.

One man with a thin black mustache stood along the right side of the path, eyes darting from me to someone at my five o'clock. He was hesitating, looking for orders. He stepped into the path, one hand behind his back.

I didn't break stride, yelled "Paulo!"

He frowned. Whether his name was Paulo or not, he wasn't expecting me to lean toward him for an embrace. Or to fake a stumble, grab the back of his neck and smash my forehead into his nose.

He melted.

I stepped over him.

"Paulo, so sorry!"

The doorman laughed when he saw us and hurried to open the back door of an idling taxi. I rolled Marcela in and slammed the door behind us.

"Promenade Barra First Hotel."

The driver dove into traffic. I put my arm around Marcela and looked back. Five men spilled out of the club, looking left and right.

Marcela caught her breath. "So you are ready to leave?"

"I was afraid my excellent dancing would be too much to resist."

"Mm, you are right. But Gil is at the hotel room." She kissed me, fingers digging into the back of my head. "And you have the fight tomorrow."

"The what?"

"You must get your rest. We will have our time after the fight. Before you fly home."

I pushed that away. All I wanted at that moment was to keep her close, feel her breathing, vibrating next to me.

What I needed was to get her as far away as possible. Before Carrasco's men caught up and moved in.

Before she found out I'd lied to her face.

———

When the hotel was in sight my phone buzzed with a text from Rubin: All clear. Her escort is ready.

Marcela was sunken into my side and didn't open her eyes. "Who is that?"

"Gil. Says to get my ass in bed."

"Mm." She burrowed closer.

What else could I lie about? Tell her drinking motor oil was healthy and country music was actually half decent. I wanted to roll on the floor of the taxi, down there with the scum and trash where I belonged.

We got out in front of the hotel. I tossed a wad of cash at the driver, who raised his eyebrows and took off before he grew a conscience and offered change. I admired his unapologetic lack of morals. Having Rubin and his men around helped keep Marcela safe from Carrasco, but not from my bullshit. She needed to get on the road and drive faster than usual before the few scruples I had fell into place and I confessed.

She stepped up into the van's driver's seat. I rolled the window down and closed the door, hard enough to tip the vehicle.

"Lock it."

She smiled, hit the button.

I said, "You don't get out of here now, you'll need more than this between us."

She leaned through the window and kissed me again. "If my uncle is awake and tells me to stay away from you, I might come right back."

Shit.

"Just leave it alone for tonight, huh? For Jairo's sake. He's had enough drama before his first fight."

She pressed a hand against my cheek. "I wish everyone knew how sweet you are behind that face."

"What face?"

She winked and pulled away, tapped the brakes and swayed into traffic. A dark sedan with mirrored windows slipped out of a parking spot and sped up to get within six car lengths of the academy van, dropped into the same lane and slowed.

I called Rubin. "That's your car?"

"Sim, two of my best. One is a woman, so we are good wherever she goes."

"You got eyes on Carrasco's men?"

"No, not yet."

"They didn't follow from the club?"

The line hummed. "We saw no one at the club. Who did you see?"

"The one with the eye patch. And at least one more."

"I think you are wrong, my friend. Relax. I let you know when they are close."

He hung up.

I stood alone in front of the hotel, surrounded by doubts and lies. The good news: I was no longer worried about what might happen to me during the Coluna.

Whatever it was, I deserved it.

I sat on a concrete bench poured as part of a retaining wall near the front of the hotel. Put in my earbuds, hit Play and did something I've never been good at—I waited for trouble to come to me.

———

It showed up around three thirty in the morning. The vehicles had changed from loud cars full of loud people to taxis stuffed with quiet drunks. I heard the footsteps behind me—one set heavy and one shuffling, rhythmic—but didn't turn around.

They'd come from the far side of the hotel, through the landscaped paths between spotlit trees and bubbling fountains. Carrasco sat at the opposite end of the bench and turned to face me. He used both hands to lift a matchstick right leg and drape it over the slightly thicker left. His black lenses reflected the taillights of the taxis as they passed like a fading flatline.

Malhar stayed somewhere behind me, hissing through his nose.

"Time?" I said.

"You are in a hurry?"

"I have things to do."

Carrasco's mouth tugged to the right. "When a man runs the Coluna da Cobra, it doesn't matter what he had planned for after. His life is different. He is either with Exu, or he is dead. But you know, this is the first time Exu's life will be different too."

"Yeah, he's gonna need some straws. Hard to chew with

no teeth."

"You do not need to talk so tough. It makes you sound stupid, arrogant. The only reason you are still alive is because I allow it. You know this."

"Bad for Exu's image if you killed me."

"It would be weak of Exu. Your choices, and the will of the spirit legion, will kill you. Not Exu's hands. This is very important. As I was saying—before you spoke of knocking my teeth out—when others run the Coluna, Exu has either another soldier, or another spirit."

He shrugged.

"Exu already has many of these, sure. They are not so valuable. But after you have given your spirit during the Coluna, Exu will have his Pomba Gira. She will come to him willingly, with her beauty, her insatiable desires."

My fingers dug into the concrete armrest.

Carrasco said, "She is the embodiment of love and sex, death and destruction. To taste her sweat will be like drinking from the well of creation."

"You won't. Ever. No matter what happens to me."

"Ah, but if you die in the Coluna? It is Exu telling everyone the Pomba Gira belongs with him, sure. It is not up to her."

Somewhere, Rubin was watching and listening. If they were half as ready as I was to see Carrasco and his Axila razed, it would be over in five minutes.

"So let's go," I said.

"No, we wait here a little longer. Exu has not said it is time."

"But it's happening. Now."

I wanted to give Rubin as much time as possible, make sure his team could get the call, load up and roll out. Carrasco watched the sparse traffic and didn't say anything.

Then: "We sit here and talk for a while, sure. So I can tell you some things. And so Exu's soldiers can look around."

I didn't like that one bit. "Look around?"

"To see if anyone is here with you. Maybe your new friend Rubin?"

I made a show of looking left, right, and remained calm even though Carrasco's threat ran through my head. What he would do if he found out I was working with Rubin.

All of it. Everything. To ashes.

"Sorry, buddy. I'm all alone."

"Exu will see. He always does. Do you have a cell phone?"

"Yeah."

"Give it to me, please."

"Why?"

"Many people ask Exu why. Not all of them get an answer."

He held his hand out. The fingers didn't extend all the way, curving into a withered cup. Or claw.

I dropped my phone into it.

He poked through the recent calls.

The last phone call I took was from Rubin.

Carrasco navigated to the text messages, where Rubin had let me know it was all clear, Marcela's escort was ready.

But the calls and texts were deleted. I didn't even have Rubin saved as a contact—I'd memorized his number. The only texts were from Gil, every half hour or so asking if I was still alive.

Carrasco scrolled through the fascinating exchange.

Gil: ok?

Me: yeah

We're a chatty pair.

Carrasco handed the phone back. "Exu will see if you are lying."

He pulled his own cell out and set it on the bench between us. It sat there like a grenade with the pin pulled.

"But Exu does not see everything, sure. Some of the spirits think Exu should fear you. They say you will be Exu's undoing."

I nodded. "Those would be the spirits of wisdom."

"They urge Exu to call upon Malhar. Let him break your skull here and now."

Malhar leaned against the concrete planter that ran along the back of the bench and tapped the head of his framing hammer against the edge. Shrapnel flew. The muscles on his bald head rippled as he chewed on something leathery. Thick brown juice ran down his chin.

I said, "Ask the spirits if Malhar has ever swallowed an elbow. I'll skip the mouth, put it right in his throat."

"Malhar lives to serve Exu. Because Exu saved him, sure. This was many years ago, in Carandiru. Do you know it?"

I kept staring at Malhar, waiting.

Carrasco said, "They call Carandiru a prison, but it is one of the many hells. Men are made to live like animals, in filth and disease and violence. Savagery. Many suffering men call upon the spirits in Carandiru, but the spirits will not go there. Except for Exu."

"You let yourself get locked up? Not very godlike."

The cell phone vibrated against the concrete. The screen lit up with a text message. Carrasco's head tilted to read it. I tried to read Portuguese upside down in a casual way.

The black lenses came back to me.

"Hm."

He pressed a button and the screen went dark. I waited for

Malhar to do whatever he thought was the first step in killing me.

Carrasco sat back. "No, I was sent to prison before Exu came to me. I was just a man, like you. My body was strong, sure. But my mind, my spirit, was nothing. I caused much harm to people. Took what I wanted and left them crying, hollow, or dead."

"Congratulations on changing zero much."

He swept a hand over his legs, the waxy scar on the side of his head. "Look at my body. Have I not changed? Take the difference you see and my spirit has changed a hundred times more. A thousand."

"So now when you steal and murder, it's for Exu."

"Yes, you see it. Not for me. For Exu."

I nodded. "It's a pretty good racket you got going."

"Racket?"

"Scam. Con. Big fat lie."

Carrasco's face twitched. "I will let you know, Exu enjoys jokes, but he does not allow disrespect. It is why he came to me in Carandiru."

"Has he told you it's time to go yet?"

My knees were bouncing. Any fighter will agree: the hardest part isn't getting into the cage. It's waiting to.

Carrasco ignored me. "I was there for a year before they told me why. Human trafficking, they said. Slavery. And killing, and burning. Like they pulled words out of a bucket and put them on me."

He shrugged.

"I did those things, sure, but they could not prove it. Still, they would let me rot in the hell of Carandiru. But I did not want to stay, so I started a riot."

Like it was a book club or a yoga class.

I said, "A riot?"

"Sure, everyone in my part of the prison. This made Exu happy. He had many followers suffering in Carandiru, unable to serve the spirits properly."

"By stealing and murdering. Kidnapping slaves."

He nodded. "Whatever the spirits asked of them. The riot went on for five days. We had guards and prisoners who worked for them, and we made them bleed and scream to get the others to open the doors and let us out. They would not. So we set men on fire, and tore them apart. Still they would not open the doors. Instead they shot at us."

"Not nearly enough."

Carrasco said, "Many of Exu's people were hurt, killed, sure. But they were not wasted. On the fifth day the guards broke through. They had armor and shields and automatic weapons, sure. What a mess they made. Even the prisoners who surrendered, they killed. They shot me here."

He touched a finger to his pelvis.

"And when I could not fight back, they dragged me to a hall-way with bars for a ceiling, so things and people thrown from above do not land on others walking. The guards had brought a rope just for this thing. They hung me from the bars and shot me again, here."

He pointed to his stomach.

"They moved along to kill more prisoners, leaving one man behind so no one could help me. I died for a while, sure. But Exu found me on the other side and wanted me to live. He came back with me, into Carandiru, into my body hanging from the bars. That was when Malhar saved me."

Malhar's eyes were half-closed, seeing it all again. He'd stopped chewing out of reverence.

I said, "What was he in for? Eating slaves?"

Carrasco smiled. "No, you don't see it yet. He was the guard."

———

I kept my face flat. "You got saved by a guard?"

Carrasco said, "He felt the presence of Exu. There was a reason he was left there with me."

"Yeah, to pull down on your feet until your neck snapped."

"Maybe. But he did not. Even then he had his hammer. The guards did not like to carry guns most normal days, sure, because it tempted the prisoners to attack them and steal the weapons. Malhar and his hammer were feared very much. So no one questioned him when he cut me down and carried me out. I rode away from Carandiru in the back of a prison vehicle, just like how I arrived. Malhar took me to the Axila da Serpente, where Exu's followers were many. They did what they could to put my body together."

"In the dark?"

He sniffed. "It does not matter what my body looks like. What it can do. Exu is not limited by these things."

"Prove it. Let's go."

Carrasco tapped the end of his walking stick on the pavement a few times, took a few deep breaths.

I said, "I'm calling bullshit. Look at you. You want your people to believe you're above all this, leaving it up to the spirits. And it pisses you off, because now you can't lose your temper anymore."

He wagged a finger at me. "Not my people. Exu's. And yes, it is a struggle, thank you for noticing."

"So what are we waiting for?"

"I am sitting here with you, telling you these things out of respect for the spirits. They think you are making foolish choices because you are ignorant."

I squinted. "Are any of these spirits named Gil?"

"They want you to know what I am. What you are opposing when you fight me. So you can make a wise choice."

"Oh, I've known what you are since Marcela first said your name."

"Ah, so Exu is working through her already. This makes him happy."

"No, she told me what you're doing, and I immediately knew you were a crazy sack of shit. And the best way to handle you is to stomp your head until you go away. One way or another."

He nodded. "And this has not changed?"

"Only because Malhar's head got added. Which is nice, because I can clunk the two together. Save my shoes."

Carrasco sprang forward, much faster than I thought possible in his condition. "Do you know what I am doing, you fucking idiot?" Spittle flew from his mouth. "I am offering you another choice. Go. Leave and never come back."

Behind us, Malhar held his breath.

I said, "Wait. Is it you offering, or Exu?"

He sat back, smoothed the front of his shirt. "Exu, of course. The spirit of the crossroads."

"Whoever it is, you're not trying to give me a choice. You're trying to scare me."

"If you are not scared, you don't have a brain."

"I'm terrified. Terrified of what will happen to Marcela if I leave. Terrified of living the rest of my life knowing I could have helped and ran away instead."

Carrasco's mouth twisted. "And for yourself? There is no fear?"

"Plenty of it. But I have a tolerance. Because here's the thing—I've had mortal fear many, many times. Each time, I beat it. And I made damn sure the source of that fear never came back."

Carrasco stared at me. I pictured that bulging, blood-filled sac of an eye behind the sunglasses. The eye of Exu. Malhar's breathing picked up speed.

The phone buzzed on the concrete again.

And again.

The screen lit up with two new messages.

Carrasco leaned over it.

I kept my voice steady. "See? Like I said, all alone."

Three more dropped into the queue. The vibration sounded like a box of angry hornets.

Carrasco picked the phone up. The screen reflected in his black lenses.

He nodded once and whispered something to Malhar, who started around the far side of the bench.

I stood up as the mortal fear closed in.

———

Malhar came around the corner. I squared up, feet spread and arms loose.

Don't punch him in the head. You'll break a hand.

Knees and elbows then.

Don't pull him into a clinch. He looks like a biter.

Check. Knees and elbows while going backward.

Malhar stopped at the corner of the bench and eased a hand

under Carrasco's right arm. Carrasco stood, most of his weight on the walking stick. He tilted and twisted his neck, the bones and tendons grinding like broken glass. A push-kick would crumple him like a sheet of newspaper.

I considered it. Might leave Malhar torn for a nanosecond— help his master or attack me—a tiny hesitation that would allow me to crush his larynx. Or at least dent his groin.

A dark SUV with bars on the front grille slid to the curb and stopped. The driver—a skinny guy in cargo shorts and a tank top with an M4 shorty hanging across his chest—got out and opened the back door.

Resisting the urge to glance around for Rubin and his men, I said, "We finally going?"

If they'd been made, would they bolt, leave me to fend for myself? Or rush in, roll up Carrasco and his men in an attempt at damage control? Either way, all I cared about was what Carrasco would do to Marcela and her family.

He took a careful step toward the SUV with Malhar's help. "I say yes, it is time."

I moved forward and tried to see inside the SUV. It was pitch-black, the interior lights covered or broken. Eye Patch could be in there, waiting to put a bullet in the back of my head as soon as the door shut. Whether Rubin had been burned or not, he'd better be on his way to the Axila.

Carrasco grabbed the open door for support, looked over his shoulder at me. "But Exu says it is not. You still have some choices to make, sure."

Malhar closed the door, scowled at me and walked around the back of the SUV. The driver got in and pulled away and left me there, flooded with adrenaline and ready for battle.

Trouble was, the only person close enough to fight was me.

———

I called Rubin.

He picked up mid-ring. "That was exciting, no?"

"Marcela?"

"My team just checked in. All quiet."

"You still here?"

"Of course."

"Nobody saw you?"

"Nobody," Rubin said. "And stop looking around. We are not hiding in the bushes or sitting in cars behind newspapers."

"You trailing Carrasco back to the Axila?"

"Eh, to the outskirts. If we get too close, things get awkward. Bullets. What are you going to do?"

"Sleep."

"Thank God. I will leave a team here to watch the hotel. The rest of us are going home. I think tomorrow is going to be a big day for us."

"You? I'll be looking over both shoulders for Carrasco while I'm getting locked in a cage with Aviso."

"Yes, and I have to keep up with you. It's like . . . hm."

"What?"

Rubin said, "It just hit me, Carrasco might be delaying on purpose."

"Yeah, he's pulling the 'Exu says' bullshit, stringing me along until he thinks the time is right."

"Yes, but I think he already knows what the right time will be. But not for the Coluna."

"The hell you saying?"

"My friend, when you are locked in the cage with Aviso, anyone watching over you will have to be there too. That means me, my teams."

My stomach tightened.

Rubin said, "If Carrasco is going to attack the Arcoverdes, go after Marcela, that is when he will do it."

"Shit."

"But she will be at the arena with you, yes? To watch Jairo fight, then you. So we can watch over everyone."

I thought about Antonio. Pictured him bringing Jairo back to the prep room after his fight, packing up their gear and leaving while I'm warming up for Aviso.

Taking Marcela with him, keeping her away from me.

Would she go?

No. Nobody could tell her what to do.

But why start a feud with the man who raised her when I was going back to Vegas on Sunday?

Back to Vegas, without her.

I could see it. She'd kiss me on the cheek, tell me good luck, she was going to talk with her uncle about us, about who was in charge of her life.

Set him straight.

She didn't want to watch me get hurt anyway, fighting Aviso.

Then she'd walk away, not seeing the pain worse than any punch or submission could cause.

"You still there?"

"Yeah."

"Marcela will be with you at the arena, yes?"

I didn't have an answer.

———

I staggered through the hotel in a daze, looking for an angle to keep everyone outside the cage safe while I was inside putting Aviso in danger.

I'd told Rubin, "If she leaves the arena, you go with her."

"No, sorry. My priority is Carrasco and his favela. Even if they go after her, we will take the Axila. We are attached to you, like it or not."

I sagged into the corner of the elevator.

One of the most important aspects of training is recovery. Recovery comes during sleep, when the body and central nervous system get repaired from the trauma and exertion of training. They rebuild, come back a little stronger, adapt to the stress.

Because of this, smart fighters protect their sleep like a piece of homemade cake in prison.

We compartmentalize everything, keep it separate from sleep.

Nothing gets through the walls to upset it.

I slipped through the hotel room door and eased it shut. Gil's snoring didn't waver. I kicked the weight of the day off with my shoes. Pushed the earbuds in and rolled the volume down to a whisper. The mantras tried to teach me secrets while I shoved everything into compartments.

Carrasco, Malhar, the Coluna.

Aviso, Eddie, Antonio.

Marcela.

She stayed free.

She wasn't weight.

She was air.

I hit the pillow face-first and breathed in her scent, let it push everything else away and pull me into quicksand sleep.

———

I dreamt of walking down the hallway to fight Aviso. The Warrior cameraman backpedaled in front of me, two red candles mounted above his camera as spotlights.

The wax ran over his lens. He grinned behind the eyepiece and kept going. "Doesn't matter anyway, right?"

I passed Jairo. He was slumped against the wall, legs outstretched, his face a meaty mess of blood and swollen flesh.

I asked him, "Did you win?"

He opened his mouth to speak and a closed fist emerged. It dropped a handful of teeth into his lap and slid back in. Jairo sobbed and began counting the teeth.

I turned the corner toward the double doors that opened on the arena, the crowd, the cage, and stopped. A snake's open mouth filled the doorway. Its fangs hung like stalactites from the top of the frame. The tongue flickered out, big as a fire hose, dancing and searching for me.

Somewhere beyond it, the crowd chanted, "*Vai morrer! Vai morrer!*"

Antonio slapped me on the back. "Go. This is what you wanted."

Gil stood behind him and covered his mouth, stifling a laugh.

The cameraman backed into the snake's mouth and kept going. The two candles grew dim, disappeared.

"Wait," Antonio said. He casually reached out and bent both of my forearms the wrong way, breaking my elbows with the ease he'd use to brush crumbs off a table. "Now go."

I took a step toward the snake's mouth. "Where is Marcela?"

Antonio tried to keep a straight face. "Where do you think?"

He turned to Gil and they collapsed into each other, giggling. "*Vai morrer! Vai morrer!*"

The snake's tongue brushed against my leg. It jumped, excited, the forks exploring my skin like antennae as I walked forward. The throat swallowed all light ten feet in. I stared into the darkness and pressed my broken left arm against one of the fangs, trying to straighten it out.

The fang swayed to the side like a wind chime. I pulled my eyes from the throat and saw the fang was Carrasco's walking stick, hanging from the snake's gums by threads of skin. Venom coursed down its length and dripped, pooling around my bare feet.

"*Vai morrer! Vai morrer!*"

I turned one last time.

Antonio and Gil were gone.

A ring of red candles burned where they had been. In the center was a hangman's noose made of long black hair. Marcela's hair, I knew. Wisps of it floated above the candles, flared, curled, and died.

I stepped into the snake's mouth and it slammed shut behind me.

———

I pushed off the bed and blinked sweat out of my eyes.

Gil stood inside the door, one foot hovering in mid-step. "I tried to be quiet."

"What's happening? Where's Marcela?"

"Easy. She's fine, at the arena with Antonio and Jairo. I came to get you."

"Why?" I stared at the clock, got tired of waiting for it to make sense. It said I'd slept until three o'clock in the afternoon.

"You need to shower, get ready."

"For what?"

"Woody, it's time to fight."

CHAPTER 14

THE ARENA WAS BEGINNING TO HUM WITH ACTIVITY, small groups of people pulled into the funnel-shaped entrance. Within an hour it would be a flood.

The cab took Gil and me around back. Texts from Rubin let me know he and his men were on-site and there was no sign of Carrasco so far, but I didn't need any Aviso fans spitting at me before I was awake enough to duck. We showed our tags to the security guard, who wrinkled his nose but let us in anyway.

"Go Aviso."

"Go to hell," I said.

Keeping up with Gil's short legs was a trial. My feet were heavy, scuffing along the concrete floor.

Gil peeked back. "You okay?"

"I think I slept too much."

"No such thing."

I shook my head to clear it, turned a corner, and ran into a Warrior camera crew. They sprang into action, lights cooking and cable wranglers poised.

The cameraman kept his eyes on the screen. "Woody, we're getting footage of fighters walking in. We'll play it back on the screens and pay-per-view feed right before your fight. Everybody boos, it's great. So look determined, yeah? But not at the camera, look over my shoulder, past me."

They started backing up and we followed into the long hallway outside the prep rooms.

My dream crashed to the front of my head. The cameraman, the hallway. I remembered Jairo sitting in his own blood, Gil tittering about some private gag between him and Antonio.

The candles, Marcela's hair noose.

And ahead, around the corner, the snake mouth.

Waiting.

"Woody, more determined," the cameraman said. "You look like you're going to the dentist, not a fight. Can you do Blue Steel?"

The dream had been so real, and it felt like I'd slept for days. Sitting with Carrasco on the bench even seemed like a dream, the details foggy, slippery.

I ran through it again—had he dosed me with something?

He'd never touched me. Neither had Malhar. The only thing . . .

I pulled my phone out and sniffed it.

The cameraman said, "Um."

I held the phone out to Gil. "Does that smell like something?"

He gave it a wary eye. "My first guess would be a phone."

"No, like herbs or incense. A potion."

"A potion?"

I sniffed it again. "What does LSD smell like?"

The cameraman said, "Can we do this again?"

"Sorry," Gil said. "We're going to work."

He pulled me through the door of our prep room and closed

it behind us.

"What the fuck was that about? LSD?"

"I don't know. I don't feel right."

Gil looked me over with a frown. "Well, we're here now. We'll start getting loose in a bit. Just take a seat, lie down. Whatever you have to do to relax."

I nodded. Glanced up and noticed there were other people in the room.

On a couch in the back right corner, Jairo sat in a sweaty green gi. He was pale, breathing hard, and looked like he was waiting for his turn in front of the firing squad.

Marcela had an arm around him, patting his knee. She shot me a worried look, went back to whispering and soothing. The dancing, smiling, laughing Marcela from the club was gone.

Antonio stood in the middle of the room, hands behind his back. He looked like the firing squad.

"Relax," I said. "Right."

———

Gil and I took the space on the left side of the room, where Jairo and I had sparred and sprawled the day before to get him back on the destroyer's path.

Between then and now he'd stepped on a landmine.

I said, "How you feeling, Jairo?"

"Don't talk to him," Antonio said. "And do not look at Marcela."

I turned my back in case he read lips.

Gil watched Jairo with a furrowed brow. He had his giant coffee poised below his mouth, but he did not drink. At his Vegas gym, Gil's coffee was our threat level indicator.

A full mug actively being slurped meant all good, everybody's green and happy.

An empty mug was condition yellow, tipping into orange. Top it off fast before it all spirals.

Spilled? Red alert, hunker down and let the mushroom cloud pass.

But a full mug not being sipped or gulped—the only word I could think of was dire.

I told Gil, "Somebody has to get him up and moving. He's tight, locked in his head right now."

"What about you?"

"I gotta shake these cobwebs. Hit the pads or do some rolling. Groundwork with Jairo would be perfect. Prep me for Aviso and calm him down."

I also needed to talk to Marcela. Touch her, hear her voice, and make sure she was staying after Jairo's fight.

I unzipped the gear bag and started dumping gloves and pads. "Come on Jairo. Let's work some drills."

Antonio turned to face me. "I said don't talk to him. You have brought shame upon him and our family. He is scared now, a coward, because of the place you took him. For his whole life, he knows only victory. Even in his sleep, he dreams of domination."

Antonio took a step toward me.

"But last night, he dreams of you. He is broken, covered in blood from his fight. His teeth are gone. And you walk right past him, like he is a ghost. Because he is one."

The image of Jairo sitting in the hallway counting his teeth doused me with ice water. Antonio moved a step closer. Behind him, a ring of short white candles burned on the table in front of Jairo.

I pointed. "What the hell is that?"

"Not your concern. We are done."

Gil said, "Antonio—"

Antonio didn't look at him. "You and I will speak when this is over."

I said, "Are those candles for Exu?"

Antonio turned away.

I stepped over the couch and around him. Got to the table before anyone could stop me and slapped the candles out with my palm. Black smoke drifted from the glowing wicks.

"Those are votive candles," Marcela said. "For Jesus."

"Oh. Were they working?"

An iron hand clamped onto my shoulder.

Pulled me around.

It wouldn't be my first fight against a senior citizen.

But I will admit: it was the first time I was nervous about it.

———

A flat-screen TV on a rolling cart stood against the center of the back wall. It ran a loop of promo footage for the Warrior event and would switch over once the live feed started.

It would also make a great bludgeon if I could get to it before Antonio got his arms around my neck.

We stood a few inches apart, breathing each other's air. His eyes were flat and bored. So that's where Jairo learned it.

"I don't want to fight you in front of your son and niece."

"She is a daughter to me."

"I don't want to fight you in front of your kids, then."

"Maybe Jairo got his cowardice from you."

"I said I don't want to. Not that I won't."

Marcela said, "Woody, calm down."

"Both of you," Gil said. "Knock it off."

Antonio cocked an eyebrow. "Your student needs to be put in his place."

"You touch him," Gil said, "you'll be fighting both of us."

Antonio blinked twice, the only indication of the shock he must have felt. He turned to face Gil. "You would challenge me?"

Gil stood frozen. His coffee mug was on the table, far from his hand and mouth—dire indeed.

Very few people can make trouble while unconscious, and this was a perfect opportunity. Antonio's left ear and the angle of his jaw were right there. One short hook with a little hip behind it and he'd go down. Roll him off to the hospital with smelling salts and ice cubes, tell him to check tomorrow's paper for how Jairo did.

Gil took a deep breath. "If you try to hurt Woody, I'll stop you."

I eased my right hand into a fist. Too quick and the tendons would pop, give him fair warning. I slid my weight to my right foot so I could push off and shift it across at impact.

Antonio snorted. "So it seems you and I are done as well."

His head turned back toward me.

Even better—combine his movement with the punch, let him jump right into it.

I braced my core and started to swing.

My right arm would not move.

Jairo's hand was wrapped around my wrist. It felt like someone had poured a concrete foundation over my hand. His fingers were freezing and his face was blotched, waxy. He stared straight ahead, shivering and watching something only he could see.

"Help me," he said.

Marcela moved closer. "What is happening to him?"

"Nerves," I said. "Pre-fight jitters."

She leaned her forehead against his shoulder. "You were like this for your first fight?"

"Sure," I lied.

Jairo's hand dropped away from my wrist. I felt my fingers again.

Antonio said, "Arcoverde blood does not allow jitters. You have infected him. Step away. Now. Or I will end your fighting career. Maybe your life."

I've heard a lot of threats. Usually as an if/then statement:

You don't step off I'ma bust yo head, son.

You ever come back here, I'll shoot you.

Look at her again, go ahead. I get my boys and we see what's up.

Most cases, it's because they don't want to progress to actual violence. Otherwise they'd shut up and get to it. Doesn't mean they should be tested or challenged, forced to make good on the threat. Just means they're puffed up, showing danger colors, time to move along before it goes sideways.

Antonio was different.

He didn't care if it progressed.

He was fine either way.

Just like me.

———

Gil push-kicked the empty couch out of his way and grabbed the front of my shirt, hauled me away from the Arcoverdes.

Because I'm an idiot and didn't want to be the one to break

the stare-down with Antonio, I didn't see the couch in our corner. Gil dragged me over the back of it and dumped me onto the cushions. I stayed there, legs draped, while he pushed down on my chest and swung his glare between me and Antonio.

"Enough! You stay over there, we'll stay over here. Now everybody just calm the fuck down and get ready to fight."

It made sense at the time.

A rap on the door made us all turn. Eddie poked his blue hair and damned face in.

"Sounds intense in here." He surveyed the room. "And it looks . . . weird."

He came all the way in.

"I'm making the rounds, checking on my fighters. How you guys feeling? Ready to blow the doors off this bitch?"

"Yup," I said from the couch, wearing my Gil scarf.

Eddie frowned at the Arcoverdes and sidled to our corner, sat on a sliver of cushion near my hip and kept his voice low. "The hell's wrong with Jairo?"

"Nothing," Gil said.

I creaked the couch leather with a shrug.

Eddie said, "He looks like complete shit. This have anything do to with the meltdown at the academy? Antonio's bullshit strategy?"

I whispered, "You know it's bad too?"

"Please. It's gonna get Jairo killed."

"Then fucking say something."

Eddie put his hands up. "I don't get between fighters and coaches. Especially when it's going to make a spectacle. Preston crushing the Arcoverde legend in Brazil? Brah, this is gold."

My right hand made a fist again. I'd punched three people on couches before, two of them while lying on my back. All of them wished it hadn't happened.

Eddie said, "Plus the footage we're running of you and Antonio almost throwing down at the academy? Everybody outside Brazil is going to hate the Arcoverdes, and everybody here is going to be rabid for revenge. I couldn't manufacture a better situation, and I sure as hell ain't gonna prevent it."

He patted my stomach and stood up, straightened his blue silk tie. "Good luck out there, boys. The world is watching . . ."

He shot his arm out and checked the heavy platinum manacle hanging from his wrist, then pointed at the TV. The loop cut to a live shot of the arena, about seventy-five percent full with fans being herded to seats.

"Now."

———

Compartments.

Seeing the live feed of the cage flipped a switch. I dumped all the tension and drama with Antonio into a bucket and slapped a lid on it. Kept the rage and adrenaline handy—some things shouldn't be contained. I used the bathroom to change into my fight gear.

Checked my phone and found a text from Rubin: Source says Coluna tonight. Carrasco wants you worn out, maybe injured from fight with Aviso.

I sent back: His mistake. Aviso is a warm-up.

Marcela is staying with you?

Don't know yet.

Keep her there. Safest place.

I dumped the phone into my bag and ran through my options

if Marcela wanted to leave the arena after Jairo's fight. Maybe to console him after a loss, mediate between him and Antonio, or ride along in the ambulance.

I beg her to stay and watch me fight, stretching her between me and her family.

But Marcela doesn't stretch.

She goes with Jairo and resents me for trying to make her choose.

Or I tell her I'm still doing the Coluna, working with Rubin to shut Carrasco and Exu and the Axila da Serpente down so she'll never have to worry about it again.

She punches me in the neck for lying and I never see her again.

I shook my head, hoping another option would tumble forward and all the noise would sift back into the damned compartments where it belonged.

Neither one happened.

"Well, shit."

I pulled a sweatshirt on and met Gil on the mats. He held focus mitts and my training gloves and wore his battered rib guard that made him look like a homeless umpire.

"Good news," I said. "I'm not sleepy anymore."

"Being an asshole wakes me up too."

"Hey."

"I didn't say it was a bad thing." He held the mitts up.

I strapped the gloves on. Jairo was on the mats across the room, sprawled in a loose push-up position. Antonio walked around him, stopping to move Jairo's ankle an inch to the right, his shoulder two inches down. Jairo looked like he was going to vomit.

Marcela paced between the couches, arms crossed.

I waited for her to see me, gave her a look: You okay?

She shook her head once and kept pacing.

I took one step toward her.

She held a hand up, shutting me down. Crossing into Arcoverde territory would only make it worse.

Gil smacked me in the face with one of the mitts. "You look like you wanna hit something."

"Good lord yes."

"These'll have to do until those fools out there put Aviso in front of you. We'll warm up, then go through the plans. A, B, C. You remember them?"

"Yeah."

He tried to smack me again. I ducked.

"Forget 'em," he said. "Right now, just hit."

Fucking genius.

———

I had a good sweat going when Javier and Edson came in with cloth grocery bags bulging with fruit and vegetables. They didn't acknowledge me—not even a scowl—and dumped the bags on Jairo's table. Oranges, apples, bananas, and clumps of greens I didn't recognize tumbled across the surface. Javier and Edson sorted them into seemingly random piles. The room took on the smell of wet cut grass and fresh garlic.

"On me," Gil said. He kept the mitts below his shoulders and flared his elbows so I could work the abdomen. It had been our plan from the day we'd signed the fight deal: Do not attack Aviso's face and head.

I'd fought Gil on it at first, standing in the Fight House cage and going over the strategy. "But this guy hates getting hit in the face."

"Right."

"And I'm really good at it."

"Yes," Gil said, "but when it happens, he goes for the take-down and the armbar. And he's better at that than you are at face punching."

His blasphemy was stunning. "Uhh, that can't be true."

"Uhh, it is."

"One solid shot to his jaw, his night is over."

Gil nodded. "One miss, your career might be over. This guy pulls arms apart like they're kindling."

"Yeah, but he's gonna give me a warning, right? The count-down thing he does."

"Right before he breaks an arm. You think those other guys just sat there and let it happen? They were fighting like wild animals and he still got 'em."

"But I really want to punch this guy in the face."

"Compromise. He shoots in, you can punch him anywhere you want to keep him away."

"Deal."

"But you keep him off and go back to squared up, walking each other down, the head's off limits again."

"Ah, piss."

But Gil was right. As much as I wanted to knock that jaw crooked, going high would make it easier for him to shoot low and take me down. So I smacked Gil's padding in the ribs, liver, belly, sternum, and kept my hips back.

He stuck a focus mitt out toward my waist. It was Aviso's head, driving in for a double-leg. I sidestepped and cracked a short hook into it, visualized it landing just behind his ear.

"Nice," Gil said. "Feel good? On to Plan B."

I shook my arms out and glanced at Jairo. He was picking through the produce on the table. Antonio stood with his back to us and pointed at pieces for Javier and Edson to cut up and stuff into a miniature blender they'd brought. Marcela rubbed Jairo's back and spoke in soft Portuguese.

I'd counted on being able to roll with him, put myself in the bad spots Aviso would look for and try our strategies to get out. Jairo wasn't as slick as Aviso, but he was stronger. Idea was, if I could yank myself out of his deathlock, I could slip out of Aviso's. We'd also wanted Javier to work the corner with Gil, dump water on me and rub an icepack wherever I needed it.

Sampling the mood in the room, I wasn't about to let any Arcoverde get his hands on me. Maybe Marcela, but the others might take the opportunity to pile on.

Two thumps on the door, then Hollywood Andersen stuck his salt-and-pepper head in. "You decent?"

"Ridiculous question," Gil said.

Hollywood was one of the top two cutmen in the fight game. When he came through the door I heard the thumping music in the arena and the white noise of the crowd cheering. The TV showed a Brazilian fighter taking his opponent's back, wrapping his legs around the guy's waist and locking him in so he could drop bombs with both fists.

The camera changed and I saw the pummeled fighter was Kuthe, the guy cutting weight on the treadmill. The round ended and the Brazilian pushed off Kuthe's back to get up. Kuthe got to his hands and knees and let blood run from his lacerated scalp onto the canvas.

The crowd screamed for more.

"That kid needs me," Hollywood said. "My man Vern'll take care of him though. I taught him right."

He dropped his tackle box on the corner of Jairo's table and patted one of the cushions, grinned at Jairo.

"Your wrap awaits, sir."

Jairo held the fruit and veggie smoothie, untouched.

"Drink it all," Antonio said.

Jairo swallowed once, then chugged the concoction. His throat bulged and fought to get it all down. Edson took the cup from him and wiped his mouth with a damp towel. Jairo shuffled to the couch, sat down and held his left hand out.

Hollywood dropped to one knee and pulled rolls of gauze and tape out of his box. "Which wrap you want? Tap-out or knockout?"

Jairo's lips were pressed together. "The tap."

"Yeah, keep it loose. Lets you grab him, keep him close, huh? You got it."

Hollywood shot a look at Gil. He'd been eye-to-eye with thousands of boxers and MMA fighters moments before they made the walk to the ring or cage. He knew what terror looked like in the prep room, and he knew what it ended up looking like in the emergency room.

He wove a tapestry of gauze around Jairo's hand and wrist, through his fingers, sealed it with a sculpture of tape, and smacked the knuckles.

"Feel good?"

Jairo closed and opened his fist, stared at his palm.

Hollywood said, "Something wrong?"

Jairo didn't say anything. I wondered if he was picturing his teeth cupped there in his hand in a puddle of blood.

"It's fine," Antonio said.

Hollywood kept his face blank and went to work on the other hand.

"Come on," Gil said to me. "He'll be fine. It's Jairo. Soon as he gets in the cage he'll puff up, pound his chest, and then pound Preston. Don't worry about him. Let's go."

Gil dropped and rolled to his back. I knelt by his feet and leaned into his full guard, a terrible spot against Aviso. Gil grabbed my right arm and pulled it close, got ready to swing his hips out and go for an armbar.

"Now what?"

Then Jairo vomited across the table.

———

Edson propped open the door to the hallway to let some fresh air in. Antonio and Javier were in the bathroom with Jairo, the sound of splashing water coming through the door.

Hollywood had made quick work of the right hand—one eye on Jairo's gray face so he could avoid a second volley if need be—then packed his tackle box and scooted, mumbling to Gil, "That boy's in trouble."

Marcela used one last handful of paper towels to wipe the table.

I squatted down next to her. "You doing okay?"

"Go find Eddie. Tell him Jairo cannot fight."

"I don't know if that's the best option."

She used the hand that wasn't holding the paper towel to tuck her hair behind her ear. "Woody, he's like a dead man. He's going to be killed out there."

"The thing is—and this is going to sound stupid—for a guy like Jairo, not going out there and fighting, even in this state, would be worse than getting his ass kicked."

"You say a lot of dumb things. Sometimes crazy. That is insane."

"You throw in the towel now, he doesn't even get a chance to get right. Give him the chance."

"The chance to die?"

"Marcela, he's a warrior. You stop him from fighting, even when he knows he shouldn't, you might as well bury him. Nobody ever said it was smart. It's just true."

"So we just let him go out there alone and be destroyed?"

She turned and walked away before I could say anything, which was good.

I don't think she'd like the answer.

———

Jairo stayed in the bathroom for close to forty minutes. I kept a light sweat going with Gil, watched the live feed, and tried to sit still while Hollywood wrapped my hands.

He pulled the gauze and tape out, said, "I'm not even gonna ask," and gave me the knockout wrap. Hard and tight, molding my fists into piston heads.

I checked my phone every five minutes. Nothing from Rubin.

After the fourth time, Marcela peeked around my arm. "What are you expecting?"

"Good luck wishes from the guys back home. Roth, Terence, you know." The lie slid out and flopped on the floor, glared up at me with one harsh eye.

"Back home." She touched my hand and walked away.

Carol and her headset leaned through the open door. "Jairo Arcoverde, walking in two minutes."

Edson darted into the bathroom.

A minute later the Arcoverde men came out. Javier first, Jairo behind him in a fresh green Arcoverde gi with his gloved hands on Javier's shoulders. His head sagged. Antonio had his hands on Jairo's shoulders and spoke to him in low Portuguese. Edson brought up the back of the train.

They filed to the door and waited.

Marcela stood with her arms crossed, shifting her weight side to side. Her desire to grab Jairo, keep him safe with her was palpable. She'd turned the TV off, saying she refused to watch this happen. To her, it must have been like watching Jairo walk blindfolded toward a thousand-foot cliff.

I checked my phone one last time.

Nothing.

I tossed it in the bag, zipped it up and said to Gil, "Follow my lead."

"Your what?"

Carol waved Javier forward. "It's time, gentlemen."

Javier plowed into the hallway, dragging Jairo, Antonio, and Edson.

Gil said, "Woody."

I ignored him and waited until the Arcoverdes cleared the door and turned right into the hallway. I winked at Marcela and caught up to Edson, put my taped hands on his shoulders and kept pace.

He turned, confused, then his eyes widened.

I held a finger to my lips and waited for Edson to make his choice: Realize I was the only hope is brother had, or succumb to ego and family pride and pull Antonio around.

Edson—not the smartest Arcoverde by a stretch—nodded once and faced forward.

So he thought it was a good idea.
Which made me think it might be a terrible one.
Too late now.

CHAPTER 15

THE CROWD SANG IN PORTUGUESE LOUDER THAN JAIRO'S entrance music and leaned over the railings along the path to the cage, trying to get a blessing of Arcoverde mystique. I caught some faces screwing from elation to confusion—outright disgust a few times—when they saw me in the convoy.

Gil stuck to my ribs and yelled something, but it was lost in the chaos of the arena. It sounded like "This is fucking crazy, what are you doing you idiot," but that couldn't be right.

We plowed into the staging area cageside. Hollywood was there, along with Vern and a couple referees to give Jairo clearance to take those last few steps. The ones that counted the most.

Preston was already in the cage, bouncing his back against the fence and taking lazy swings with both arms. He frowned at me and I waved back. The referee was Brubaker, considered by most fighters to be the best one in the business for letting a fight go right to the point when it needed to be stopped.

Good and bad. If Jairo got in a tough spot he'd take a hell of a beating, but the ref would give him plenty of time to get out of it.

Javier pulled Jairo's black belt and gi top off and folded them over his arm. Jairo tried to untie his gi pants but his hands shook too much. Javier yanked the heavy canvas cord and scooped the pants up after Jairo stepped out of them. He wore tight mid-thigh fight shorts with the Arcoverde logo on one leg, no other sponsors.

Antonio spun him around for one last look, eye to eye.

Jairo saw me and Gil. His mouth fell open.

Antonio turned. Fury pulled his face toward the center. The crowd rampaged around us. I could barely hear the Portuguese he spat but it made Edson take a step back. Antonio pointed toward the prep rooms.

I shook my head.

He moved closer. "Go back!"

I stepped next to Jairo, told him, "Don't think. Don't wait. Destroy him."

Antonio tried to push me away and did a damn fine job of it. I slammed into the cage apron and had to grab the outside of the fence to stay standing. Gil caught my arm and held a palm toward Antonio, who was still coming.

"Hey, assholes!" Eddie's teeth were clenched hard enough to fuse together. "What the fuck is going on?"

"A fight," I said.

The crowd sang and stomped and cheered. Somewhere underneath the racket I heard Jairo's music start over.

Eddie leaned into the tension between Antonio, Gil, and me. "What are you two doing out here?"

I said, "I'm cornering Jairo."

"You're fighting next, jackass."

"Right."

Eddie asked Gil, "You're okay with this?"

Gil kept his eyes on me, nodded.

"I am controlling this," Antonio said. "I am the cornerman. It is not up to him."

Eddie glanced at all three of us, then studied Jairo. He looked like someone had stripped him and pushed him out into sub-zero weather, even worse than when Eddie had seen him in the prep room.

"You're right," Eddie said. "It's not up to him." He waved Jairo over and held two fingers up, shouted, "You get two cornermen. Who's it gonna be?"

Jairo found another shade of pale.

"I am all he needs," Antonio said.

"He gets two," Eddie said.

Jairo pointed at me.

His father lunged again and messed up Eddie's faux hawk before Gil could wrap Antonio up.

Eddie put a finger in his face. "I'll have security drag your ass out of here, Antonio."

Javier and Edson flanked Antonio.

A half-dozen brutes from Warrior security moved in behind Eddie.

The crowd likely had no clue what was happening, but they could see Banzai Eddie disrespecting a national treasure. He may as well have pulled one of the massive Brazilian flags out of the crowd and pissed on it. The arena shattered into boos and war cries, oaths of vengeance and blood feuds.

In the center of it all, I put my arms around Jairo and spoke into his ear.

Antonio must have realized he was on the verge of getting kicked out. He shrugged Gil off and smoothed his shirt, pulled his shoulders back and regained his regal posture. He said something to Javier and Edson, who struggled to break the stare-down with security before carrying the Arcoverde banner around the perimeter of the cage to Jairo's corner.

Eddie said, "Well, that was some bullshit." He turned to Hollywood. "Fix my hair."

I finished talking and gave Jairo a squeeze. The bear hug he gave back pushed the air out of me and threatened a few ribs. He bowed to Antonio and stepped onto the launching pad.

Vern rubbed Vaseline onto Jairo's eyebrows and cheeks so he wouldn't get cut early in the fight, before he was slick with sweat. The refs checked behind his ears for pre-existing damage—sponsors didn't like ears getting torn off on live TV—scanned his tape and gloves, fingernails and toenails.

Verified his cup and mouthguard.

The ref held a hand toward the open gate. "Fighter is ready."

We'll see.

———

The fighter announcements were a blur. The arena hated Preston and loved Jairo, I know that much. The deafening sound of it crashed around the civil debate Antonio and I had below Gil, Javier, and Edson, who draped Jairo's banner over the fence and shot worried glances down at us.

"You say nothing to him," Antonio said. He had a handful of my sweatshirt.

"I'll tell him what he needs to hear. Long as you don't tell him to stop and wait, he'll be fine."

"Don't tell me what is right for fighting."

"Just go wait outside."

"What? You want to go outside? Let's go! I leave you there!"

"Calm down."

"Don't tell me what to do! Don't tell my son what to do!"

"Let go of my shirt."

He released with a stiff shove. "Go to hell, you and your shirt."

It may have been the first time I'd heard Antonio swear. Small victories.

Jim Lincoln, the Warrior announcer, pointed into our corner and cycled up to a bellow as the crowd chanted "AR-CO-VER-de."

"Ladies and gentlemen, making his debut in the Warrior cage. . . . He's a worldwide Brazilian jiu jitsu legend, six-time Brazilian Champion, and four-time Abu Dhabi Champion. Fans of Brazil, it is Jairo . . . Arcoverde!"

Antonio huffed in my face while the crowd went insane.

"You're missing it," I yelled.

He blinked. Gazed up at his son bathed in the lights and the adoration of thousands as he stood alone, preparing to fight another man who had trained specifically to do him great harm.

Antonio put his hand on me again. I didn't mind—it was the only thing keeping him upright.

The guys packed up the banner and dropped off the apron next to us.

Gil said, "I can do this instead. You go get ready."

I shook my head.

"I figured. We'll be close by."

Javier and Edson hugged their father, followed Gil to the small cageside corral for trainers.

I could barely hear Antonio muttering resentment at me while Brubaker walked into the center of the cage and pointed at Preston.

"Fighter, are you ready?"

Preston nodded.

I realized Antonio was saying prayers, and they weren't for me.

"Fighter, are you ready?"

Jairo nodded.

"Fight!"

———

Preston launched from his side of the cage with his hands low. Jairo stepped to his left and waited, glanced over his shoulder at Antonio, who barked something in Portuguese.

Jairo stepped to his right.

This was alarming. If Jairo moved to his right it would let Preston set up the distance and timing to unleash that crushing overhand.

I cupped my hands and yelled, "Go left."

Antonio jostled against my shoulder and snapped a command. It didn't seem possible Jairo would hear us over the crowd noise, but he must have. Because he froze.

Preston moved in, right hand cocked. He seemed eager to engage but wary of a trap. Jairo stepped back and bumped against the cage. Preston angled to his right, setting up the punch.

This is how it would go.

Preston crushes Jairo with the overhand right.

Jairo goes down and Preston hammerfists him until the ref jumps in.

Or, Preston rushes in after the overhand and clinches Jairo against the cage, gets into some dirty boxing until he drags him down into side-control with his body perpendicular to Jairo's, all his weight sunk onto Jairo's chest.

Then it's butcher shop time—short, heavy punches and elbows until the ref decides it's enough or Jairo taps.

Either way, Jairo gets hurt and the Arcoverde name is stained forever.

I gave zero fucks about the legacy. But between getting some new scars or having his family sullied, Jairo would start cutting.

"Move left! Left!"

Antonio took a deep breath and opened his mouth. I hit him under the ribs with a quick left hook and heard the wind come out in a rush. It was a sneaky punch, slipped between us and the apron. Invisible from behind unless you had X-ray vision.

Antonio grunted and gaped at me with shock and accusations.

I ignored him and yelled when Jairo sidestepped to his left. "Keep going, circle, circle."

Jairo skipped sideways around the cage. Preston followed and threw a few right jabs that fell short.

Antonio clutched my arm and wheezed, "I'm going to kill you."

"Save it. After the fight." I was going to need a spreadsheet to keep track of all the Brazilians who wanted to throw me a beating.

Preston lunged right and cut into Jairo's path, sending him back the other way. As soon as Jairo stepped right, Preston returned to stalking with his fist cocked.

Even with his wrestling pedigree it was obvious Preston wanted to keep the fight standing. He'd had plenty of opportunities to shoot in for a takedown and dismissed every one.

As always, the strategy came down to two options: Figure out what you're better at and force him into that fight. Or figure out what he wants to do and beat him to it.

Both Jairo and Preston were better off with the first one. It was going to come down to which man could force the other into the fight he didn't want.

So far, Jairo was in a fight no one would want and Preston had done pretty much everything he'd wanted to.

Then it got worse.

———

Preston landed the overhand right.

It smashed Jairo in the left temple and pulled his legs up like a curtain. He landed on his right hip and splashed onto his back, arms flopping.

Antonio gasped and reached toward the fence like he was going to climb it and drop down between Preston and his son, absorb the impending punches so Jairo wouldn't have to.

He'd never make it.

Preston dove in and knelt between Jairo's dead legs. The first hammerfist glanced off Jairo's cheek and spent most of its impact against the canvas. The second landed flush against his ear.

Brubaker crouched next to them, poised to intervene, and yelled, "Do something, Jairo. Defend yourself."

My brain panicked, flooded with what Jairo needed to do. "Cover up! Roll! Wrist control!"

Worse than worthless.

Jairo's eyes were pinched shut, arms flailing to defend his face from the machine-gun strikes from Preston. I doubted he heard my chaotic cues or could even think straight.

Antonio pulled a white towel out of the corner bucket.

I nodded even though he didn't consult me.

Then Jairo's legs clamped around Preston's waist. His ankles crossed and he bucked Preston forward, off balance.

I twisted to my right and snatched at the trailing corner of the white towel as Antonio hurled it into the cage. It fell onto the apron in front of us. Antonio swiped at it and I pinned the cloth down.

"Wait!"

We watched Preston tilt forward and post his hands on Jairo's chest to keep from falling. Jairo grabbed both of his wrists and held them there like they'd been welded. His face was swollen, red, and completely calm.

I grinned.

With that overhand right, Preston had done the one thing Jairo needed to turn off his damned brain.

Now Jairo Arcoverde was working on pure muscle memory.

Poor, poor Preston.

———

Preston tried to push his way out of Jairo's guard, found himself locked in concrete. He pulled his feet in and stood up, stacking Jairo onto his shoulders and the back of his head.

Preston was in a good spot to drop punches if he could get a hand free. He yanked and tugged, lifting Jairo off the canvas a few inches and dropping him down. I feared a powerbomb was imminent—that Preston would haul Jairo all the way up into the air and slam him on his head—then Jairo released Preston's left wrist and reached for his left ankle.

Preston wasn't stupid. He saw a leg- or anklelock coming and stuck his left leg out like a kickstand beyond Jairo's grasp.

Jairo was moving before his foot hit the canvas. He pulled his legs into a butterfly guard, knees outside Preston's hips and the tops of his feet against Preston's inner thighs. His right sole scraped down Preston's left leg and held it up, stopped just above his knee and drove it back. Jairo lifted with his left foot, torqued to his right, and captured Preston's left wrist again as it came down to stop the fall.

Jairo kept the sweep going, rolled into a full mount with his knees clamped against Preston's ribs and his head tucked under the brawler's chin, facing away from us.

It was a blur of technique that took less than one second, start to finish.

The crowd went berserk. Antonio thumped a fist on the apron and grabbed a handful of my sweatshirt, though he didn't seem to notice.

Preston kicked his legs and tried to roll left, right, but Jairo didn't give him an inch of space. He locked in and sank his weight onto Preston's chest. I've been in that spot with Jairo before. It feels like treading water in a riptide, then someone hands you a sack of cannonballs.

Being a former wrestler, Preston liked being on his back about as much as crocodiles like being tickled. He shoved Jairo's shoulders and tried to punch his face and head, but Jairo was too close to allow a good shot. His hands fought for control of Preston's wrists, and Preston managed to land a few short right hooks that wouldn't do any damage but were enough to make Jairo turn his head to face us.

His eyes found me, flicked over to Antonio.

And waited.

Antonio froze, his fist still full of my sweatshirt while he studied the position.

Preston bucked and slapped punches into Jairo's ear.

Brubaker had to yell so they could hear him. "You guys gotta work. Do some work or I'll stand you up."

Great. Another chance for the overhand right to make an appearance. If Preston got back on his feet, he'd work his ass off to make sure he stayed there.

Antonio squinted, moved his head up and down, examining the angles and tension, then shouted, "Apenas lutar! Lutar!"

I said, "What's that?"

Antonio glanced at me. "I tell him just fight. Fight."

Jairo winked at us, then caught Preston's left wrist with his right hand, rocked up into a kneeling position, and slammed his left fist into Preston's face. The crowd detonated a nuclear weapon somewhere in the upper deck.

Jairo punched again and again. Preston turned his head side to side and tried to cover up with his forearms. Jairo still had the left wrist, and when Preston lifted his head off the canvas Jairo looped his right arm behind the head and dragged Preston's left arm around his own neck and trapped it there, leaving Preston's reddening face exposed.

Jairo landed heavy lefts onto Preston's mouth, nose, and brow. Preston's right hand and forearm blocked some of them. Then Jairo dropped a crushing elbow that made the arena howl.

I nudged Antonio. "I taught him that."

Brubaker had a keen eye on Preston, watching for the moment when he could no longer intelligently defend himself. Jairo punched him three more times, ripped Preston's left arm tighter around his neck, and fell forward to plant all of his weight on the triceps.

Preston's legs kicked, stomped, and sagged.

Jairo let go and stood up.

Brubaker waved Jairo back into the fight, then saw Preston's glazed eyes staring up at the lights.

I heard Davie Benton, the Warrior color commentator, screaming, "He choked him out with his own arm!"

Jairo raised a fist as the crowd shook the building apart.

Antonio slapped me on the back and touched a thumb to his puffed chest. "I taught him that."

———

I followed Antonio toward the cage doorway. Edson and Javier jumped the steps, pulled their father up, and ran to Jairo. I was right behind them when Gil caught my arm.

"You gotta get your gloves on! You're next!"

Ah, shit.

Aviso.

I took a moment to watch the Arcoverdes celebrate the victory, then ran with Gil up the aisle to the prep rooms.

Under the crowd's elation for Jairo and the singing of Eu Sou Brasileiro, the chant was already starting.

"*Vai morrer! Vai morrer!*"

———

Marcela had tears on her cheeks as she grabbed Gil and me, gathered us into a group hug that blocked the space just inside the prep room door.

Some suit from the fight commission came in without

knocking and ran into my back.

"Official business," he apologized, then peered at my wrapped hands, hefted the gloves waiting for me on the table and poked his finger inside each one before grunting and moving to the corner. He pulled out his phone and ignored us, though I'm sure he would have spoken up if I slipped on a pair of brass knuckles before I picked up the gloves.

Marcela released us and ran a sleeve over her face, waved a hand at the TV showing replays of Preston's punch and Jairo's resurrection. "I turned it on and off twenty times. I couldn't watch, then I couldn't stand not knowing. I wanted to come out and be strong for Jairo, but with his getting sick, and my uncle . . . it was too much. He is okay?"

I tugged one glove on. "This is probably the best moment of his life."

"He's fine," Gil said. "But we should all be prepared—his machismo will now grow exponentially."

"This is not possible." Marcela helped me with the second glove.

The commission guy kept one eye on us while Gil tightened the laces and tied them off, then presented a focus mitt. I tagged it a dozen times with each hand.

"Feels good."

The official produced a roll of blue duct tape from his pocket and slapped a strip around each of my wrists, covering the laces and edges of sewn leather. He signed his work with a black Sharpie so everyone would know I hadn't re-wrapped my hands with lead strips and kryptonite.

"Good luck," he said, then left.

Gil walked to the mats. "Let's get you warmed up again."

"I'm ready."

"You loose?"

"Just another Saturday."

"Let's have some fun."

I smacked the pads around, Gil moving to check my footwork and angles, making sure I wasn't defaulting away from the Aviso strategy. This was my thirtieth professional MMA fight and my third with Warrior. The previous two had been against disparate opponents: Junior Burbank, a poster-boy powerhouse and the only guy I'd fought who hit as hard as me, and Zombi, a Japanese robot sent by the Yakuza to infect Warrior.

Burbank wanted to break my will and leave me a bloody mess before he put me down for good.

Zombi took everything I threw at him and kept coming forward to choke me unconscious—at least.

I knocked them both out. Beyond the victory, there is something powerful in turning the lights off on another man. You steal a slice of time from him. You take a bit of his soul, his presence.

Aviso had never been knocked out. Hell, I hadn't seen any footage of him taking a solid punch. He was slippery and elusive and an expert at avoiding punishment.

But he was about to get locked in a cage with me.

And I am punishment.

———

The Arcoverde brothers boiled through the door, hugging and hopping and laughing. Antonio followed with his hands behind his back, beaming with pride. Cameras flashed from the hallway and a Warrior media crew nosed into the room to feed live footage to the TV.

Gil and I stepped out of the way.

Marcela ran her hands over Jairo's face and hugged him. Javier and Edson wrapped them up and within a few seconds they were all crying and laughing with relief and joy.

Gil sniffed and used the hood of his sweatshirt to wipe his eyes. Sweat ran into mine and I had to blink a few hundred times to keep things clear. It also made my throat thick and my nose run.

Antonio approached, his face blank.

Gil put a hand out. "Congratulations. Your son was incredible."

Antonio stopped, his mouth a thin line while he studied Gil. He turned and walked away toward the Arcoverde corner, disappeared behind his sons.

Gil's hand hung out there like a puppy in the cold. More tears fell, but they weren't for Jairo and they weren't happy.

I scrambled for something to say or do, came up with nothing. It didn't seem like the right moment to put Antonio through a wall, but I've never been good at reading a room.

Antonio reappeared, stepped around his family and walked toward us with his weathered satchel. He stopped in front of Gil, reached into the satchel, and pulled out a carefully folded strip of cloth. It had wide, alternating stripes of black and red, similar to a coral snake. I'd seen one like it before, the first time Jairo came to Gil's dojo in Vegas and Gil held a welcoming ceremony.

It was a seventh-degree black belt in Arcoverde jiu jitsu.

Antonio bowed his head and held the belt out to Gil with both hands. Behind him, Jairo stood with his arms around Marcela, Javier, and Edson. They were all still crying while they watched in silence.

Gil's mouth was open. He took an unsteady step back and pulled a deep, shuddering breath, then shook his head and sobbed.

He bowed to Antonio and slid his palms beneath the belt.

Antonio gripped Gil's forearms. "You have taught me much, my friend. My son. I do not know if I am worthy to give you this, but you are worthy of it."

They fell into a fierce embrace. The rest of the Arcoverdes piled on and Marcela hauled me in. I rubbed Jairo's head and slapped backs and kissed lips I'm pretty sure were Marcela's.

All in all, it was a lot more hugging than I'm used to before a fight.

We broke apart. The Warrior media crew extracted themselves and Carol stuck her head in the door.

"Woodshed Wallace, walking in five minutes."

She closed the door.

Gil stared down at the belt, still folded in his hands.

I said, "Do I have to call you 'professor' now, or 'master'?"

"Actually, you shouldn't be talking to me at all anymore."

"Sounds about right."

Antonio turned to me, his posture rigid. "Thank you for helping my son."

"Hey, Arcoverde blood won that fight. We just needed to get out of his way."

He nodded. "You are still not good enough for Marcela."

"I know."

Marcela's jaw clenched.

Antonio held a palm toward her, then winked. "But it is only because no one is."

He offered the hand to me.

I shook it.

"You are ready for Aviso," he said.

"Yes."

"I think you are. You are calm."

"Right."

"We saw this with Jairo. The calm fighter has an advantage, he wins. Because he knows what is going to happen next, yes?"

"Sure."

"And you are calm because you know what you are doing."

"Damn right. I'm getting into a fight."

Marcela puffed her cheeks and patted my arm.

The hallway crew thumped on the door.

"We're in business," Gil said. He grabbed the bucket with all his cornerman gear.

Marcela kissed me hard, put her forehead against mine. "I love you."

"I love you."

"Oh!" She pulled back and ran to my bag. "During Jairo's fight your phone would not shut up, but I was pacing too much to care or make it stop."

She checked the screen.

"Your guys back home say, 'They are here. Where are you?'" Marcela frowned. "The next one says, 'Where is Marcela?' These are just from a number, no name. 'They are coming.' Who is this from? Who are they?"

A fist pounded the door again.

Gil found my mouthguard and held it up, made a display of putting it in the bucket so I'd know it was ready. He walked around the couches.

"Somebody let poor Carol in."

He opened the door.

Carrasco stood there with Malhar and Eye Patch.

"It is time, sure."

CHAPTER 16

THE ROOM WAS DEAD SILENT. MY STOMACH SHRANK AND fell between my feet.

Carrasco smiled at Marcela. "Hello, Pomba Gira."

"Why are you here?"

"For your man, sure. Oh, maybe he did not tell you this was happening. From your face, I think so. Is too bad. I will never lie to you, Pomba Gira."

The Arcoverde men lost their elation and turned into a tense pride of lions, staring and snorting at Carrasco's crew. Eye Patch lifted the butt of a cut-down shotgun out of his bag, just enough to show everyone, and shook his head.

Marcela turned to me. "What is happening?"

"I didn't have a choice. I'm sorry."

"He lies," Carrasco said. "Exu gave him choices. Chances to go away. He chose to stay, to run the Coluna da Cobra, sure."

Marcela said, "Tell me."

I felt ridiculous standing in my sandals, shorts, and gloves against men with guns, grenades, and fuck knows what else. I took

Marcela's hands, slipped the phone out of her loose grip and let it fall to the carpet, nudged it under the couch to keep Rubin's messages away from Carrasco.

"I couldn't leave. I couldn't walk away knowing he'd come for you. You and your family."

"So you will kill yourself instead. Then what? He still comes, and I am heartbroken."

Carrasco looked concerned. "No no. Exu will heal you, Pomba Gira."

"Shut up."

Malhar puffed at the insult. He took a step forward. Carrasco tilted his walking stick across the doorway. Malhar stopped, the veins in his head throbbing as he scanned the Arcoverdes with pig eyes. He grinned and nodded, eager to take on the whole room. He spat something in Portuguese and squeezed his crotch.

Carrasco said to me, "Exu gave you choices. Now you have another. The Coluna is ready. The snake is hungry, sure. And it is time for your little fight, with rules and music to make people happy for the violence. Which one do you choose?"

"I'll make the fight quick."

Carrasco shook his head. "Not quick enough. Exu's people are ready. If you break your oath to Exu, if you do not feed the snake, they will be angry. And scared. They will want to make Exu happy."

"How?"

He shrugged. "Climb into the Arcoverde estate and take everything, burn it to the ground. Leave only ash and bones, I think."

Jairo and his brothers cursed and shouted. Antonio's chest heaved.

Carrasco tilted his glasses down and stared with his red, bulging jellyfish eye until the noise died. "In this room, Exu kills everyone and takes Pomba Gira to her new home."

I said, "Somebody cut these gloves off me."

Gil said, "Woody, wait."

"Cut 'em off or I'll chew 'em off."

Marcela put a hand on my chest. "You are not going."

I gnawed at the duct tape around my right wrist.

"Wait," Marcela said. "Even if you live, your fight career is over. Eddie will never forgive this."

"Fuck him. Fuck Warrior. This is you. This is family."

"I won't let you through the door."

I told Gil, "Keep her out of my way."

She grabbed Gil's hand. "Make him stop. Choke him unconscious. Jairo, all of you. Help me."

"Anyone who interferes with Exu's will," Carrasco said, "angers him."

Eye Patch poked the barrel of the shotgun through the open zipper and leveled it at the room. I held my hands out to Gil, who pulled a pair of medical shears out of the cornerman bucket.

He couldn't look at Marcela but told her, "I tried to take him home."

He slid the shears in.

"No," Marcela said. She turned to Carrasco. "Let him fight. Let him go out there, and afterward I will go with him for the Coluna."

"Don't listen," I said shoving my gloves at Gil again. He pulled the scissors away.

Carrasco said, "Pomba Gira, the Coluna is very dangerous."

"Yes. And if he does not survive it, I will already be there. I will come to Exu willingly."

Carrasco gasped a prayer in Portuguese. "This makes Exu very happy. He accepts."

"Bullshit he does," I said.

Marcela pulled my head down, pressed her cheek against mine, and whispered, "You have fought alone for so long, and now you are willing to do this. I cannot take it. Don't you see? It is too much. I will go with you. If they want to hurt you, they have to go through me. And if they want to hurt me, they must face you. Tell me—who in the world will be safer than us?"

She looked me in the eye.

I saw truth.

"Make a path, make a path." Carol and her headset elbowed between Malhar and Carrasco. Eye Patch's shotgun disappeared into the duffel like a turtle's head. Carol eyeballed the three men blocking the doorway like they were bird shit on a bible. "Woody, we're walking."

I stared at Carrasco's dark lenses and waited.

He backed away. Malhar and Eye Patch followed, clearing the exit.

Carrasco said, "Good luck out there."

———

"*Vai morrer! Vai morrer!*"

The chant was louder than my entrance music. Brazilian fans tilted over the barricades lining the path to the cage, flailing and spitting and clutching. Flags slapped me in the face.

"*Vai morrer! Vai morrer!*"

You will die.

Gil had a hand on my shoulder. His mouth was moving but I couldn't hear a word of it. All I could think about was being dropped at the top of the Axila da Serpente with Marcela. Tried

to picture it, what kind of shape I would be in after this fight
with Aviso.

"*Vai morrer! Vai morrer!*"

Ideally, this would be over quickly.

Let me save energy.

"*Vai morrer! Vai morrer!*"

I had a feeling Aviso wouldn't play along. Something else
huddled in the corner of my mind, a black crusty thought I hadn't
paid attention to in years. Maybe ever.

"*Vai morrer! Vai morrer!*"

It was the worst thing a fighter could carry into the cage. I
survived the gauntlet and stopped at the base of the stairs, stripped
off my sweatshirt, kicked off the sandals, and started up.

Gil yanked me back and yelled into my ear: "Easy, Woody.
Easy. They gotta check you."

He slapped my mouthguard in and wrapped me in a bear hug.
Behind him, Antonio stood with the bucket of gear. He nodded
and pulled me close when Gil stepped away.

"You are calm. You are ready."

I nodded. The surreal moment of having the grandmaster of
Arcoverde jiu jitsu as a cornerman was wasted on me—everything
was focused on ignoring the black thought.

It was stretching, shaking off the dust.

"*Vai morrer! Vai morrer!*"

Vern spun me around and did his thing. I barely felt the
smeared Vaseline, relied on muscle memory to tap my cup and
show him the mouthguard.

He held a hand toward the cage entrance. "Fighter may enter."

I ran up the steps, trying to shake the thought loose and leave
it behind.

It was dug in and swelling, like it had tapped an artery.

The one thought a fighter can never have.

And the one I needed to obey if Marcela and I were going to survive the Coluna.

Don't get hurt.

———

Aviso came in to something with bongos. He cha-cha'ed his way down the runway to the crowd's deafening rendition of Eu Sou Brasileiro, slapping palms, kissing women, and posing for photos.

I paced my corner.

Don't think about getting hurt.

That doesn't work, idiot.

Think about the strategies.

I sorted through the noise in my head, couldn't find them.

Shit.

Gil and Antonio leaned over the top of the cage, holding a banner with the Fight House logo and our sponsors'.

I yelled, "What are the strategies?"

Gil held out a water bottle.

"No, the strategies. I forgot them."

"Yeah, you got this."

So much for that.

Aviso sprang into the cage with his hands in the air like he'd already won. He skipped around, blowing kisses to the crowd. When he got near me he shook a finger in my face and pointed to his chest, then grabbed my left arm, tapped the elbow, and yelled, "This belongs to me! It is mine!"

I shoved him away.

He pulled a face and waved a hand in front of his nose, cartwheeled to his corner, and bowed to the arena.

Jim Lincoln introduced us, his voice drowned out first by chants that I would die, then that they were Brazilian. At least the crowd was consistent. Gil and Antonio pulled the banner and dropped away.

The ref, a stocky guy named Hector, walked to the center of the cage and pointed at me.

"Fighter, are you ready?"

I don't fight carefully.

I don't fight scared.

Hell, I don't even fight smart.

I fight hard.

I care more about hurting the other guy than I do about getting hurt.

Knowing Carrasco and his Coluna waited for me and Marcela, I couldn't do that.

I nodded anyway.

Hector turned to Aviso. "Fighter, are you ready?"

Aviso posed like a matador and nodded.

"Let's go!"

———

Aviso strolled out of his corner. I stomped out of mine and we met in the center of the cage. As soon as Aviso was in striking distance he dropped into a loose crouch, hands wheeling in front of his bobbing head.

I kept my hips back, away from any takedown attempts, and threw a straight right. Aviso danced away. My fist came back with no sweat or blood on it.

What's the goddam strategy?

Destroy his face, slosh his brain around, paint the canvas with him.

No, the other strategy. The smart one.

Gil was yelling something.

Aviso skipped to his right, toward my cocked left hand, crowding it. I cut him off and tried a left hook. Aviso ducked. As my arm swiped above his head he slapped the elbow, shoved me away, and laughed.

"Not yet, man. Not yet!"

I glanced at Gil, who pointed at his own head and shook it while he yelled.

No attacks to the head—that was the strategy.

No wonder I didn't want to remember it. Every muscle fiber in my body wanted to do just that.

Couldn't punch him in the head or he'd take me down.

Couldn't attack the legs or he'd catch a kick and take me down.

What was left?

Just the blocky abs with their highlights and shadows on all the Aviso billboards. A liver tucked in there somewhere, hoping to be overlooked. I had my hands up near my jaw, covering against incoming strikes. But Aviso doesn't throw punches worth a damn, especially to the face.

I took a deep breath.

Get your shit together.

You trained this for months.

Forget about what's next.

This fight is in front of you now.

I dropped my hands to chest height, like Gil had drilled over and over. Aviso punched me in the face and sprang back out of reach. It happened so fast I tried to deny it, but the sting around my left eye objected.

Aviso grinned.

Well, fuck all that.

I drove in, chin tucked and fists pumping. It didn't matter what they hit—shoulder, biceps, ribs, referee—the aftershocks would shake something loose. Aviso leaned back and slid his feet around. My thumb knuckle grazed the top of his head, and that's the closest I came before he shot in, hooked an ankle with his leg and pulled it out from under me.

I tried to pry him off as I went down but he was a tumor, latched around my abdomen and weaving himself into me.

I landed on my back in the center of the cage with Aviso on top of me.

During training, this was referred to as The Worst Thing Possible.

——

Aviso's knees dug into my sides and his hips dropped onto my belly. I tried rolling right but someone had stacked wet sandbags around me.

He stuck the top of his head under my chin and shoved forward, trying to get me to reach up and push him away, exposing my arms. I kept my elbows tucked, found his wrists between our chests and grabbed both of them.

Aviso shouted, "You ready? You ready?"

He pulled a hand free and smacked me in the ribs a few times before I caught it again.

"I think you might be. I gonna break your arm, man."

The crowd was a distant roar, surf crashing while I fought for my life on shore.

Aviso popped up, yanked his hands free and looped both fists into my head. The strikes were fast, but I'd hesitate to call them punches. I'd taken worse in light sparring at the Fight House.

I let Aviso have his slap fight and hammered a short left into his abdomen, twisting my whole body into it. The ribs flexed in and out like an aluminum can. Aviso grunted and came back down to put his head under my chin.

I asked him, "Didn't like that, huh?"

"That's the arm I gonna break for you. But first I cook you, man. Get you nice and soft."

He fought to get his left hand loose and patty-caked it into the side of my head a few times. I took the opportunity to bash his ribs with my right, one solid thud for every three taps.

"You relax for one blink, man, I snap it. Maybe I go now, huh?"

Hector the ref barked at us. "Get busy, gentlemen."

Aviso landed a few more punches, a bit of weight behind them. My skull finally noticed we were in a fight.

Rolling with Jairo, I'd been on my back plenty of times. He had a brutal, smothering strength. It was like being mauled by a crocodile with gorilla arms. Aviso was just as strong, which surprised me, but his strength was different—wiry, steel cables cinching tight. I'd move to create space between us and he'd ratchet tighter, closing the gap and claiming that space as his own. We were in trench warfare, and I was losing ground.

Without intending to, I'd kept my left arm out of the action. Beyond Aviso's head, up near the lights, Carrasco and his Coluna hovered.

Don't get hurt.

My feet kicked around. Hips rocked side to side, trying to dump Aviso off. He was a leech.

"You simmering now, huh? I gonna turn up the heat."

He sat back and dropped two quick hammerfists onto my face and crashed back down before I could counter.

"Why don't you just get up? Don't they teach you how to get up? It's so easy, man. You cooking yet?"

My left arm moved a fraction, a sliver of light between my ribs and elbow. Aviso dove on it. I tensed, panicked, and never saw the right elbow he slammed into my eye socket.

My head bounced off the canvas, again, again.

The scar tissue split apart. Blood ran over the bridge of my nose into my left eye.

"Defend yourself," Hector yelled.

I rolled into the next elbow, caught it between the eyes and kept going. Because Aviso's right arm was busy chopping my face he couldn't post out to that side and stop me. His thighs dug in but I was sweaty, slick, and managed to get onto my knees and elbows.

I never like giving a guy my back—especially a master grappler like Aviso—but it was better than Hector stopping the fight or Aviso smashing my head until he could rip my arm off and take it home with him.

Don't get hurt.

Now I had to worry about a rear-naked choke as well as Aviso scooping the arm from behind in some jiu jitsu wizardry. He tucked his head behind mine and tried to wedge his right forearm across my throat.

"Hey, you know how to count in Portuguese? Ready? Três . . ."

His left arm snaked over my left shoulder and grabbed my wrist.

What the fuck is he doing?

"Dois."

I felt him take a deep breath against my back, loading up for something.

Choke?

Armbar?

Well don't sit here waiting for it.

I stood up. Aviso clung to my back and wrapped a long leg around my stomach, hooked the other knee over that ankle and crushed my guts in a body triangle. Everything rose against my diaphragm and cut off half my lungs. He let go of my arm and focused on getting the rear-naked choke.

I faced the center of the cage and leaned back.

Aviso and his coaches must have watched my fight against Zombi. When that cyborg had me in a similar pickle, the black curtains closing from no blood getting to my brain, I dove head-first into the canvas, knocking myself for a loop and Zombi out cold.

I widened my stance for maximum torque while Aviso scrambled for the choke. I pulled his wrists away and blinked blood out my eyes, then rocked forward.

Aviso sprang off my back. I tucked into a shoulder roll and came up facing the cage, turned and wiped blood from my eyes.

Hector leaned in. "Can you see?"

"Just fine."

Aviso stood in the middle of the canvas, waving me forward. "You almost done, man. I cook you first, then I burn you up."

I closed the distance, hands near my shoulders.

The crowd noise was there, drowned by the racket in my head.

Don't get hurt.

Straight right toward his solar plexus.

He dodged.

I followed.

Don't get hurt.

Left push-kick to the belly that missed and almost got caught as he sidestepped.

I stalked him around the perimeter.

Don't get hurt.

"I making you look stupid, man. Slow."

He changed directions.

I plodded after him.

"Don't get hurt, now."

Hearing the voice out loud made me hesitate, then dive in with a right uppercut followed by a gunshot left hook.

Aviso leaned away from the first and ducked the second. He came in behind it and found me on one foot, off-balance, and took me down easier than Jewish Christmas decorations.

I worked to get him in full guard on the way to the canvas, claimed a small victory in achieving half. I was on my back with his left leg trapped between mine.

"Let's see how your jiu jitsu is, huh?"

He did something to my knee and twisted his leg out, slid into full mount like we were making a how-to video.

"I don't think it's so good, man. Now I count for you in English. You ready?"

I welded my left arm to my ribs.

Aviso fought for it, got his fingers around the wrist and started to pry it away.

"One."

He put another elbow into my face, planted it across my throat and ground it in.

"Two."

The horn blasted.

End of round one.

Hector pulled Aviso off and waved him toward his corner.

I rolled onto my hands and knees, watched the fat drops of blood splash onto the canvas below me.

One.

Two.

Three.

———

I dropped onto the stool. The way things were going, it should have scooted out and let me fall on my ass.

"Terrible," I said.

Gil dumped water in my mouth. "Nah, he's running scared."

"I can't hit him."

Hollywood pushed something into the cut over my right eye—his thumb or a compact car—while Antonio slapped an ice pack on the back of my neck to slow the blood flow.

"You will," Gil said. "It's working. Just keep it on the feet. Control the distance."

I shook my head.

"Hold still," Hollywood said.

I told Gil, "He's gonna keep running and pick his shots."

"We know what to do about that. We worked it. Patience. Don't go headhunting. Work the body. We got two rounds to break him down."

Which was Gil code for, "You left skid marks on the canvas because you fought like a creeping pile of shit."

We have a policy at the Fight House: No lying in the cage.

Not to yourself, your coach, your fighter.

Lying to the ref and doctor is okay—they aren't real people.

Gil was on the verge of breaking that code by telling me I had a chance against Aviso.

We both knew I was outmatched.

I loved him for hiding it and hated myself for how badly I was going to let him down.

He saw it. Put a hand on my shoulder. "You're okay. You're fine."

Antonio touched Gil's arm, moved it aside, and knelt in front of me. Pressed his palms against my cheeks. His eyes bored into mine, searching.

"What is your mind saying?"

The truth was shameful. But I couldn't lie.

And he already knew.

"Don't get hurt."

Antonio nodded. "Because of Marcela. What you have to do after."

"Yes."

"Your head is racing around, too much happening. Not good for fighting. We know this. We saw it with Jairo, eh? So you simplify. What do you want for Aviso?"

"To hit him. Hard."

"But you can't reach him."

"I'm too slow."

"Very much, yes. What does Aviso want?"

"To rip my arm off."

Antonio grabbed my left elbow, pulled himself close to me. "To do this he must be close. Here. Tight."

"Okay."

He looked from me to Gil, couldn't believe we didn't get it.

"Give him the arm."

"Uh," Gil said.

"Give it to him. Then you are close enough to hit him as much as you want. You can defend the armbar, yes?"

Gil and I shared a silent panic.

"Simplify," Antonio said. "What is in your head?"

"Don't get hurt."

Saying it out loud again felt just as bad as it had the first time.

"Now simplify," Antonio said. "Remove the negative."

This took longer than it should have.

"Get hurt," I said.

"Okay, you are hurt. You are bleeding. Aviso tried to choke you. You are still alive, yes?"

"Yes."

"Simplify. Only this moment, the present. What are you going to do?"

"Hurt."

"Who?"

"Aviso."

The whistle blew.

Antonio stood. "So do it."

———

"Come on man, back to the cooking."

Aviso waited in the center of the cage, hips shaking and fingers wiggling.

Give him the arm.

Everything Gil and I had trained, out the window.

I knew some armbar defenses. Mostly because, early on, I kept getting caught in armbars during training.

All right—no lying in the cage—early on, recently, and currently.

But the primary defense against Aviso was to tap before he snapped my elbow.

If I gave him the arm, would I be able to shut his lights off before that happened?

Simplify.

I pushed Marcela and Carrasco away. Rubin and Malhar, the Coluna. Shoved it all into the corner on top of the black scab that had pried itself loose and infected my thoughts.

Bottom line: Would my desire to hurt my opponent override my fear of getting hurt?

You're goddam right it would.

———

Aviso skipped to his right, arms loose.

I pivoted and followed. Tried a right cross that fell short by a bus length.

Aviso grinned. "What you swinging at? You soft yet? You cooked?"

"I'm getting there."

He laughed. "Yeah, you close, man. You close."

I cast a left hook out, fishing for anything. In a flash he dug in and planted a front kick into my stomach, sending my hips back and my feet out. I landed on one knee, hands up to protect my face.

Aviso bull-rushed, landed an elbow against my forehead and bowled me backward, then latched his right heel behind my left knee so I couldn't put a kickstand out. I landed on my back, Aviso in the full mount again, slamming fists into my face.

This was going great.

He came down with some elbows. I caught them with my head.

I peeled my left hand away from my ribs and hooked it behind his neck, pulled him close to stop the leveraged strikes.

"Man, I don't need to break your arm. I gonna beat the shit out of you, huh? I gonna knock you out instead."

This crossed the line.

He could talk shit all day about choking, submitting, breaking, whatever.

But knockouts were my world.

I provided them quickly and brutally, free of charge if you were begging for one.

And I'd never been on the receiving end of one.

Aviso pissing in my yard was too much.

I shoved him away and put everything behind a left missile aimed for his chin. I'd knocked guys out from my back before.

Happy to do it again.

The fist rose, broke through the atmosphere, and landed right in Aviso's trap.

As soon as my arm was nearly straight Aviso clamped the wrist with both hands and dropped off to my left side as his right leg whipped over my face and smashed it against the canvas.

His left leg was across my chest, my left arm between his legs. The only thing stopping him from falling back, pulling my arm with him, and popping his hips up against my elbow to snap it was my hand position.

In order to make sure he would break my arm, Aviso needed to pull toward my pinkie. Ideally, he'd have it pressed against his chest with my thumb pointing toward the ceiling when he fell back. This would open my elbow and leave it vulnerable to easy hyperextension and breakage.

Too bad for him, I had my knuckles pressed against his throat while I tried to knock him out with one-centimeter punches under his jaw.

He torqued my wrist, trying to turn the pinkie toward him. "It's coming man. You ready? Three . . ."

He'd fuck around for only so long before he rocked back and did it the hard way, a vicious yank and hip bridge that would leave my forearm hanging by the skin.

I rolled left and brought my right hand over. I needed to grab my left wrist, hand, whatever I could to keep him from extending it beyond straight. Aviso blocked my right hand with his left foot—his goddam foot—and twisted my pinkie closer to his chest.

"Two . . ."

He was getting the arm whether I gave it to him or not.

With brute force, a dollop of terror, and a flash of shock on Aviso's face, I twisted right, lifted him off the canvas, and pulled my left hand closer to my right until I clasped them together, palm to palm.

"One."

Aviso yanked.

———

He dropped back and pulled with everything, the cords on his neck strumming against the light fixtures above the cage.

I welded my hands together and roared into the back of his knee, the tendons slicing into my face and choking what little air I could find. Something in my left elbow popped.

Aviso eased a fraction of the tension and yanked harder, trying to shock my grip apart.

I tried to crush my hands into one lump. The bones ground against each other. The damn gloves were slick with sweat, and I felt my fingers slip.

Aviso leaned forward and slammed his right fist into my eyebrow, splitting the cut open. I kicked my feet in protest.

He snaked that hand through the crook of my left elbow and got his forearm against mine, pulled again and found some good bone-on-bone agony. The elbow joint seemed to stretch, pull apart.

"We still on one, man. I feel it going."

My fingers slipped again. Something in the elbow clunked. I had no strength in my left arm—the grip was the only thing keeping Aviso from snapping it.

"I gonna break it now. And you never even hit me."

I released my grip.

In one movement—no one would call it graceful—I jerked my left thumb toward Aviso's right hip like a spastic hitchhiker, popped my left shoulder up against the backs of his legs and pulled my right shoulder underneath me.

If Aviso was going to break my elbow, he'd have to get the arm straight—wrist, elbow, and shoulder aligned. Then he'd force the elbow into an unnatural peak in the middle of that straight line, breaking the joint and pushing it the wrong way.

By hitchhiking and lifting my shoulder, I took the arm out of alignment and raised the level Aviso would have to exceed to break my elbow.

But I wasn't done.

I kept my left hand near his hip, faced his feet and started running along the canvas, pivoting clockwise on my right shoulder. This gave the escape its name—the coffee grinder—one of Gil's favorites because it reminded him to buy more coffee.

Aviso scrambled to pull my wrist up and straight and tried to block my progress with his legs, but I kept going, spinning so my head was tucked beneath his hamstrings, kept going until it popped out the other side.

Aviso still had my left arm between his legs, my wrist clamped in his hands, but now I was up on my left knee, my right leg posted out and my chest crushing his left hip, trapping him against the canvas.

Best of all, my right hand was free.

And his face was exposed.

"You ready?"

———

The first punch felt so good I sighed.

After chasing, missing, defending, panicking, I smashed my knuckles into his face and felt the solid, satisfying impact, like chewing steak after years of pudding.

Aviso's face screwed shut.

I hit him again and again, six times in two seconds.

He scrambled and let go of my wrist to cover up.

I sank against his side and hammered everything above the

shoulders. My left arm was dead from the elbow down, so Aviso only got the right. Blood fell between his gloves onto the canvas. He rolled onto his knees and elbows, showed me his back and exposed neck.

I smelled another trap.

He was baiting me, offering a chance at a choke so I'd stop smacking him around. If I went for it, we'd be back in his world.

I punched him in the neck, the ear, and the neck again.

He got the memo—I wasn't interested in any chokes.

Aviso wrapped his forearms around his head and got a foot under him, drove forward to push me off-balance. I let the momentum lift me onto my feet and stepped back. Aviso followed, stood up and immediately shot for a takedown.

The coffee grinder escape wouldn't work again. I was slightly baffled it had worked the first time. My other escapes weren't half as good, and Aviso wouldn't give me the time to try them anyway. In the brief window I'd had to land punches, I'd closed his left eye, split that cheek open, and squirted blood out of his right ear. If he got me down again and got hold of my dead arm, he'd take it home with him.

So I retreated, let him come in for the double-leg.

I planted my right foot.

Speared a left knee into his belly hard enough to feel vertebrae against my patella.

Aviso's arms came down from his face. His mouth gaped, pulled down in the universal mask of someone who'd been gutshot.

My left elbow wouldn't work. The fist dangled at the end like deadweight.

Or a wrecking ball.

I threw the left hook, all hips and shoulder.

It landed on Aviso's square, stubbled jaw, kept going as his head cranked sideways and eventually turned, tugging his body around in a ragdoll spin as he crumpled to the canvas.

I didn't bother following him.

———

Gil managed to get a t-shirt over my head, slipping the left arm through first and stretching it around everything else. He and Antonio squeezed and poked the soft tissue around the elbow while a crowd of officials woke Aviso up, got him on a stool, and asked him about current events.

The crowd roiled and sang and chanted, got louder when Jim Lincoln announced me as winner by knockout and Davie Benton stuck a microphone in my face.

"Woody, leading up to this fight Aviso said he was going to break your arm. It looks injured—did he break it?"

I tested the elbow. It didn't move and sent a hot twang up to my neck. "It's fine."

"Fine or not, you knocked him out with that hand."

"That's correct."

Davie waited for more, then said, "All right, well, there were rumors before this fight that if you won, you'd be next in line to fight for the belt. After this impressive performance, do you think your next fight should be for the heavyweight championship of Warrior?"

The correct answer: I'll leave that up to Mr. Takanori and the matchmakers. I'll fight whoever they put in front of me.

What I said: "Yup."

Davie's eyebrows popped. "Well, you seem content letting

your fighting do the talking, but is there anything you'd like to say to Aviso and his fans?"

"I'm glad I knocked his ass out. And he smelled great. Like sandalwood."

CHAPTER 17

C ARRASCO, MALHAR, AND EYE PATCH WAITED OUTSIDE the prep room. The Arcoverde brothers stood inside the door, sizzling on the verge of violence.

Marcela was stuck to my left hip, helping me hold that arm against my ribs.

Carrasco smiled at her. "Hello, Pomba Gira." He turned to me and dropped the smile, thumped his walking stick on the floor. "You won. Congratulations. Exu appreciates this. Now we go."

Antonio stepped close to Marcela and put a hand on her shoulder.

Gil tried to push me into the prep room. "We need to look at his elbow."

"No," Carrasco said.

"It might be broken."

"If so, it is what Exu wishes."

"I don't give a shit," Gil said. "His arm's broken and his face is busted up. He needs medical attention."

"You are delaying?"

"He can't go like this."

Carrasco said something to Eye Patch, who pulled a phone out of the duffel and hit a button, held the phone so we could see the screen.

It was an image of the Academia de Arcoverde. The street was dark and deserted. The broken glass on the sidewalk glittered from the flames inside the shattered windows.

Gil swore.

Antonio grunted like he'd been kicked in the gut.

Marcela hardened against my side.

Eye Patch swiped the screen, showed us again.

This one was shot through the gate of the Arcoverde estate, showing the driveway, dim landscape lighting, and front door. The photo caught the silhouette of a woman walking past one of the windows.

Along the bottom of the shot were the backs of at least fifteen heads. They belonged to people kneeling outside the gate, waiting to break it down.

"We are done delaying," Carrasco said.

I held my hands out to Gil. The left arm stayed bent at the elbow. The hand shook. "Cut 'em off."

———

Marcela hugged her uncle and cousins and pressed her cheek against theirs. Their tears mixed as they whispered in choked Portuguese.

I scanned the hallway for Rubin, any of his men. Warrior and arena staff hustled by and didn't give us a second glance.

Carrasco waited until she was finished. "You are ready, my

Pomba Gira?"

Marcela cuffed her cheeks, put an arm around my waist, and nodded.

Carrasco turned to me. "You?"

"Let's go."

His mouth twitched in a smile. "You have not said your goodbyes."

"I'm not saying goodbye. I'll see them in a few hours."

"Maybe so. If Exu wills it."

He limped away. Malhar and Eye Patch stayed, our escorts.

Gil said, "Woody."

I couldn't look at him. Or Jairo or Antonio. Any of them. "I'll see you soon."

We started walking. Away from our family, away from the phone with Rubin's unanswered warnings. I told myself he and his men were in motion, rolling heavy toward the Axila da Serpente.

Marcela looked up. "Are you praying?"

I kissed her forehead. "I'm not sure."

"It's okay. I will pray for both of us. I will keep us safe."

The weight of what she was doing landed against my chest, knocked the breath out and locked my legs. I could not face Gil and the Arcoverdes to tell them goodbye, but I had no trouble looking each man in the eye when I turned and said, "She is safe. They won't touch her."

It didn't feel like a lie at the time.

———

They took us through the loading dock to a waiting Suburban. The driver helped Carrasco into the passenger seat. Malhar pointed

Marcela and me to the rear bench, then climbed with Eye Patch into the seat in front of us.

The Suburban had been police or military at one time. A tight steel mesh ran to the ceiling behind our headrests, blocking access to the back doors and cargo area. I peeked back and saw metal rings bolted to the floor with handcuffs looped through.

Malhar caught me looking and grinned, nudged Eye Patch. If we wanted out, we'd have to get through them.

The Suburban rolled into traffic.

No one spoke.

Marcela touched my left elbow. "How is it?"

"Fine."

"Don't lie to me."

"Bad."

She stuck two fingers into my palm. "Squeeze. Go, now."

"I am."

She muttered in Portuguese. "Can you straighten the arm?"

I tried. Pain lanced from the elbow to my neck. My face twisted like a wrung towel.

"Woody, you can't use it."

"Hold on." I tried the shoulder, got full range of motion. Slapped my right palm against the left elbow a few times.

No pain.

I slammed the elbow into the headrest behind Eye Patch. He turned, his one eye huge, and raised the suppressed Mac-10.

"Just checking something."

Malhar scowled over the back of the seat and chewed something stringy.

When they relaxed and faced forward again I nodded to Marcela.

"We're good."

"Good?"

I put my mouth against her ear and whispered, "We get there, we find a safe place and we hide."

She frowned. "No. We have to get down the hill."

"We don't want to go down there. Trust me. We'll be fine. We hide, and we wait."

"For what?"

Eye Patch turned again. "Shut up. No talking."

Marcela said, "Why not?"

He blinked his eye. "Just be quiet."

I squeezed Marcela's hand with my good one. We rode in silence through swift traffic, along darkening streets, and finally cut along a narrow road with abandoned buildings on the left and black jungle on the right. The empty windows watched us pass.

Through the windshield I caught a glimpse of the four Dumpsters on the right, filled with concrete and rebar blocking the base of the Axila da Serpente.

The armpit of the snake.

One of the pickup trucks nosed out of the alley on the left. The men in the bed confirmed who was inside our Suburban. A horn blasted twice.

Two rusty and dented forklifts emerged from somewhere within the Axila. They scooped up the middle Dumpsters and hauled them aside, then idled, waiting. A man ran over and folded the Suburban's side mirrors back, making us about a foot skinnier.

The Suburban turned into the narrow entrance, killed the headlights, and began to climb.

———

The Suburban's running lights cast a yellow glow onto the road ahead. Road was too classy—this was more of an uppity goat path. Illumination scraped along the edges of the trash heaped in the gutters and the rickety buildings yawning toward each other.

The driver knew the route, probably could have driven it blindfolded. I pressed my face against the window and held my breath, scanned for landmarks, choke points, bunkers we could duck into.

Every light in the Axila was blacked out.

Except the damn candles.

A red one burned in every black window we passed. It gave the favela a sense of great expanse, endlessness, cramped alleys stretching away from the road and changing their shape in the flickering shadows.

A face rushed out of the darkness and hovered on the other side of my window, invading my reflection and turning it into a mongrel's. The face belonged to a young, hungry-looking man with too many scars for his age. He stared at me, chin forward as if marking me or demanding I remember him when we met again, then tapped a short piece of steel pipe against the window.

He drifted into the Suburban's taillights, chin out and pipe ready.

Another man stood at the window. His breath puffed a brief veil across the glass. He tapped it with a wooden club and stepped back as the Suburban crept on.

"Woody." Marcela slid away from her door, closer to me.

A fat man with an aluminum baseball bat across his shoulders had his tongue pressed against her window. It sounded coarse and left a gluey streak. The man next to him tapped the fluid with an ax handle.

Ahead, the Suburban's running lights showed legs and feet lining the road, waiting for us to pass, like we were touring a deep-sea cave of butchers. I checked the back window. As the red lights crawled forward the men were peeling away, diving into the shadows to claim their favorite nook for beating someone to death.

The hierarchy intrigued me. Did seniority mean you got a spot near the top, action more likely, or was that for the unproven who wanted to show what they could do?

I got my answer when the Suburban cut a hard left, crept across the face of the hill, and pulled into a tight 180-degree switchback that angled up as we spiraled closer to the top.

The red candles winked and danced, beckoning.

One by one, the men along the road rapped the windows, but most of them didn't have pipes or chains or machetes.

They tapped with bare knuckles.

These were Exu's true killers. And they'd be the first ones we faced coming down the spine of the cobra.

Marcela breathed deep and slow next to me.

Getting ready.

Eye Patch turned in his seat. "Heads down. Between your knees."

"Why?"

"This part, only Exu's people can see."

"I can't see anything."

"Put your fucking heads down. And no talking."

We bent, foreheads touching. I reached for her hand, found it searching for mine.

The thumps against the windows stopped.

The Suburban swayed, dipped, and climbed, then the engine howled as we tilted to what felt like a forty-five-degree angle. We accelerated into the slope, then rocked forward onto a plateau. Level ground felt alien. The tires crunched over some kind of stone and the brakes whined once as we eased to a stop.

The driver killed the engine.

I squeezed Marcela's hand, listened her breathing.

Carrasco said, "Welcome home, Pomba Gira."

———

We stepped out of the Suburban into a wide, circular area covered with pale crushed concrete. The night sky was overcast, like the moon and stars took a vote and decided they didn't want to see any of this.

Malhar stood at the edge of the concrete, his back to the route we'd come up. The road was so steep the space behind him dropped into nothing. Far beyond that were the warm lights of Rio, none of them concerned with what was about to happen. The thick hush of the favela pressed in from all sides. It set off primal alarms, and I couldn't zero in on it.

Eye Patch stayed near the Suburban. He had the Mac-10 out and pointed at the ground near our feet.

I said, "Are we supposed to run now?"

Nobody answered.

I rolled my neck and shoulders, tried to bend the left elbow again.

Nothing.

I squeezed that hand into a fist and told it to stay.

Marcela wound her hair into a tight bun with some strands spouting. Hugged herself a few times and moved her hips in circles.

She put her hands on my chest. "Ready?"

"I'm with you."

We walked toward the edge. Malhar grinned, his greasy lips sliding over pointed teeth.

If he was the first obstacle, it was going to be a long fucking night.

"Wait," Carrasco said.

He was walking away from us, grinding his walking stick into the crushed concrete with each step toward the black house at the top of the Axila da Serpente. The mural at the bottom, in the room where Carrasco and Exu had offered my first no-choice choice, had depicted the place as a black skull with red eyes.

The artist hadn't done it justice.

The house was three levels in the center and sprawled out into a wing on each side, dipping to two stories, then one at the extremities, like it was melting into the mountain. Every window was sealed with cinderblocks except two on the top level. These were open, a dozen red candles burning in each, their sills draped in hardened red wax like tumorous scabs.

Three wide steps led to a deep porch—almost a stage—built across the bottom level like a jutting jawbone. There was no furniture, but the floor was littered with offerings to Exu. Knives, rum, cleavers, dead chickens, hatchets. Flies buzzed and the stench wriggled through the air and stuck to my upper lip.

Carrasco put one foot on the bottom step. "Come. We will invite Exu to be here for this."

"I thought you were Exu."

He barked a laugh and struggled to the next step. "I am Carrasco. The Hangman, remember? Exu works through me when it is his desire, sure. And he desires to be here when his Pomba Gira comes to him."

"Well, I think he's here already. I can smell him. Let's get this over with."

Carrasco made it to the stage and leaned on his stick, took a few deep breaths and turned to face us. "You will know when he is here, sure. And you will want him here, I promise you."

He limped toward the black wooden door, which opened for him. Red candlelight danced within.

"You will want him here. Because when you see him, and he sees you, it will make you run very fast. Faster than you would ever believe, sure."

———

Eye Patch followed us up the stairs.

I scanned the offerings to Exu, but none of the blades were close enough to snatch up before I got a Mac-10 tattoo across my back. From the platform I could see rings of canvas and leather strewn across the floor and hanging from nails driven into the front of the house. Those on the floor had a red candle in the center and what looked like scraps of furry fabric. The wall offerings had the swatches nailed inside the rings.

Marcela saw them and covered her mouth, and I finally realized why the silence bothered me so much.

There were no dogs barking.

Even in Vegas, you step away from the racket of the Strip and at least one dog is yapping somewhere nearby. But in the Axila da Serpente, where watchdogs and scavengers and litters of feral puppies should have been barking and howling, there was nothing.

The rings of canvas and leather had been collars at one time, and the scraps within probably still had the velvet texture that made dogs' ears perfect for rubbing. I couldn't help picturing Malhar, his hands and that damned framing hammer matted with blood and fur, grinning while he pounded the nails into the wall.

I glanced back at him, still standing in the middle of the crushed concrete.

He had the hammer out, flipping it head over handle and catching it without looking.

He licked his greasy lips, tilted his head back, and howled at the sky. He cut the mournful sound off with a high-pitched yelp.

He was still laughing about it when Marcela and I entered the Black House.

————

The room had a bare wooden floor and scarred plaster walls of an unknown color. The hundreds of red candles cast a shifting, simmering coat over everything.

Carrasco stood across the room with his back to us, facing an altar crowded with more candles, photos, dog collars, blades, and sticky bottles of rum. It covered the entire wall and spilled around the corners toward us.

Closed doors led left and right. A hole in the center of the ceiling sprouted frayed wires from the light fixture that had been torn out. From somewhere in the house above us came the thump of a constant drumbeat and female voices chanted in a language I didn't know.

Carrasco said, "Pomba Gira, I know what you are wishing. After seeing Exu's soldiers, what they are going to do to this man, you want another choice. You wish for Exu to offer to let this man go home, unharmed, and in return you will stay with Exu."

I scoffed. Looked at Marcela to share a good eye roll.

She stared at the floor.

"You don't have to say anything," Carrasco turned to face us. "I know. Exu knows. And he is offended. For you to realize you must be with Exu only after you see for yourself this man is going to die—it is an insult. And for that, Exu will kill this man. He will die badly, Pomba Gira. With blood and screams in his mouth."

The drums and chanting got louder. Now it came from the same floor, maybe the next room. Carrasco's black lenses studied me, drifted to Marcela. He took the sunglasses off. His left eye was swollen with blood, pulsing and sliding across the top of his cheek.

"But Exu is not cruel. He will not make you go with him down the Coluna da Cobra, to see him die. You will stay here with Exu, sure."

Marcela took a step forward, her head still down. Another. "You will not let him go?"

"It is not me, Pomba Gira. Exu." Carrasco shook his head, so very sad. "Exu will not let him go."

Marcela moved closer to him. She lifted her head so she could look him in his dead eye. "Neither will I. Never. Do you see that now? Do you realize it?"

The drums and chanting stopped.

Marcela stepped back, cracked her knuckles, and spat a bullet against the wall.

"Now get your stupid Exu here so he can watch me kiss my man before we walk down your little hill."

———

Carrasco's breathing took on a harsh, ragged rhythm. His fingers opened on the head of his walking stick, wrapped around it, and squeezed. He fought to keep his lips from snarling.

The door on the left opened and four women dressed only in long, flowing silk headscarves walked through. Each scarf was a solid color—blue, green, yellow, purple—and matched the smears of paint slashed across their bodies.

An ancient black man with a full head of white hair and a knife in his teeth hunched into the room behind them, hugging a large handmade drum to his belly. He squatted against the wall near the end of the altar and started thumping the skin, the same beat we'd heard descending from somewhere in the upper floors of the Black House.

The women flowed around Carrasco, turning and skipping and chanting. They started fast, picking up where they'd left off in the next room, and within seconds jumped to a frenzied pace, wild-eyed with teeth bared.

The drummer pounded a manic beat, his head rocking back and forth like the blade in his mouth could sever the final strings anchoring the room to reality. Carrasco stood in the center of the spinning ring with his head tilted back and mouth open. His bulging left eye throbbed, the blood and fluid within it swirling.

I reached for Marcela, and we squeezed each other's hand, making sure the other was still there in the red, dancing light.

Carrasco's head tipped forward. He was panting. The hunger and promise of violence in his face as he stared at Marcela made my hackles jump. His gaze slid to me, and I realized my impotent fury was feeding him just as much as her flesh would when he finally got his hands on her.

He knew we were scared and wanted to catch a glimpse of

it—flick his tongue out and sample the stench of it. His right eye rolled up and he started to chant with the four frenzied women.

The door on the right opened. Malhar stepped through with a white rooster trapped between his outstretched hands. He carried it straight to Carrasco like it was too hot to hold. The rooster knew what was coming. He kicked and thrashed and squawked, pecked Malhar's hands hard enough to hear above the chanting.

The women parted for Malhar, who held the rooster out to Carrasco and bowed his head.

Carrasco stood trembling, leaning his full weight on the stick with his eyes flashing white and red. He flung the stick aside and snatched the head off the rooster with one hand. He pulled the twitching body away from Malhar and held it up, letting the blood splash across his upturned face. It seeped into his white linen suit and spread like an infection.

He crushed the rooster's body, wringing every drop he could get, then tossed it over his shoulder onto the altar like a rag. It landed among cigars and glasses of rum, and even in death it wasn't sure how to interact with such foreign things. One wing rested above a candle and started to smolder.

The four women started again, chanting and clapping toward the ceiling. It sounded grateful, and it terrified me. The man they surrounded stood unbroken, chest lifted and arms out to his sides. His grin was wide and even—no more internal wires yanking it to one side—and his right eye was closed so he could glare at us with that pulsing, bloody sac.

Carrasco was gone.

Exu was here.

This thing laughed a deep, guttural bellow that spewed blood onto the floor.

"Run," it said.
We ran.

CHAPTER 18

W E JUMPED OFF THE PORCH LITTERED WITH sacrifices and kept going.

The area in front of the Black House was empty. The Suburban was gone. The crushed concrete ran to the edge of the plateau and dropped off into nothing. Rickety buildings with red candles in the windows rose from the darkness and leaned away from us, pulling us down the Coluna da Cobra.

Marcela sprinted for the road.

I snatched her wrist, cut in front, and pulled her to the right. The road was a funnel into a drain clogged with the grease and bones of everyone Carrasco—Exu—had murdered in the Axila.

Even though the light coming from the Black House was dim, it cast enough of a shadow to make the ground past the lip of the plateau a dark pool.

We jumped in.

We landed on a steep slope of wet, ripe trash that shifted beneath us and slid down itself like skin shedding off a snake. I kept my left arm tucked and held my breath against the thick, sweet odor, some primal instinct telling me most of it came from rotting meat on slippery bones.

Marcela coughed, gagged, and grunted when we hit feet-first against the foundation of a two-story building constructed from sheet metal and tarp. Black House trash piled against our backs and flowed over our shoulders.

We burst out of it. I banged against the metal with my left shoulder, felt a pang as my elbow tried to straighten to catch me. The framing beneath the metal groaned, leaned away, and rocked back again. I'd never moved a multi-story building with just bodyweight and momentum before. I ignored the obvious lack of structural integrity and took the credit.

"Come on."

Marcela followed close along the wall away from the road. "Where are we going?"

"Away from the action. Into the jungle. Hell, into the sewers if we can find one."

"Sewers?"

We got to the corner and stopped. Beyond it was a sheer rock wall rising to the second story of a house that had been built as close as possible to the mountain. But the sag and lean of the house created a narrow gap we could squeeze into. A black, silent gap hiding fuck knows what.

I held my breath again and listened.

Nothing.

I put my lips against Marcela's ear. "Rubin and his men are at the bottom of the mountain. They're going to storm the favela. Armor, machine guns, grenades. He isn't going to arrest anyone."

She pulled away, searched my face in the darkness. "This is why you agreed to run the Coluna?"

"Carrasco's done. Exu, all of it. You and your family won't have to worry about it anymore."

She looked around, wide-eyed. "Starting when?"

Fair question.

"Like I said, we hunker down, stay out of it until Rubin sweeps through."

"He knows we are here?"

I thought about my phone, his messages unanswered, unread as far as he knew. "Sure."

"And he knows it's started? The Coluna?"

"Yes," I hoped.

A man screamed from the top of the mountain. It had to be Exu. I pictured him standing on the edge of the stage, bellowing with blood falling from his mouth, calling his disciples to arms.

Footsteps splashed across the crushed concrete.

Lots of them.

I pulled Marcela around the corner into the dark gap, straight into a deathtrap.

———

The man was standing right around the corner, listening. Waiting for the right time.

I brought the right time to him, ran smack into the top of the ax he had in his outstretched arm like an antenna, probing the space in front of him. When it pressed into my belly he tried to pull it back.

I caught it below the blade in my right hand, crouched and yanked him forward, drove my forehead into the shadows. I stayed low—none of these urchins would be as tall as me. My forehead crushed something hot and wet. Blood sprayed. A heavy sack slumped against the wall to my left and slid down.

Poor guy would never walk around in the dark again, if he ever got up at all. It was like running full-speed in the black of night and going face-first into a tree trunk. Though a tree trunk wouldn't reach down, find the leaky head, and stomp on it three times.

I would, and I did.

Then I felt around, plucked the ax out of the mess, and handed it to Marcela. I only had one hand, and I wanted to be able to grab things. Mostly throats.

We stepped over the body and squeezed between the metal paneling and the mountain. I felt along the face for handholds, roots, cracks, ridges—the stone was rough but had nothing big enough to grip.

Marcela leaned close. "What are you doing?"

"Maybe we can climb. Get over the top and into the jungle where it's safe."

I said this with confidence, having never been in a jungle.

"Uh," Marcela said.

Voices rolled around the top of the mountain, shouting and calling, whispering.

Hunting.

My eyes were getting used to the dark. Artifacts still floated around—possibly due to having used my head as a blunt instrument—but I could see shapes in my peripheral vision. The gap we were in led out to a three-way junction. Left or right. Ahead was another two-level structure, no doors or windows visible, sheathed in odd shapes of particle board.

I peeked left.

The road was there, past the depth of the two buildings, glowing red. Something ran past in a blur, downhill.

We went right.

When we got to the next corner we went around it low, ready. Nobody home.

It was another gap, sheer mountain on the right, but slightly wider. I started forward.

Marcela tugged my shirt. When I turned, she pointed up.

I shook my head. "Nothing to grab."

"Watch."

She dropped the ax and pressed her back against the particle board, put one foot on the stone, then the other, wedging herself between the two. Walked her shoulder blades up the wood, paused, and brought her lowest foot higher.

I looked up. Dark foliage sagged over the top of the cliff. We could get close enough to grab it, pull ourselves over and run like hell. I smacked her butt when it shimmied past.

"Not now."

I walked ten feet away from her and started up. My left shoulder and upper arm did a decent job bracing against the wood, but having my left hand available would have been nice. When I pushed my full weight against the house it grumbled and tilted away from the mountain. Moisture seeped out of the damp, squishy paneling.

Marcela hissed at me. "Don't make me fall."

"I think it's good."

I tried to keep the racket to a minimum, stomping and sliding and grunting my way up. Marcela looked like a ballerina floating up a curtain. She was near the top as I rose above the first level and someone whistled from the road in front of our building.

Once, high-pitched. A signal.

I froze. Whispered, "Go. Get over."

Marcela eased one hand out, reached for a gnarled coil of roots above her feet, and yanked on them. They held strong. She pressed her butt hard against the wood, stretched her other hand higher into the roots, then let her body dangle against the cliff. Executing a perfect pull-up, she hooked one leg over the edge and rolled into the underbrush.

She was out.

Low male voices spoke somewhere close. Footsteps thumped away, but the voices stayed.

Sending someone to bring everyone?

Let them find no one.

I ground my way higher.

Marcela appeared above me, a finger to her lips.

Yeah yeah.

I was halfway up the second level. A thick root sagged over the cliff near my left foot. I stretched with my right hand, couldn't reach. I worked my shoulder blades left, brought each foot behind, one at a time, pushing hard against the stone. I reached again and brushed the root with my fingers.

"Paulo!"

The voice was right under me.

I quit breathing. Marcela's eyes were huge across the gap.

"Paulo, *onde está você?*"

So the guy I'd headbutted into sleepy time was Paulo. The man looking for him came around the corner to my left, took a few steps into the gap, and stopped below me.

I did not look down.

He'd feel my eyes.

"*Você os viu?*"

He took a step, paused, then ran forward. I let the corner of my vision slide toward him. He stooped and picked something up off the ground.

Paulo's ax.

"*Eles estão aqui!*" He disappeared around the corner, running toward Paulo. "*Aqui!*"

Voices and whistles and war cries rose from the street. Footsteps flooded toward us.

So much for silence.

Marcela reached down for me.

I braced my ass against the particle board, lunged for the root, and exploded myself backward through the soggy wall into the second level of the building.

It was not empty.

———

I landed on my back in a thick cloud of mold and sawdust. I tried to keep my left arm pressed against my ribs but the elbow still tried to straighten and break my fall. The pain shot up and across the back of my neck, added a high-pitched finale to the impact grunt.

I scanned the room from my dominant position. A man stood at the open street-side window, silhouetted by a red candle burning on the sill. His head was cranked around to see what the hell had just happened. His body didn't seem to believe it yet—it still faced the window.

I pulled my knees into my chest and rolled toward him over my right shoulder.

The lookout came around with a long meat cleaver in one hand.

I rose, closed the distance before he could wind up and kicked him out the window. The candle went with him, leaving me in darkness. He hit the hard-packed road and didn't bounce. The half-dozen men headed for the back of the building dodged away, pointed up at me, shouted, and ran for the front door.

I whirled around, looking for the top of the stairs so I could face them one at a time and found Marcela standing behind me.

"What the hell?"

"I'm not hiding in the jungle while you get butchered. How long until Rubin gets here?"

I listened for gunfire, bullhorns, authority. Heard feet stomping up rickety stairs.

"A while."

"We can't stay here," she said.

"Nope."

The building had no interior wall panels—just the soggy particle board tacked to the outside of crooked studs. I stuck my head out the window and glanced right. The next structure downhill had two levels as well, but the slope of the mountain put its flat roof level with our floor.

Wood splintered somewhere on the staircase. A man cursed. Metal clanged. Footsteps got closer.

I put a foot waist-high into the wall on the downhill side, sent a chunk of wood flying. Again, higher. Marcela joined me and kicked a large section, which hung like a loose tooth for a moment and then dropped. We squeezed between the studs, jumped to the next house, and kept going.

The roof was made of something spongy covered in tarpaper. It felt like running on a waterbed.

A man yelled behind us.

The next house was covered by a ragged tarp, sagging against the erratic framing beneath it like mummified skin over a twisted skeleton. We were both moving too fast to stop.

Someone landed on the roof behind us as we jumped.

Marcela spread her weight over four points of contact, her body making no sound when she lit upon the tarp. I crashed spread-eagle between two pipes, caught myself with my left arm and both knees against the steel tubing. The tarp purred along the frame, coming apart like a zipper.

Behind us, a man on the sloshy roof worked to keep his balance while he cocked an arm back, ready to throw a knife as big as his face.

"Drop!"

I shoved Marcela into the flapping tarp and followed, pulled my feet off the framing and used my left hand like a clamp on the pipe as I dropped so I wouldn't land on her.

The pain of yanking my elbow straight made me scream, and I fell on her anyway. We landed in a tangle on a floor crowded with sour-smelling blankets and clothes.

"Up, up. They know we're in here."

We stood up into a web of rough hemp rope strung back and forth across the room. Sheets hung from it to create rippling walls. It was impossible to gauge the size or shape of the room. Red candles burned in the windows facing the street, so at least we had a shitty compass.

A man yelled from the uphill roof.

"Where is Rubin?" Marcela said.

"Not here. Not yet. Come on, we gotta move."

I ripped the sheet next to us down.

Eye Patch was there, already swinging his machete.

———

I recoiled and felt the tip of the machete pluck the front of my shirt as it whickered past. The weight of the swing carried Eye Patch's right arm across his body and I dove in behind it, elbowing him in his left eye hard enough to tilt him off his feet and ragdoll him into a pile of mismatched shoes.

Two more men stepped around him.

One had a short wooden club and the other had a meat hook.

They were both smiling.

That made three of us.

Four if you count Marcela's grimace as a smile, which I do when it isn't aimed at me.

She came from their right with a dank sheet and threw it in their faces. I ducked under a strand of clothesline, gauged the bulges of the man on the right, and punched where I figured his windpipe would be. He squawked in confirmation so I kicked him in the groin and smacked his screaming face away.

Marcela had the guy with the wooden club in a clinch, her right shoulder shoved into his right armpit so he couldn't swing. He tried to shake her off once, then dropped the club from his right hand into his free left and cocked back for a nasty blow to her kidneys.

I snatched his wrist with my right hand and ripped his arm straight, pulling him and Marcela into a free fall, then dislocated his elbow over my knee. When she sprang away I stomped his neck and face until he stopped complaining.

Marcela pushed a strand of hair out of her eyes. "Where is

the one with the patch?"

I checked the pile of shoes.

Vacant.

"No!" Her eyes popped at something behind me.

I turned in quicksand and watched Eye Patch bring the machete down with both hands. I noticed his left eye was swollen shut, that whole side of his face puffed up like a sweaty cinnamon roll, and realized he was swinging blind.

It was a damn good guess—the blade was just a sliver as it came toward my forehead.

I dropped. Begged gravity to speed up for just a sec and pull me to the ground faster than usual. Marcela's fingers scrabbled at my arm, trying to haul me out of the arc of the blade, but it was too late.

It came down, held firm in both of Eye Patch's hands, his full weight behind the straight arms full of corded muscles until it hit the clothesline, hung frozen for a beat, then catapulted back over his head.

He staggered, his face a twisted mess of confusion and rage.

I grabbed the clothesline with both hands, ignoring the pain in my elbow, and lifted my feet of the floor. I planted them in his chest and shot him backward as the rope tore free of its anchors, clearly designed to hold a middleweight at best.

Eye Patch bounced off a wall and dropped the machete. He staggered forward, reached into his waistband, and pulled the Mac-10 out, no suppressor needed. He yelled something garbled and pulled the trigger, spraying the walls, roof, shoes, and two men at his feet.

I was behind him, curled over Marcela. I recalled Carrasco saying something about no guns but calling a time-out seemed petty.

The Mac-10 clicked.

My ears rang but I heard muffled voices on the uphill roof yelling, scrambling away. And I still had the clothesline in my hands.

I wound it around Eye Patch's neck, once for each time I saw him at the Arcoverde Academy and each time he threatened to hurt Marcela, her family, her students. Added a half-dozen more for all the good times we'd had then shoved him out the window overlooking the street.

More anchors snapped loose, but eventually the weight was distributed evenly and the rest of the clothesline held. It trembled and jerked in time with the heels drumming against sheet metal somewhere near the first level.

Marcela blinked and took her hands away from her ears.

Men yelled on the tarpaper roof. Voices answered from below.

"We're trapped," she said.

"That's their problem."

I grabbed her hand, stepped to the window Eye Patch dangled from, and jumped.

———

The road had been just wide enough to let Carrasco's Suburban squeak through with its mirrors folded back. The building across from us yawed into the street, cutting the distance to five feet.

Easy jump.

It was a one-story jumble of stacked cinderblocks with a sloped roof made of lumpy thatched grass. The slope ran downhill. In a heavy rain it would act like a waterslide, and as if to prove this the building adjacent was a washed-out pile of de-barked logs and frayed tarps.

Marcela touched down like a cat on the thatch. I did my best not to cave the roof in. We slid down the grass and dropped into the debris. Somehow nobody twisted an ankle.

Men ran around and cursed inside the building we'd left.

The tarpaper roof above it was empty.

Eye Patch hung against the wall of the building, his neck twice its usual length.

We ran away from the scene, away from the road, further into the twisted maze of the Axila da Serpente. Red candles danced from the windows as we passed. We didn't worry about left or right—just tried to get distance between us and the hunters we knew were somewhere behind us.

We followed a wall made of ribbed sheet metal and came to a wide path that had been a road before the shanties and lean-tos crept inward from its edges like plaque in an artery, congesting any flow to single-file.

The cramped area was still.

It didn't feel silent.

It felt coiled.

I peeked left around the corner—uphill—to see how far we'd gone. The Black House loomed, almost close enough to touch. We hadn't even gone a Mayberry block.

Marcela leaned close to my ear. "What are we doing?"

"Hiding. Waiting."

"For Rubin?"

I nodded.

"He is coming?"

Somewhere close, metal scraped against stone.

I pulled Marcela across the path through a doorway covered

with a floral shower curtain. A man stood to our left, bent over a red candle to light the crumpled cigarette in his mouth. He leered at Marcela and squinted at me while reaching for the aluminum bat leaning near the doorway.

Where the hell were the guys who'd tapped the Suburban glass with just knuckles?

I smashed his face into the candle, cupped the back of his head and held it still so I could crush some knees into it. His legs gave out. I slammed his head against the windowsill on the way down. He fell into the corner. I hit him with the bat—awkward right-handed swings—until it splashed instead of thumped, then dropped the bat onto him and inched the shower curtain aside. I didn't see anyone, but they were out there.

"Woody."

"Huh." I stepped around Marcela, looking for another exit. She caught my arm and pulled me around.

"What is this? Who are you?"

"What?"

She tilted her head toward the man in the corner but didn't look at him. "He was out after the first knee. He—"

"Would have woken up pissed off with a good idea where we might be. He and the rest would kill me and drag you back to Carrasco. I had to put them down."

She grabbed my face, looked into my eyes. "I know what this is. The times when I say I wish I'd known you longer, from when you were younger, so we could be together then and now. You tell me no, I would not have loved you then. I didn't believe you. But this is what you were like then, isn't it? Before Gil found you."

I didn't answer.

"But you were alone then. You aren't anymore."

"What do you think I'm fighting to protect?"

She nodded, tears in her eyes, and glanced at the mess in the corner. "But this . . . the men back there."

I kissed her forehead and pulled her close.

Sad for her. Miserable.

But not sorry.

Because Rubin wasn't coming, and Carrasco wasn't the only one with a demon running around inside, chewing on the wiring.

———

We slipped out a window opposite the shower curtain into an alley so narrow I couldn't turn around. No one had bothered to light any red candles. It smelled like wet shit and slimy fruit. Our shoes began to sink.

I had my left shoulder aimed downhill and started to slide, had to sidestep to keep from falling. Marcela had room to twirl and could have faced forward but the footing was better sideways.

Our feet slurped in and out of the muck. Weak starlight gave up somewhere in the ivy of wires and limp laundry hanging above us, leaving the bottom of the alley a well of dark blue shapes.

Waist-high lumps of garbage blocked the path ahead.

I reached a toe out, probing for solidity.

The lumps stood up.

Two men, waiting.

Quiet.

Professional.

They chose this spot knowing it was too narrow to run away.

Too tight for any weapons longer than a knife.

I realized it was also too cramped to turn and get my right

arm forward.

They were both lean enough to square their shoulders, and they came forward with a strategy. One returned to a crouch, arms in front to absorb any knees or kicks. The other stood tall and reached over his buddy's shoulders. They were like a locomotive of clutching hands in a black, stinking tunnel, and they were going to drive me back, wrap me up and take me down into the sludge.

After that it would probably get all stabby and chokey.

I shuffled uphill to control the distance.

Marcela pulled on my right arm.

Our feet slipped and the men followed. The only sounds they made were quick snorts of air.

There's a reason most of my scars are on the front.

I'm just not good at retreating.

My left foot slid out and I dropped to my right knee. I shoved Marcela uphill, barely registered the sound of her running away.

The crouching man lunged.

I leaned back to make his body a blockade for the guy behind him, lifted my crooked left arm and caught his right thumb coming in and bent it flat. He hissed. His left hand found my face. Rough, calloused fingers scurried toward my eyes. I bit one hard enough to make it squirt.

With the broken thumb and gristly finger, I had both of his hands occupied.

He bit down on my left knuckles to get me to let go.

I did, then used that hand to fishhook his cheek and slam his head into the wall on the right. He sagged for a fraction and drove forward, forcing his shredded finger into the back of my throat.

I fell back.

The second guy reached down and grabbed my ears, pulled

my head forward.

I started to choke on finger and blood.

They were too close to bring my foot up and push them away. I got a knee between me and the crouching one, tried to buck him but he brushed the knee off and shoved his gushing finger deeper.

The second man wrapped both hands behind my head and pulled.

I gagged and choked and willed my left arm to work, tried to find the eyeballs of the crouching man. He pinned my wrist between his head and shoulder, used the fingers of his right hand to cinch it there.

My eyes welled and I tasted copper and bile.

Like dying ought to taste.

My body jolted in spasm, some hard-wired response to suffocation designed to shake me free of whatever pinned me down, send me to the surface of flowing rapids, roll me out of the quicksand.

It didn't work.

The two men snorted and grunted and watched me dying.

Some people don't like the sound of aluminum bats. I happen to think it's beautiful, especially when the bat is brought straight down in a two-handed swing onto the skull of a man focused on killing me.

Marcela had gone back for the bat, and now she put all of her hundred-plus-a-sandwich pounds behind it. It bounced off the standing guy's head. His arms went stiff and his hands fell away.

She hit him again. It sounded squishier than the first blow.

He tilted back and disappeared.

The crouching man pulled his finger out of my throat, held both hands above his face for protection. I grabbed the front of his shirt and held him still for Marcela.

She smashed the bat through his hands into his upturned face. Once was enough.

He sagged over my arm. I let him go.

Marcela pulled me out from under him, helped me up.

"I'm sorry," she said.

I spat blood and calluses. "Don't apologize to them."

"I'm not. I'm apologizing to you, for saying you didn't have to do what you did to those men before. After these two . . . I see it now."

"Oh. Accepted."

"I don't like it down here. The roofs were better."

"Agreed."

We stepped on the bodies in search of higher ground.

———

The alley dumped into a roundish courtyard the size of a parking space and lined with mismatched lawn chairs. I didn't want to meet anyone who spent a moment there relaxing.

Alleys led left and right. The ground was level, a plateau somewhere on the face of the mountain. We tried left—away from the road, I was almost sort of certain, but maybe not—and hit a dead-end within ten steps. There was nothing to climb that wouldn't topple over.

The alley to the right took us along a hard dirt path between concrete walls adorned with graffiti and bullet holes. We dodged through a rank of fifty-five-gallon drums filled with stagnant rainwater and empty plastic bottles. A chest-high wall of paper concrete bags had been stacked and soaked in place to form a barricade against something. The paper was brittle and flaked under our hands as we climbed over.

The path ended on the other side of the barricade in a cramped space with high cinderblock walls. Empty black doorways led left, straight, right.

A man shouted somewhere ahead, or above. It could have been behind.

Marcela said, "Which way?"

I went through the door on the right and stepped out of the opening so I wouldn't be a big fat silhouette to club.

The air was stale, dusty.

I tried the doorway straight ahead.

A slight breeze hit my face, carrying a scent so faint it might have come from the molecules already lodged in my nose.

I pulled Marcela close. "What do you smell?"

She inhaled. "Smoke. Candles."

We took the door on the left. It was pitch-black inside. Marcela gripped the back of my shirt. Our shoes crunched grit against uneven concrete. Air pushed from somewhere ahead. I found a wall and felt along it to the right, expecting to touch sweaty, waiting flesh instead of cinderblock.

My fingers curled around a sharp corner.

A doorway.

Wind brushed my knuckles.

We went through the gap and found gray light spilling through another doorway on the right at the end of a short hallway. Our footsteps were much too loud as we approached. I turned the corner in a crouch, hands up and ready.

Marcela stepped next to me, searching for threats. When she saw the far side of the room she pulled up with a gasp.

The wall was missing.

We eased closer. The floor extended out into space, past the walls, some delirious engineer's notion of a balcony or the result of someone not being able to count concrete blocks. We kept a safe distance from the edge, tucked in the shadows, and took in the view.

The gaping hole faced downhill, displaying the clustered sprawl of the Axila da Serpente. It looked like a jagged stairway of crooked, sagging roofs held together with a spider web of electrical wire and clotheslines.

Red candles pricked the darkness like infectious fireflies. The road was a narrow scar a half-dozen structures to our right. Black shapes darted.

Far below us—past the candles and swaths of darkness, the piles of rubble and honeycomb hovels—the first lights of Rio marked the border of civilization.

It could have been on Jupiter.

Marcela pointed even beyond that. "Look."

Her statue rose out of the landscape. The Redeemer, bathed in light from below, his arms outstretched. Marcela leaned against me. I put my arm around her and tried to see what she did, what made the tears run down her cheeks.

He had his back to us.

Yeah, no shit.

I slid my arm off and leaned past the edge of the floor for a look. A sheet-metal roof was ten feet below.

Marcela cuffed her eyes dry, saw the roof, and nodded. Her voice was thick. "We wait here for Rubin. One door in. If anyone comes, we deal with them. If there are too many, we jump and take our chances."

"I say we jump now. Keep moving."

"No, it is better to hide in a safe place, to not get to the bottom. You said this."

"Marcela, they aren't coming."

"But . . . "

"I know. I'm sorry."

I took her hand. We faced the drop. The Axila uncoiled below us, waiting.

Off to the right and below us a man started to sing in scratchy, guttural Portuguese.

"What song is that?" I said.

"It isn't a song. He's just singing, 'Where are you, dead man? I want your heart. Where are you?' Over and over."

Another voice joined in, closer.

"Ready?"

She wiped her eyes again and nodded.

We stepped to the edge and had an excellent view of the first flare jumping into the sky from the bottom of the favela.

———

The flare rose like a sizzling firework, paused at its apex, and drifted down beneath a pale parachute. Sparks lanced away from the core and faded.

It was military grade and illuminated most of the rooftops below our balcony. Spread across them were at least two dozen men, watching and waiting for us. More joined them, scrambling up to gape at the flare and point downhill.

Another flare popped out of the darkness at the base of the mountain, this one on a much tighter angle. It skimmed across the rooftops and dropped into a nest of colorful tents, which caught fire immediately.

More flares followed, some high, some arcing into different areas of the favela and blossoming into white flames. Three shots from an assault rifle smacked the silence and rolled up the mountain. A man screamed.

Marcela said, "Is it Rubin?"

"It better be."

The Axila became an anthill. Men poured into the narrow street and scurried downhill. Whatever rules had been assigned to the Coluna no longer applied—every man carried some kind of gun. The roof lookouts distributed AK-47s and AR-15s, dropped heavy duffel bags at their feet, and got ready to repel the invaders.

Single gunshots were answered, then the favela broke into full-out war.

Marcela pulled me toward the back wall. "Get down! Come, we wait here, in the hall."

As I turned I caught a glimpse of a group of men running uphill, against the current. They carried buckets and jugs with liquid slopping over the rims. Something about their expressions and the way they were lit with flickering orange light made me stop.

I pulled free from Marcela and leaned around the corner, kept going until I saw the top of the mountain.

The Black House was engulfed in flames.

Set from within by Exu's candles or from above by Rubin's flares, it was an inferno blazing hot enough to make my eyes water. The center of the house collapsed, tumbling burning chunks of wood into the piles of trash and houses below. These lit up in turn like they'd spent decades waiting for the opportunity.

The men with buckets of water would only succeed in

making steam.

The Axila da Serpente was burning from the top down, erupting like a volcano of filth while Exu's soldiers flowed down toward Rubin and his take-no-prisoners private army.

We were somewhere in the middle.

"Woody?" Marcela stood by the door to the hallway. Wisps of her hair stirred in the hot wind pushing through. The fire was close already, greedy, eating its way down the slope. She coughed and staggered away from the rancid smoke filling the hallway.

I reached for her.

She took my hand and we jumped.

———

We hit a roof made of garage doors, rolled, and kept moving down. Jumped onto a wobbly pile of car tires and picked our way across until we looked over a short drop to the next roof.

It was made of tarpaper and solid enough to hold two men with assault rifles. They scanned the street a few buildings to the right and the area below, waiting for anybody with a badge to show up. Probably happy to practice on me if they got the chance.

My eyes watered in the steady rush of air being sucked up toward the hungry flames. The flow had a hum, close to becoming a howl. It would carry away for cremation any sound in my approach.

The guy on the left pointed and said something.

The one on the right moved closer to him, so I grabbed the back of his pants and dumped him over the side, then kicked the one on the left between the shoulder blades. They made a racket when they landed.

Automatic gunfire erupted somewhere along the street, aimed downhill but close enough to send us scampering left. We dropped over a dozen more roofs like a pair of shoes tumbling down a staircase until we came to a ring of structures tilted around a pool of darkness. The flares danced light across the upper floors of the buildings, but the bottom was deep enough to remain in shadow.

I pulled Marcela to the right, skirting the blackness, then she grabbed my left wrist and yanked me down. I bit the inside of my mouth to keep from squawking about the elbow.

A door had opened in the darkness. Heavy steel swinging on oiled hinges, spilling a rectangle of yellow light across the bottom of the circle.

A lean man stood in the doorway, head cocked.

Listening.

He hit a switch and a string of halogen lights bolted to the buildings buzzed to life. The area looked like a large courtyard, walled-in on all sides with a few crooked, narrow alleys leading away. The ground was covered in crushed concrete. A gray tarp covered a lumpy shape in the center.

The man stepped into the courtyard and hustled toward the shape.

I recognized him.

Carrasco's driver.

He ripped the tarp off. Underneath was a matte black armored car with slits for windows, sinister gunports, and a raised turret on the roof. We could see the passenger side and the two armored doors on the back. A large white skull was stenciled on the passenger side with the words POLÍCIA MILITAR next to it.

Marcela crushed my arm. "A Caveirão," she whispered. "Only the police should have these."

One of the back doors had BOPE stenciled beneath the small window.

Batalhão de Operações Policiais Especiais.

Rubin's unit.

The driver ran to the wall in front of the armored car's iron-plated bumper, tossed a small plastic table aside, and started popping levers. The wall was a gate. He pushed the doors open onto a cramped dirt road choked with weeds and dripping with vines.

I put my mouth next to Marcela's ear. "He starts it up, we're taking it."

She nodded.

The man disappeared around the driver's side, then a diesel engine grumbled awake.

We circled left to get behind the vehicle, hopefully a semi-blind spot, and slipped over the edge of the roof. The building was made of pocked cinderblocks, some of them stacked on the side to make ventilation holes.

Or firing ports.

We hurried down.

The crushed concrete was loose and crunchy beneath our shoes as we moved in a crouch to the back doors of the armored car.

I put a hand out toward Marcela: Wait.

The door the driver had come through was still open. It showed ten feet of a concrete tunnel lit with caged yellow construction bulbs, then the passageway cut ninety degrees left. If we went after the driver our backs would be on display for anyone coming out.

The gunfire along the Coluna was muted within the courtyard but remained constant. Flakes of ash as big as my palm drifted down around us like ancient butterflies.

We gave the driver two seconds to hurry his ass back into the tunnel and make our lives easy.

He didn't accept.

Marcela nodded and went around the passenger side. I counted to three and hugged the armor around the driver's side. The door was open. I could see the man's legs. My back puckered, exposed and vulnerable to the tunnel.

I heard Marcela rap on the passenger window.

The driver grunted, then gave a little sigh when I pulled myself through his door by the handle mounted next to it and elbowed him below the left ear. He oozed out of the seat like grease down a drain.

Marcela tried to open her door.

Locked.

I was reaching across to open it when something stabbed me in the left thigh. I screamed, came around and saw Malhar grinning a few feet away. The clawed side of his hammer was buried in my leg.

From the tunnel, Carrasco said, "You taking my ride, man."

———

Malhar dragged me out with the hammer, tugged it loose, then shoved me against the side of the armored car. He raised the framing hammer with his right hand, the claws still facing me.

My left arm wouldn't do much to stop it, but I lifted it anyway.

Marcela came around the front bumper and leaped at him, hitting him full-force and barely putting a wrinkle on his greasy head. She bounced off and stumbled across the crushed concrete toward Carrasco, who caught her.

"My Pomba Gira, don't be so clumsy."

He had on his dark lenses and a fresh white suit. If Exu was still around, he was in low-profile mode.

Malhar put his left hand around my throat to keep tabs while he watched Carrasco and Marcela. He squeezed hard enough to keep me from swallowing, but I could wheeze. My left leg shook and bled. I tried to put pressure on it with that hand and my elbow gave out.

Marcela stepped toward me.

Malhar squeezed and bounced the side of his hammer off my head without looking. It was all wrist, just hard enough to put black spots on everything. He cocked the hammer again.

Marcela stopped, her fists white and trembling.

"Yes, Pomba Gira," Carrasco said. "Come back. You are here with me now. If you interfere Malhar might have to hurt you, and that would make me sad, sure. Come, stand next to me. Be with me and I will tell Malhar to make it quick. Quicker than your man deserves, sure, for bringing these murderers to my home."

Carrasco leaned on his stick and waved Marcela toward him.

"Come. I won't even make you watch. I will sing to you so you won't hear him dying."

Marcela stared at me, her tan eyes shining. Eyes that looked at me, saw me, in a way I never understood. Since I'd met her, I'd tried to be what she saw.

She took another step.

I shook my head.

Waved her back.

Away from me.

Her head fell. She shuffled backward, arms limp.

Malhar dismissed her. He let go of my neck and grinned, the

jagged spine of a small animal tucked into his cheek. He sucked on it and squared up for a forehand swing.

"Hey."

My voice was thick and ragged.

"If you're busy killing me, who's protecting your god?"

Malhar frowned and turned just in time to see Marcela punch Carrasco in the left eye.

———

Blood exploded behind the shattered lens of his glasses. Carrasco stood rigid, stunned, while more blood and a thick yellow fluid ran from his deflated eye toward his slack mouth.

I kicked Malhar in the balls hard enough to crack my back. The bones in his mouth jutted out. I stuffed them back in with a right fist and gave them a few broken teeth for company.

He went cross-eyed and swung the hammer. I stepped in, caught his forearm on my shoulder, and put a right elbow into the bridge of his nose. I hooked my left hand behind his neck, turned and slammed his face into the edge of the open driver's door. He staggered back and waved the hammer in front of him like he was fending off wasps.

Carrasco reached for Marcela. "Pomba—"

She hit him with two quick lefts, pak-pak. His jaw clacked around and his suit got bloody again, then Exu must have decided he didn't like his physical vessel getting his ass kicked.

The monster from the Black House came back.

Carrasco's right eye glared at Marcela. His body shook and he bellowed, strands of fluid fluttering away from his lips.

Malhar recovered enough to aim a hammer swing in my

general direction. I stepped right, away from it and into a brutal left I never saw. I covered up and heard the dull thud of a hammer hitting flesh. My knees wobbled and I tilted back, watching from underwater while Carrasco—Exu, whatever he was—screamed in Marcela's face and pulled a chrome pistol from his waistband.

Even in slow motion she was a blur.

She kicked his walking stick out and drove her forehead into his nose when he fell forward. She cracked his arm against the door frame once, twice. He dropped the gun. She crossed her wrists, grabbed the lapels of his white jacket and ripped them across his throat in a scarf choke.

Carrasco fell to his knees, his face bulging with trapped blood while he struggled to breathe.

Malhar saw this and turned away from me. He staggered toward Marcela's back with his hammer raised.

Something came out of my mouth—a war cry, a sob, maybe Latin. I had blood in my eyes and couldn't feel anything from the hair down, so I forgot about the holes in my leg, the arm that didn't work, whatever damage Malhar had done with his hammer.

I launched forward, hit him in the ear with a left hook from the coast of Chile.

He went sideways.

I stayed behind him and grabbed the hammer with both hands and twisted.

He wouldn't let go.

I cranked hard enough to go airborne. Tendons popped like bubble wrap.

He let go.

I hit him with the hammer until he went to his knees, then I kicked him in the head until he went flat. After that I stomped all of him until my leg stopped working.

Marcela stood with her back against the steel door. She was barely out of breath. Carrasco lay near her feet, coughing and pawing at his throat.

"We have to kill them."

I didn't recognize my voice, but I agreed with it.

She shook her head. "I can't. I'm done. Let's just go home."

"He'll come after you. Your family."

I shuffled toward Carrasco's pistol. Sporadic bursts and cracks of gunfire still rolled through the Axila. No one would notice two more.

"Woody, don't. Please. You don't have to."

"I do. You aren't safe if they're alive."

I lifted the gun off the crushed concrete. It was heavier than I'd expected.

"This is murder," Marcela said. "Look."

She waved at the black smoke drifting into the night sky, the flames jabbing after it and spilling over rooflines.

"The fire will take care of it."

"I have to be sure."

"Woody—"

"Go into the armored car for me. Please. I don't want you to see it."

She closed her eyes. "I don't want your heart to carry this."

I didn't say anything, just waited until she walked toward the armored car.

Away from me.

I pulled the slide back until brass gleamed. Carrasco already had a round chambered.

I pointed the pistol at the side of his head. He watched with his right eye.

"She won't love you after this," he whispered. "Pomba Gira cannot love a murderer. Trust me, I know this. You will lose her. You will be alone."

"And she'll be safe," I said.

I watched Marcela climb into the driver's seat, moving like she was sleepwalking. She closed the door and put her hands over her ears.

"From me," Carrasco said. "And safe from you too."

I squeezed.

"Hey, thank you very much. It is nice when others collect evidence for me."

Rubin walked out of the darkness from the dirt road, grinning wider than the gate.

———

Rubin carried a short carbine with a powerful flashlight mounted along the barrel. He wore black body armor , POLÍCIA emblazoned across the front, strapped over a white button-up and an unbuckled helmet pushed back on his forehead. His face was streaked with sweat and gunpowder.

His approach was casual, just another day in the favela, but his eyes were wide and ready in case I moved the pistol away from Carrasco toward him. I must have looked like something fresh out of hell—beaten, rolled in trash, covered in several blood types, and ready to pull a trigger with a shaking finger.

Rubin walked in front of the idling armored car and rubbed the fender, shook his head. "I've been looking for this." He glanced through the driver's window and waved at Marcela. "You are okay?"

She nodded but didn't open the door.

Rubin stepped next to me. "Here, let me see that."

His voice was calm, his hand loose. His eyes stayed hard.

I couldn't wait to give him the damn thing.

Rubin dropped the magazine and worked the slide, stuck it all in a pouch on his vest and nodded at Carrasco. "How you doing?"

Carrasco swore and concentrated on breathing. Malhar twitched on the crushed concrete like his brain was doing a systems check.

Rubin looked for a bloodless spot on my shoulder, patted it with two fingers. "Congratulations my friend. You survived the final Coluna da Cobra of the Axila da Serpente."

"You got everybody?"

"Those who stayed to fight are dead." He made a face. "Or arrested. The fire will do the rest. Remember what I said about dropping Napalm at the top, watching it roll down? Man, I didn't think my flares would do this, but it's all right. And hey, the fire don't care if we're with Exu or not, so let's get moving."

He waved Marcela out of the armored car.

She checked with me. I nodded. She popped the door and came to me, wrapped my right arm over her shoulders and pulled me away from Carrasco.

Rubin tilted his head and listened to the sporadic gunfire. Whatever it told him, he tugged on a radio mic strapped to his shoulder and spoke in Portuguese. A man's voice responded with something brief.

I asked Rubin, "Everybody else—Gil, Antonio—they're safe?"

"Yes, my men escorted them back to the estate."

The Arcoverde estate. I flashed on the picture Carrasco showed us, Exu's soldiers waiting to storm the gate and slaughter the innocents inside.

Marcela's grip tightened. "My home. My family."

Rubin shook his head. "It is unfortunate. Carrasco had some of his people there. But I also had some of mine, in place since before the sun went down. His people were trapped and should have surrendered, but would not. They are dead. Everyone else, your family? They are fine."

Marcela squeezed me even harder.

Rubin brightened. "Hey, do you like the Caveirão? It's good to have it back. So embarrassing, to have one go missing. This Carrasco, man. Come on, get in. We will drive you down. I have a trauma station set up and buddy, I think you need it."

Two of Rubin's men emerged from one of the alleys, guns and flashlight beams sweeping every surface. They wore heavier armor and had black balaclavas on under their helmets.

Rubin spoke with them in a low voice. They opened the back doors on the armored car and helped me and Marcela into the jump seats, facing each other, then walked around and got into the cockpit.

Rubin stood below us, hands on the doors. "I'm happy you two are safe."

"You coming with us?"

He winked. "Just a couple things left to do."

He closed the doors and we rolled away. Marcela reached for my hands and found them searching for hers. We leaned forward into each other and shared uneven, hitching breaths. She put her head on my right shoulder and I turned toward her neck, smelled her hair.

When I opened my eyes I could see through the rectangular

window in the door. Rubin stood over Carrasco, who was trying to crawl into the tunnel.

Rubin had the chrome pistol out, reloading it.

We tipped over the edge of the courtyard and bumped down the mountain. Branches and vines scraped along the armor.

The gunshots were louder than the others, closer, but otherwise no different.

CHAPTER 19

THE SURVIVING MEMBERS OF EXU'S ARMY KNELT ALONG one of the abandoned buildings across from the Dumpsters with their hands zip-tied behind their backs and their heads pressed against the cinderblock walls.

If the cops had a bus, they would only need one trip.

The medics at the trauma station asked if I'd been hit by a car. "Close enough."

They poked at my elbow, rubbed our cuts with alcohol pads and cut away my pant leg to get a look at the holes in my thigh.

"Claw hammer," I said.

The lead medic shrugged. "Seen it before. What happened to your face?"

"He's like that always," Marcela said.

He grunted. "Your head is lumpy too. Hammer?"

"Mostly."

He told Marcela, "Watch him for a concussion. The elbow is badly sprained with a partial tear in the biceps tendon. Don't let him use it for a while."

He wrapped my arm in a sling and kicked us out to make room for a policeman who'd been shot in the foot.

Two uniformed officers, male and female, approached.

The woman said, "You are Mr. Wallace and Miss Arcoverde?"

"Yes," Marcela said.

"Detective Rubin sent us. We are to take you home."

———

Brazilians know how to hug. And they love to show it, even when you're busted up and whimpering with every embrace. I made several rounds through the Arcoverde family with Gil glued to my side. He established a pattern of one hug from an Arcoverde, one from him.

When I crossed paths with Marcela we would ask, "You okay?"

Answers were muffled in arms and shoulders.

Antonio bawled like he was performing an opera. Jairo draped a dishtowel over his shoulder and Antonio threw it across the room with glee. Javier and Edson sang something in Portuguese.

At three in the morning Marcela kissed me goodnight. The celebration had dwindled to some sniffing and laughing.

"I am falling over," she said.

"Long day."

"You are okay?"

"Great. You?"

She nodded. "You aren't supposed to sleep. You might have a concussion."

"Oh, I'm gonna sleep."

She rolled her eyes. "After all of this, don't die from going to bed, okay?"

"I'll do my best."

She kissed me again and padded away, exhausted.

I hit the pillow and had the most well-earned sleep of my life.

———

Everyone was up before me. Easy enough when you sleep until eleven. Our flight to Vegas was at three.

I had work to do before then.

I rolled out of bed and every cell in my body stomped the brakes. My elbow was checked out, not even interested in moving. The perforated thigh responded to increased blood flow by convulsing and clacking my knees together. All the cuts, lumps, and bruises piped up, not to be ignored.

Fuck all of 'em.

I swore and staggered my way into the kitchen.

Someone gasped about it.

Antonio's wife Cecilia had a spread of ham, fruit, and cheese on the counter. I clear-cut it on my way through, carried the plate around with my right hand and tilted it to slide the food into my mouth while I Frankenstein's Monstered my way around. I finally found Marcela sitting on the bench near the pond, overlooking the green hills rolling down toward Rio.

She had some scrapes on her forehead and knees, her knuckles were swollen, and one ankle was wrapped with a compression bandage.

"You look gorgeous."

She stole the rest of my ham and swung her feet.

"I have to leave today."

Her mouth was full. "I know this."

"Come with me."

"Woody . . ."

"You can't tell me we don't belong together. After everything."

"We do. You are life to me. I think about you and have to pull my knees up to my chest because my stomach won't hold still. But I can't come with you."

"Before, you said—"

"Yes, before they burned our academy to the ground. Everything I said then is still true, and now we must rebuild. That academy is our family. I am the reason it was destroyed."

"No way. You can't think that."

She shrugged. "It doesn't matter what I think. I can't leave everyone else to clean up our mess."

We stared at the trees. All I could see was an unacceptable future.

"What about after?"

She leaned against my shoulder. "There is no after. You will go home, I will stay here, and things will change."

"No."

"I will be here, running the academy, all sweaty and smelly with many children trying to choke me. You will find some ring girl or dancer with a perfect nose and nothing to say."

"Hell no."

"I will miss you every day. And I will be sad, not having a next time to look forward to. Not planning what I will do when I first get to see you again, touch you again."

"But that could be every day," I said. "Come with me. The next time we see each other will be every morning."

"How I would love that. But I can't. I'm sorry." She sniffed and wiped her eyes on my sleeve. "You know what I will miss the most?"

I used the other sleeve. "Everything."

She nodded.

We watched the trees and saw nothing until it was time to go.

———

Gil met us at the back door of Antonio's house. He winced at the shuffling approach of broken hearts.

"Eddie's here."

"What the hell for?"

Gil shrugged and sipped his coffee. "I ever start understanding Eddie, something has gone horribly wrong." He put his arm around Marcela. "I'm sorry I have to steal him from you."

She slumped a punch into his ribs, hard enough to jostle his mug.

"Damn, be careful. I deserve it but the coffee didn't do a thing."

Eddie stood in the kitchen with Jairo and Antonio. When he saw me limping in his mouth fell open. "Aviso did all of that?"

"Sure, why not. I thought you were leaving last night."

"Brah, did you see what happened last night? Yeah. The place was crazy. Because of you two."

Jairo popped his eyebrows and biceps.

Eddie slapped two stacks of paper on the table. "We've been working all morning on this."

Gil said, "One of those better be a title shot for Woody. After Aviso, there is no argument against him being the top contender."

"Not an argument," Eddie said, conducting the room. "An opportunity."

Gil closed his eyes. "Ah, fuck me."

"Blood Brothers," Eddie said. He let it hang for a moment. "Two friends, practically brothers. They trained together, they lived together. Hell, one even loves up on the other's sister."

Portuguese outrage made him retreat.

"All right, maybe we'll leave that part out. Probably not. But we already have the footage of Woody wanting to fight Antonio, Jairo telling him to get the hell out. The foundation is set, gentlemen."

Jairo frowned.

Antonio's head tilted forward. His jaw muscles rippled as he chewed Eddie's bullshit and tried to spit it out.

"We hype it up," Eddie said. "Woody trains at the Warrior-Dome in front of the whole world. Jairo trains here in his family's sanctuary, like a goddam warrior monk. In a few months, maybe half a year, we make you two the main event in Las Vegas. Winner fights for the championship. I know we just had Jairo's first fight, but he brings enough history to make it legit."

"And enough Brazilian fans," Gil said.

Eddie shrugged. "Don't hurt."

"No way in hell," I said. "I'm not fighting Jairo."

"Okay, let me remind you. Your contract states if you refuse a fight, I can terminate the agreement altogether. You're out. Maybe you don't think it's fair for Jairo to get a shot at the belt alongside you, but tough shit. At least this way you get a chance to beat him out for it. You don't fight him, I'll give him another top contender. You can watch him fight for the title from the undercard. Or the street, whatever."

Marcela looked like she was going to choke him with his own legs.

"We all need to talk about this," I said.

Eddie shook his head. "No time. If Blood Brothers is gonna

happen we'll leave a crew here, start filming today." He slid one of the contracts toward me, one over to Jairo. "Bleed some ink, brothers."

I turned to Gil.

He shook his head.

Eddie saw it. "Jairo? You want to be the man here and show these guys how to be a professional fighter? A true Warrior?"

Jairo chewed his lip, whispered with Antonio, and finally said, "I will do what my brother does."

"Fuck's sake," Eddie said. "Woody, just sign the damn thing. Woodshed versus Arcoverde. Bragging rights over the most famous martial arts family in the western hemisphere. A chance to fight for the heavyweight championship. This is what you've been fighting for your whole life, isn't it?"

He was right.

I looked Antonio in the eye, nodded at Jairo.

Hugged Gil.

Kissed Marcela and felt her breathing against me.

Pulled the contract close, found the spot for my signature at the bottom. Tore the whole thing to shreds and dropped them at Eddie's feet.

"Everything worth fighting for is in this room, and I already have it. I'm done. I'm staying here."

Then I tried out one of the Portuguese phrases I'd been listening to the whole trip.

"*Vá se foder.*"

Go fuck yourself.

END OF ROUND 3

ABOUT THE AUTHOR

Jeremy Brown is a novelist working in many genres, including crime thrillers, murder mysteries, and military thrillers. He has worked as a narrative designer and lead writer for a massively popular video game and enjoys kettlebells, stockpiling firewood, and using coffee as a delivery system for cream. He lives in Michigan with his wife, sons, and various animals.

For more information and to sign up for the

Reader Club, please visit

JEREMYWBROWN.COM